About the author

Michael Moorcock was born in London in
1939. He published his first fantasy story at
the age of sixteen and has since earned
himself a reputation as a master of science
fiction. Editor of sf's foremost magazine *New
Worlds* and of the anthologies *New Worlds
1–6*, he is also the author of numerous short
stories, poems and novels, including *The
Shores of Death*, *The Blood Red Game*, *The
Winds of Limbo* and *Behold the Man*, the
story which won him the 1968 Nebula Award.

Also edited by Michael Moorcock and available from Sphere Books

NEW WORLDS 1
NEW WORLDS 2
NEW WORLDS 3
NEW WORLDS 4
NEW WORLDS 5
NEW WORLDS 6

The Ice Schooner

MICHAEL MOORCOCK

SPHERE BOOKS LIMITED
30/32 Gray's Inn Road, London WC1X 8JL

First published in Great Britain by Sphere Books Ltd 1969
Reprinted September 1972, March 1974
Copyright © Michael Moorcock 1969

The *Ice Schooner* was originally serialized in *SF Impulse* magazine.
It is published here for the first time in book form.

Printed in Great Britain by
Hazell Watson & Viney Ltd
Aylesbury, Bucks

ISBN 0 7221 6221 9

THE ICE SCHOONER

CHAPTER ONE

KONRAD ARFLANE

When Konrad Arflane found himself without an ice ship to command, he left the city-crevasse of Brershill and set off on skis across the great ice plateau; he went with the intention of deciding whether he should live or die.

In order to allow himself no compromise, he took a small supply of food and equipment, reckoning that if he had not made up his mind within eight days he would die anyway of starvation and exposure.

As he saw it, his reason for doing this was a good one. Although only thirty-five and one of the best known skippers of the plateau, he had little chance of obtaining a new captaincy in Brershill and refused to consider serving as a first or second officer under another master even if it were possible to get such a berth. Only fifteen years before Brershill had had a fleet of over fifty ships. Now she had twenty-three. While he was not a morbid man, Arflane had decided that there was only one alternative to taking a command with some foreign city, and that was to die.

So he set off, heading south across the plateau. There would be few ships in that direction and little to disturb him.

Arflane was a tall, heavy man with a full, red beard that now sparkled with rime. He was dressed in the black fur of the seal and the white fur of the bear. To protect his head from the cut of the cold wind he wore a thick bearskin hood; to protect his eyes from the reflected glare of the sun on the ice, he wore a visor of thin cloth stretched on a seal-bone frame. At his hip he had a short cutlass in a sealskin scabbard, and in either hand he held eight foot harpoons which served him both as weapons and as ski-poles. His skis were long strips cut from the bone of the great land whale. On these he was able to make good speed and soon found himself well beyond the normal shipping routes.

As his distant ancestors had been men of the sea, Konrad Arflane was a man of the ice. He had the same solitary habits, the same air of self-sufficiency, the same distant expression in his grey eyes. The only great difference between Arflane and his ancestors was that they had been forced at times to desert the sea, whereas he was never away from the ice; for in these days it encircled the world.

As Arflane knew, at all points of the compass lay ice of one sort or another; cliffs of ice, plains of ice, valleys of ice and even, though he had only heard of them, whole cities of ice. Ice that constantly changed its colour as the sky changed

7

colour; ice of pale blue, purple and ultramarine, ice of crimson, of yellow and emerald green. In summer crevasses, glaciers and grottoes were made even more beautiful by the deep, rich, glittering shades they reflected, and in winter the bleak ice mountains and plateaux possessed overpowering grandeur as they rose white, grey and black beneath the grim, snow-filled skies. At all seasons there was no scenery that was not ice in all its varieties and colourings and Arflane was deeply aware that the landscape would never change. There would be ice for all eternity.

The great ice plateau, which was the territory best known to Arflane, occupied and entirely covered the part of the world once known as the Matto Grosso. The original mountains and valleys had long since been engulfed by the ice and the present plateau was several hundred miles in diameter, gradually sloping at its farthest points and joining with the rougher ice that surrounded it. Arflane knew the plateau better than most men, for he had first sailed the ice with his father before his second birthday and had been master of a staysail schooner before he was twenty-one. His father had been called Konrad Arflane, as had all in the male line for hundreds of years, and they had all been masters of ships. Only a few generations back, members of the Arflane family had actually owned several vessels.

The ice ships—trading vessels and hunting craft for the most part – were sailing ships mounted on runners like giant skis which bore them across the ice at great speed. Centuries old, the ships were the principal source of communication, sustenance and trade for the inhabitants of the eight cities of the plateau. These settlements, situated in crevasses below the level of the ice, all owned sailing craft and their power depended on the size and quality of their fleets.

Arflane's home city, Brershill, had once been the most powerful of them all, but her fleet was diminishing rapidly these days and there were now more masters than ships; for Friesgalt, always Brershill's greatest rival, had now risen to become the pre-eminent city of the plateau, dictating the terms of trade, monopolising the hunting grounds and buying, as had recently happened to Arflane's barquentine, ships from the men of other cities who were unable to compete.

When he was six days out of Brershill and still undecided as to his fate, Konrad Arflane saw a dark object moving slowly towards him over the frozen white plain. He stopped his skis and stared ahead, trying to distinguish the nature of the object. There was nothing by which he could judge its size. It could be anything from a wounded land whale, dragging itself on its huge, muscular flippers, to a wild dog that had lost its way far from the warm ponds where it preyed on the seals.

Arflane's normal expression was remote and insouciant, but

at this moment there was a hint of curiosity in his eyes as he stood watching the object's slow progress. He debated what to do.

Moody skies, immense, grey, and heavy with snow, rolled above his head, blotting out the sun. Lifting his visor, Arflane peered at the moving thing, wondering if he should approach it or ignore it. He had not come out on to the ice to hunt, but if the thing were a whale and he could finish it and cut his mark on it he would become comparatively rich and his future would be that much easier to decide.

Frowning, he dug his harpoons into the ice and pushed himself forward on his skis. His muscles moved beneath his fur jacket and the pack on his back was jostled as he went skimming swiftly towards the thing. His movements were economical, almost nervous. He leaned forward on the skis, riding the ice with ease.

For a moment the red sun broke through the layers of cold cloud and ice sparkled like diamonds from horizon to horizon. Arflane saw that it was a man who lay on the ice. Then the sun was obscured again.

Arflane felt faintly resentful. A whale, or even a seal, could have been killed and put to good use, but a man was of no use at all. What was even more annoying was that he had deliberately chosen this way so that he would avoid contact with men or ships.

Even as he sped across the silent ice towards the man, Arflane considered ignoring him. The ethics of the icelands put him under no obligation to help, he would feel no pang of conscience if he left the man to die. For some reason, though he was taciturn by nature, Arflane still found himself continuing to approach. It was difficult to arouse his curiosity, but, once aroused, it had to be satisfied. The presence of men was very rare in this region.

When he was close enough to be able to make out details of the figure on the ice, he brought himself to a gradual halt and watched.

There was certainly little life left in the man. The exposed face, feet and hands were purple with cold and covered in frostbite swellings. Blood had frozen on the head and arms. One leg was completely useless, either broken or numb. Inadequate tatters of rich furs were tied around the body with strips of gut and leather; the head was bare and the grey hair shone with frost. This was an old man, but the body, though wasted, was big, and the shoulders were wide. The man continued to crawl with extraordinary animal tenacity. The red, half-blind eyes stared ahead; the great, gaunt skull, with its blue lips frozen in a grin, rolled as the figure moved on elbows and belly over the frozen plain. Arflane was unnoticed.

9

Konrad Arflane stared moodily at the figure for a moment, his strong, tanned face frowning heavily. Then he turned to go back. He had an obscure feeling of admiration for the dying old man. He thought that it would be wrong to intrude on such a private ordeal. He poised his harpoons, ready to push himself across the ice in the direction from which he had come, but, hearing a sound behind him, he glanced back and saw that the old man had collapsed and now lay completely still on the white ice. It would not be long before he died.

On impulse, Arflane pushed himself round again and slid forward on the skis until he was able to crouch beside the body. Laying down one harpoon and steadying himself with the other, he grasped one of the old man's shoulders in his thickly-gloved hand. The grip was gentle, virtually a caress. "You are a determined old man," he murmured.

The great head moved so that Arflane could now see the frozen face beneath the ice-matted mane of hair. The eyes opened slowly; they were full of an introverted madness. The blue, swollen lips parted and a guttural sound came from the throat. Arflane looked broodingly into the insane eyes for a moment; then he unslung his bulky pack and opened it, taking out a flask of spirit. He clumsily removed the cap from the flask and put the neck to the puffy, twisted mouth, pouring a little of the spirit between the lips. The old man swallowed, coughed, and gasped, then, quite levelly, he said: "I feel as if I burn, yet that's impossible. Before you go, sir, tell me if it is far to Friesgalt . . ."

The eyes closed and the head dropped. Arflane looked at the old man indecisively. He could tell both from the remains of the clothing and from the accent, that the dying man was a Friesgaltian aristocrat. How had such a one come to be alone on the ice without retainers? Once again, Arflane considered leaving him to die. He had nothing to gain from trying to save the man, who was as good as dead. He had only contempt and hatred for the grand lords of Friesgalt, whose tall ice-schooners these days dominated the frozen plains. Compared with the men of the other cities the Friesgaltian nobility was soft-living and godless. It openly mocked the doctrine of the Ice Mother; it heated its houses to excess; it was often thriftless. It refused to make its women do the simplest manual work; it even gave some of them equality with men.

Arflane sighed and then frowned again, looking down at the old aristocrat, judging him. He balanced his own prejudice and his sense of self-preservation against his grudging admiration for the man's tenacity and courage. If he were the survivor of a shipwreck, then he had plainly crawled many miles to get this far. A wreck could be the only explanation for his presence on the ice. Arflane made up his mind. He took a fur-lined sleeping sack from his pack, unrolled it and spread it out.

10

Walking clumsily on his skis, he went to the man's feet and got them into the neck of the sack and began to wrestle the rest of the body down into it until he could tie the sack's hood tightly around the man's head, leaving only the smallest aperture through which he could breathe. Then he shifted his pack so that it hung forward on his chest by its straps and hauled the sleeping sack on to his back until the muffled face was just above the level of his own broad shoulders. From a pouch at his belt, he took two lengths of leather and strapped the fur-swathed old man in place. Then, with difficulty even for someone of his strength, he heaved on his harpoons and began the long ski-trek to Friesgalt.

The wind was rising at his back. Above him, it had cut the clouds into swirling grey streamers and revealed the sun, which threw the shadows of the clouds on to the ice. The ice seemed to be alive, like a racing tide, black in the shadow and red in the sunlight, sparkling like clear water. The plateau seemed infinite in extent, having no projections, no landmarks, no indication of horizon save for the clouds which seemed to touch the ice far away. The sun was setting and he had only two hours or so in which to travel, for it was unwise to travel at night. He was heading towards the west, towards Friesgalt, chasing the great red globe as it sank. Light snow and tiny pieces of ice whirled over the plateau, moved, as he was moved, by the cold wind. Arflane's powerful arms pumped the tall harpoons up and down as he leaned forward, partly for speed, partly because of the burden on his back, his legs spread slightly apart on the tough whalebone skis.

He sped on, until the dusk faded into the darkness of night and the moon and stars could occasionally be seen through the thickening clouds. Then he slowed himself and stopped. The wind was falling, its sound now like a distant sigh; even that faded as Arflane removed the body from his back and the pack from his chest and pitched his tent, driving in the bone spikes at an angle to the ice.

When the tent was ready he got the old man inside it and started his heating unit; a precious possession but one which he mistrusted almost as much as naked fire, which he had seen only twice in his life. The unit was powered by small solar batteries and Arflane, like everyone else, did not understand how it worked. Even the explanations in the old books meant nothing to him. The batteries were supposed to be almost everlasting, but good ones were becoming scarcer.

He prepared broth for them both and, with some more spirit from his flask revived the old man, loosening the thongs around the sack's neck.

The moon shone through the worn fabric of the tent and gave Arflane just enough light to work by.

The Friesgaltian coughed and groaned. Arflane felt him shudder.

"Do you want some broth?" Arflane asked him.

"A little, if you can spare it." The exhausted voice, still containing the traces of an earlier strength, had a puzzled note.

Arflane put a beaker of warm broth to the broken lips. The Friesgaltian swallowed and grunted. "Enough for the meantime, I thank you." Arflane replaced the beaker on the heater and squatted in silence for a while. It was the Friesgaltian who spoke first.

"How far are we from Friesgalt?"

"Not far. Perhaps ten hours journey on skis. We could move on while the moon is up, but I'm not following a properly mapped route. I shan't risk travelling until dawn."

"Of course. I had thought it was closer, but . . ." the old man coughed again, weakly, and a thin sigh followed. "One misjudges distances easily. I was lucky. You saved me. I am grateful. You are from Brershill, I can tell by your accent. Why . . .?"

"I don't know," said Arflane brusquely.

Silence followed and Arflane prepared to lie down on the groundsheet. The old man had his sleeping sack but it would not be too cold if, against his normal instincts, he left the heating unit on. The weak voice spoke again. "It is unusual for a man to travel the unmapped ice alone, even in summer."

"True," Arflane replied.

After a pause, the Friesgaltian said hoarsely, evidently tiring: "I am the Lord Pyotr Rorsefne. Most men would have left me to die on the ice—even the men of my own city."

Arflane grunted impatiently.

"You are a generous man," added the principal Ship Lord of Friesgalt before he slept at last.

"Possibly just a fool," said Arflane, shaking his head. He lay back on the groundsheet, his hands behind his head. He pursed his lips for a moment, frowning lightly. Then he smiled a little ironically. The smile faded as he, too, fell asleep.

CHAPTER TWO

ULSENN'S WIFE

Scarcely more than eight hours after dawn Konrad Arflane sighted Friesgalt. Like all the Eight Cities it lay beneath the surface of the ice, carved into the faces of a wide natural crevasse that was almost a mile deep. Its main chambers and passages were hollowed from the rock that began several hundred feet below, though many of its storehouses and upper chambers had been cut from the ice itself. Little of Friesgalt was visible

12

above the surface; the only feature to be seen clearly was the wall of ice blocks that surrounded the crevasse and protected the entrance to the city both from the elements and from human enemies.

It was, however, the field of high ships' masts that really indicated the city's location. At first sight it seemed that a forest sprouted from the ice, with every tree symmetrical and every branch straight and horizontal; a dense, still, even menacing forest that defied nature and seemed like an ancient geometrician's dream of ideally ordered landscape.

When he was close enough to make out more detail, Arflane saw that fifty or sixty good-sized ice-ships lay anchored to the ice by means of mooring lines attached to bone spikes that had been hammered into the hard surface. Their weathered fibreglass hulls were scarred by centuries of use and most of their accessories were not the original parts, but copies made from natural materials. Belaying pins had been carved from walrus ivory, booms had been fashioned of whale bone, and the rigging was a mixture of precious nylon, gut and strips of sealskin. Many of their runners were also fashioned of whale bone, as wore the spars that joined them to the hulls.

The sails, like the hulls, wore of the original synthetic material. There were great stocks of nylon sailcloth in every city; indeed their very economy was heavily based on the amount of fabric that existed in the storechambers of the various cities. Every ship but one, which was preparing to get under way, had its sails tightly furled.

Twenty ships long and three ships deep, Friesgalt's docks were impressive. There were no new ships here. There was no means, in Arflane's world, of building new ones. All the ships were worn by age, but were nonetheless sturdy and powerful; and every ship had an individual line, partly due to the various embellishments made by generations of crews and skippers, partly because of the cuts of rigging favoured by different captains and owners.

The yards of the masts, the rigging, the decks and the surrounding ice were thick with working, fur-clad sailors, their breath white in the cold air. They were loading and unloading the vessels, making repairs and putting their craft in order. Stacks of baled pelts, barrels and boxes stood near the ships. Cargo booms jutted over the sides of the vessels, being used to winch the goods up to deck level and then swung over the hatches where they dropped the bales and barrels into the waiting hands of the men whose job it was to stow the cargo. Other cargoes were being piled on sledges that were either pulled by dogs or dragged by hand towards the city.

Beneath the lowering sky, from which a little light snow fluttered, dogs barked, men shouted, and the indefinable smell of shipping mingled with the more easily distinguished smells of oil and skins and whale flesh.

Some distance off along the line a whaler was crewing up. The whaling men generally kept themselves apart from other sailors, disdaining their company, and the crews of the trading vessels were relieved that they did so; for both the North Ice and the South Ice whalers were more than boisterous in their methods of entertaining themselves. They were nearly all large men, swaggering along with their ten foot harpoons on their shoulders, careless of where they swung them. They wore full, thick beards; their hair was also thick and much longer than usual. It was often, like their beards, plaited and held in place by whale grease, fashioned into strange barbaric styles. Their furs were rich, of a kind only normally worn by aristocrats, for whale men could afford anything they pleased to purchase if they were successful; but the furs were stained and worn casually. Arflane had been a whaling skipper through much of his career, and felt a comradeship for these coarse-voiced North Ice whaling men as they swung aboard their ship.

Aside from the few whalers, which were mainly three-masted barques or barquentines, there were all kinds of boats and ships on the oil-slippery ice. There were the little yachts and ketches used for work around the dock, and brigs, brigantines, two-mast two-topsail schooners, cutters and sloops. Most of the trading ships were three-mast square-rigged ships, but there was a fair scattering of two-mast brigs and two-mast schooners. Their colours for the most part were dull weather-beaten browns, blacks, greens.

The hunting ships of the whaling men were invariably black-hulled, stained by the blood of generations of slaughtered land-whales.

Arflane could now make out the names of the nearer craft. He recognized most of them without needing to read the characters carved into their sides. A heavy three-master, the *Land Whale*, was nearest him; it was from the city of Djob-habn, southernmost of the Eight, and had a strong resemblance to the one-time sea-mammal which, many centuries earlier, had left the oceans as the ice had gradually covered them, returning once again to the land it had left in favour of the sea. The *Land Whale* was heavy and powerful, with a broad prow that tapered gradually towards the stern. Her runners were short and she squatted on them, close to the ice.

A two-masted brig, the *Heurfrast*, named for the Ice Mother's mythical son, lay nearby, unloading a cargo of seal-skin and bear pelts, evidently just back from a successful hunting expedition. Another two-master—a brigantine—was taking on tubs of whale oil, preparatory, Arflane guessed, to making a trading voyage among the other cities; this was the *Good Wind*, christened in the hope that the name would bring luck

14

to the ship. Arflane knew her for an unreliable vessel, ironically subject to getting herself becalmed at crucial times; she had had many owners. Other two-masted brigs and schooners and two- or three-masted schooners, as well as barques were there, and Arflane knew every ship by its name; he could see the barquentine *Katarina Ulsenn* and its sister ships, the *Nastasya Ulsenn* and the *Ingrid Ulsenn*, all owned by the powerful Ulsenn family of Friesgalt and named after Ulsenn matrons. There was the Brershillian square-rigger, the *Leaper*, and another three-master from Brershill, the slender hunting barque *Bear Scenter*. Two trading brigs, small and bulky, were from Chaddersgalt, the city closest to Brershill, and others were from Djobhabn, Abersgalt, Fyorsgep and Keltshill, the rest of the Eight Cities.

The whale hunting craft lay away from the main gathering of ships. They were battered looking vessels, with a spirit of pride and defiance about them. Traditionally, whaling ships were called by paradoxical names, and Arflane recognised whalers called *Sweet Girl, Truelove, Smiling Lady, Gentle Touch, Soft Heart, Kindness* and similar names, while others were called *Good Fortune, Hopeful, Lucky Lance* and the like.

Also to one side, but at the other end of the line to the whaling ships, stood the ice-clippers, their masts towering well above those of all the surrounding craft, their whole appearance one of cruel arrogance. These were the fast-running, slim-prowed and stately queens of the plateau that, at their best, could travel at more than twice the speed of any other ship. Their hulls, supported on slender runners, dwarfed everything nearby, and from their decks one could look down on the poop of any other ship.

Tallest and most graceful of all these four-masted clippers was the principal ship of the Friesgaltian fleet, the *Ice Spirit*, with her sails trimly furled and every inch of her gleaming with polished bone, fibre-glass, soft gold, silver, copper and even iron. An elegant craft, with very clean lines, she would have surprised her ancient designer if he could have seen her now; for she bore embellishments.

Her bow, bowsprit and forecastle were decorated with the huge elongated skulls of the adapted sperm whale. The beak-like mouths bristled with savage teeth, grinning out disdainfully on the other shipping, witnesses to the skill, bravery and power of the ship's owners, the Rorsefne family. Though she was known as a schooner, the *Ice Spirit* was really a square-rigged barque in the old terminology of the sea. Originally all the big clippers had been fore-and-aft schooner rigged, but this rig had been proven impracticable soon after ice navigation had become fully understood and square rig had been substituted; but the old name of schooner had stuck. The Rorsefne flag flew from above her royals; all four flags were large. Painted in black, white, gold and red by some half-barbaric artist, the Rorsefne standard showed the symbolic white hands of the Ice Mother, flanked by a bear and a whale, symbols of courage and vitality, while cupped in the hands was an ice ship. A grandiose flag, thought Arflane, hefting his near-dead burden on his back and skimming closer to the great concourse of craft.

As Arflane approached the ships, the schooner he had noticed preparing to leave let go its moorings and its huge sails bulged as the wind filled them. Only the mainsail and two fore-stay sails had been unfurled, enough to take the ship out slowly until it was clear of the others.

It turned into the wind and slid gracefully towards him on its great runners. He stopped and saluted cheerfully as the ship sailed by. It was *The Snow Girl* out of Brershill. The runners squealed on the smooth ice as the helmsman swung his wheel and steered a course between the few irregularities worn by the constant passage of ships. One or two of the sailors recognised him and waved back from where they hung in the rigging, but most were busy with the sails. Through the clear, freezing air, Arflane heard the voice of the skipper shouting his orders into a megaphone. Then the ship had passed him, letting down more sail and gathering speed.

Arflane felt a pang as he turned and watched the ship skim over the ice towards the east. It was a good craft; one he would be pleased to command. The wind caught more sail and *The Snow Girl* leapt suddenly, like an animal. Startled by the sudden burst of speed, the black and white snow-kites that had been circling above her squawked wildly and flapped upwards before diving back to the main gathering of ships to drift expectantly above them or perch in the top trees in the hope of snatching tit-bits of whale meat or seal blubber from the carcasses being unloaded.

Arflane dug his lances deep into the ice and pushed his overloaded skis forward, sliding now between the lines and hulls of the ships, avoiding the curious sailors who glanced at him as they worked, and making his way towards the high wall of ice-blocks that sheltered the city-crevasse of Friesgalt.

At the main gate, which was barely large enough to let through a sledge, a guard stood squarely in the entrance, an arrow nocked to his ivory bow. The guard was a fair-haired youngster with his fur hood flung back from his head and an anxious expression on his face which made Arflane believe that the lad had only recently been appointed to guard the gate.

"You are not of Friesgalt and you are plainly not a trader from the ships," said the youth. "What do you want?"

"I carry your Lord Rorsefne on my back," said Arflane. "Where shall I take him?"

"The Lord Rorsefne!" The guard stepped forward, lowering his bow and pulling back the headpiece of the sleeping sack so that he could make out the face of Arflane's burden. "Are there no others? Is he dead?"

"Almost."

"They left months ago—on a secret expedition. Where did you find him?"

"A day's journey or so east of here." Arflane loosened the straps and began lowering the old man to the ice. "I'll leave him with you."

The young man looked hesitant and then said: "No – stay until my relief arrives. He is due now. You must tell all you know. They might want to send out a rescue party."

"I can't help them," Arflane said impatiently.

"Please stay—just to tell them exactly how you found him. It will be easier for me."

Arflane shrugged. "There's nothing to tell." He bent and began dragging the body inside the gate. "But I'll wait, if you like, until they give me back my sleeping sack."

Beyond the gate was a second wall of ice-blocks, at chest height. Peering over it, Arflane saw the steep path that led down to the first level of the city. There were other levels at intervals, going down as far as the eyes could see. On the far side of the crevasse Arflane made out some of the doorways and windows of the residential levels. Many of them were embellished with ornate carvings and bas reliefs chiselled from the living rock. More elaborate than any cave-dwellings of millennia ago, these troglodytic chambers had from the outside much of the appearance of the first permanent shelters mankind's ancestors had possessed. The reversion to this mode of existence had been made necessary centuries earlier when it had become impossible to build surface houses as the temperature decreased and the level of the ice rose. The first crevasse-dwellers had shown forethought in anticipating the conditions to come and had built their living quarters as far below ground as possible in order to retain as much heat as they could. These same men had built the ice-ships, knowing that, with the impossibility of sustaining supplies of fuel, these were the most practical form of transportation.

Arflane could now see the young guard's relief on the near-side ramp leading to the second level to the top. He was dressed in white bearskins and armed with a bow and a quiver of arrows. He toiled up the slope in the spiked boots that it was best to wear when ascending or descending the levels, for there was only a single leather rope to stop a man from falling off the comparatively narrow ramp into the gorge.

When the relief came the young guard explained what had

17

happened. The relief, an old man with an expressionless face, nodded and went to take up his position on the gate.

Arflane squatted down and unlaced his skis while the young guard fetched him a pair of spiked boots. When Arflane had got these on they lifted the faintly stirring bundle between them and began carefully to descend the ramp.

The light from the surface grew fainter as they descended, passing a number of men and women busy with trade goods being taken to the surface and supplies of food and hides being brought down. Some of the people realized the identity of the Lord Rorsefne. Arflane and the guard refused to answer their incredulous and anxious questions but stumbled on into the ever-increasing darkness.

It took a long time to get the Lord Rorsefne to a level lying midway on the face of the crevasse. The level was lighted dimly by bulbs powered by the same source that heated the residential sections of the cavern city. This source lay at the very bottom of the crevasse and was regarded, even by the myth-mocking Friesgaltian aristocracy, with superstition. To the ice-dwellers, cold was the natural condition of everything and heat was an evil necessity for their survival, but it did not make it any the less unnatural. In the Ice Mother's land there was no heat and none was needed to sustain the eternal life of all those who joined her when they died and became cold. Heat could destroy the ice, and this was sure proof of its evil. Down at the bottom of the crevasse the heat, it was rumoured, reached an impossible temperature and it was here that those who had offended against the Ice Mother went in spirit after they had died.

The Lord Rorsefne's family inhabited a whole level of the city on both sides of the crevasse. A bridge spanned the gorge and the two men had to cross it to reach the main chambers of the Rorsefne household. The bridge, made of hide, swayed and sagged as they crossed. Waiting for them on the other side was a square-faced middle-aged man in the yellow indoor livery of the Rorsefne.

"What have you got there?" he asked impatiently, thinking probably that Arflane and the guard were traders trying to sell something.

"Your master," Arflane said with a slight smile. He had the satisfaction of seeing the servant's face fall as he recognised the half-hidden features of the man in the sleeping sack.

Hurriedly, the servant helped them through a low door which had the Rorsefne arms carved into the rock above it. They went through two more doors before reaching the entrance hall.

The big hall was well-lit by light tubes imbedded in the wall. It was overheated also, and Arflane began to sweat in mental and physical discomfort. He pushed back his hood and loosened the thongs of his coat. The hall was richly furnished,

Arflane had seen nothing like it. Painted hangings of the softest leather covered the rock walls; and even here, in the entrance hall, there were chairs made of wood, some with upholstery of real cloth. Arflane had only seen sailcloth and one wooden artifact in his life. Leather, no matter how finely it could be tanned, was never so delicate as the silk and linen he looked at now. It was hundreds of years old, preserved in the cold of the store-chambers no doubt, and must date back to a time before his ancestors had come to live in the ravines of the south, when there was still vegetation on the land and not just in the warm ponds and the ocean of blasphemous legend. Arflane knew that the world, like the stars and the moon, was comprised almost wholly of ice and that one day at the will of the Ice Mother even the warm ponds and the rock-caverns that sustained animal and human life would be turned into the ice which was the natural state of all matter.

The yellow-clad servant had disappeared but now returned with a man almost as tall as Arflane. He was thin-faced, with pursed lips and pale blue eyes. His skin was white, as if it had never been exposed above ground, and he wore a wine-red jacket and tight black trousers of soft leather. His clothing seemed effete to Arflane.

He stopped near the unconscious body of Rorsefne and looked down at it thoughtfully; then he raised his head and glanced distastefully at Arflane and the guard.

"Very well," he said. "You may go."

The man could not help his voice—perhaps not his tone either—but both irritated Arflane. He turned to leave. He had expected, without desiring it, at least some formal statement of thanks.

"Not you, stranger," said the tall man. "I meant the guard."

The guard left and Arflane watched the servants carry the old man away. He said: "I'd like my sleeping sack back later," then looked into the face of the tall man.

"How is the Lord Rorsefne?" said the other distantly.

"Dying, perhaps. Another would be—but he could live. He'll lose some fingers and toes at very least."

Expressionlessly, the other man nodded. "I am Janek Ulsenn," he said, "the Lord Rorsefne's son-in-law. Naturally we are grateful to you. How did you find the Lord?"

Arflane explained briefly.

Ulsenn frowned. "He told you nothing else?"

"It's a marvel he had the strength to tell me as much." Arflane could have liked the old man, but he knew he could never like Ulsenn.

"Indeed?" Ulsenn thought for a moment. "Well, I will see you have your reward. A thousand good bear skins should satisfy you, eh?"

It was a fortune.

19

"I helped the old man because I admired his courage," Arflane said brusquely. "I do not want your skins."

Ulsenn seemed momentarily surprised. "What *do* you want? I see you're," he paused, "from another city. You are not a nobleman. What . . .?" He was plainly puzzled. "It is unheard of that a man—without a code—would bother to do what you did. Even one of us would hesitate to save a stranger." His final sentence held a note of belligerence, as if he resented the idea of a foreigner and a commoner making the gesture Arflane had made; as if selfless action were the prerogative of the rich and powerful.

Arflane shrugged. "I liked the old man's courage." He made to leave, but as he did so a door opened on his right and a black-haired woman wearing a heavy dress of fawn and blue entered the hall. Her pale face was long and firm-jawed, and she walked with natural grace. Her hair flowed over her shoulders, and she had gold-flecked brown eyes. She glanced at Ulsenn with a slight interrogatory frown.

Arflane inclined his head slightly and reached for the door handle.

The woman's voice was soft, perhaps a trifle hesitant. "Are you the man who saved my father's life?"

Unwillingly, Arflane turned back and stood facing her with his legs spread apart as if on the deck of a ship. "I am, madam —if he survives," he said shortly.

"This is my wife," said Ulsenn with equally poor grace.

She smiled pleasantly. "He wanted me to thank you and wants to express his gratitude himself when he feels stronger. He would like you to stay here until then—as his guest."

Arflane had not looked directly at her until now and when he raised his head to stare for a moment into her golden eyes she appeared to give a faint start, but at once was composed again.

"Thank you," he said, looking with some amusement in Ulsenn's direction, "but your husband might not feel so hospitable."

Ulsenn's wife gave her husband a glance of vexed surprise. Either she was genuinely upset by Ulsenn's treatment of Arflane, or she was acting for Arflane's benefit. If she were acting, Arflane was still at a loss to understand her motives; for all he knew she was merely using this opportunity to embarrass her husband in front of a stranger of lower rank than himself.

Ulsenn sighed. "Nonsense. He must stay if your father desires it. The Lord Rorsefne, after all, is head of the house. I'll have Onvald bring him something."

"Perhaps our guest would prefer to eat with us," she said sharply. There was definitely animosity between the two.

"Ah, yes," muttered Ulsenn bleakly.

Wearying of this, Arflane said with as much politeness as he could muster "With your permission I'll eat at a trader's lodging and rest there, too. I have heard you have a good traveller's hostel on the sixteenth level." The guard had told him that as they had passed the place earlier.

She said quietly, "Please stay with us. After what—"

Arflane bowed and again looked directly at her, trying to judge her sincerity. This woman was not of the same stuff as her husband, he decided. She resembled her father in features to some extent and he thought he saw the qualities in her that he had admired in the old man; but he would not stay now.

She avoided his glance. "Very well. What name shall be asked at the traveller's lodging?"

"Captain Konrad Arflane," he said gruffly, as if reluctantly confiding a secret, "of Brershill. Ice Mother protect you."

Then, with a curt nod to them both, he left the hall, passing through the triple doors and slamming the last heavily and fiercely behind him.

CHAPTER THREE

THE ICE SPIRIT

Against his normal instincts, Konrad Arflane decided to wait in Friesgalt until the old man could talk to him. He was not sure why he waited; if asked, he would have said it was because he did not want to lose a good sleeping sack and, besides, he had nothing better to do. He would not have admitted that it was Ulrica Ulsenn who kept him in the city.

He spent most of his time wandering around on the surface among the big ships. He deliberately did not call at the Rorsefne household, being too stubborn. He waited for them to contact him.

In spite of his strong dislike of the man, Arflane thought he understood Janek Ulsenn better than other Friesgaltians he had encountered. Ulsenn was not typical of the modern aristocracy of Friesgalt who belittled the rigid and haughty code of their ancestors. In the other poorer cities the old traditions were still respected, though the merchant princes there had never had the power of families like the Rorsefnes and Ulsenns. Arflane could admire Ulsenn at least for refusing to soften his attitudes. In that respect he and Ulsenn had something in common. Arflane hated the signs of gradual change in his environment that he had half-consciously noted. Thinking was looser, the softening of the harsh but sensible laws of survival in the icelands was even illustrated by his own recent action in helping the old man. Only disaster could come of this trend towards decadence and more like Ulsenn were needed in positions of

21

influence where they could stop the gradual rejection of traditional social behaviour, traditional religion and traditional thinking. There was no other way to ensure their ability to stay alive in an environment where animal life was not meant to exist. Let the rot set in, Arflane thought, and the Ice Mother would lose no time in sweeping away the last surviving members of the race.

It was a sign of the times that Arflane had become something of a hero in the city. A century earlier they would have sneered at his weakness. Now they congratulated him and he in turn despised them, understanding that they patronised him as they might have honoured a brave animal, that they had contempt for his values and, indeed his very poverty. He wandered alone, his face stern, his manner surly, avoiding everyone and knowing without caring that he was reinforcing their opinion that all not of Friesgalt were uncouth and barbarian.

On the third day of his stay he went to look, with grudging admiration, at the *Ice Spirit*.

As he came up to the ship, ducking under her taut mooring lines, someone shouted down at him.

"Captain Arflane!"

He looked up reluctantly. A fair, bearded face peered over the rail. "Would you like to come aboard and look around the ship, sir?"

Arflane shook his head; but a leather ladder was already bouncing down the side, its bottom striking the ice near his feet. He frowned, desiring no unnecessary involvement with the Friesgaltians, but deeply curious to set foot on the deck of a vessel that was almost a myth in the icelands.

He made up his mind quickly, grasped the ladder and began to climb towards the ivory-inlaid rail far above.

Swinging his leg over the rail he was greeted with a smile by the bearded man, dressed in a rich jerkin of white bear cub's fur and tight, grey sealskin trousers, almost the uniform of Friesgaltian ship's officers.

"I thought you might be interested to inspect the ship, captain, as a fellow sailor." The man's smile was frank and his tone did not have the hint of condescension Arflane half expected. "My name's Petchnyoff, second officer of the *Ice Spirit*." He was a comparatively young man for a second officer. His beard and hair were soft and blond, tending to give him a foolish look, but his voice was strong and steady. "Can I show you around?"

"Thanks," said Arflane. "Shouldn't you ask your captain first?" He, when commanding his own ship, was firm about such courtesies.

Petchnyoff smiled. "The *Ice Spirit* has no captain, as such. She's captained by the Lord Rorsefne under normal conditions,

22

or by someone he has appointed when he's unable to be aboard. In your case, I'm sure he'd want me to show you over the ship."

Arflane disapproved of this system, which he had heard about; in his opinion a ship should have a permanent captain, a man who spent most of his life aboard her. It was the only way to get the full feel of a ship and learn what she could do and what she could not.

The ship had three decks, main, middle and poop, each of diminishing area, with the two upper decks aft of them as they stood there. The decks were of pitted fibreglass, like the hull, and spread with ground-up bone to give the feet better purchase. Most of the ship's superstructure was of the same fibreglass, worn, scratched and battered from countless voyages over countless years. Some doors and hatch-covers had been replaced by facsimiles fashioned of large pieces of ivory glued together and carved elaborately in contrast to the unadorned fibreglass. The ivory was yellowed and old in many places and looked almost as ancient as the originals. Lines—a mixture of nylon, gut and leather—stretched from the rails into the top trees.

Arflane looked up, getting the best impression of the ship's size he had had yet. The masts were so high that they seemed almost to disappear from sight. The ship was well kept, he noted, with every yard and inch of rigging so straight and true that he would not have been surprised to have seen men crawling about in the top-trees measuring the angle of the gaffs. The sails were furled tight, with every fold of identical depth; and Arflane saw that the ivory booms, too, were carved with intricate pictorial designs. This was a show ship and he was filled with resentment that she was so rarely sailed on a working trip.

Petchnyoff stood patiently at his side, looking up also. The light had turned grey and cold, giving an unreal quality to the day.

"It'll snow soon," said the second officer.

Arflane nodded. He liked nothing better than a snow-storm. "She's very tidily kept," he said.

Petchnyoff noted his tone and grinned. "Too tidy, you think. You could be right. We have to keep the crew occupied. We get precious little chance of sailing her, particularly since the Lord Rorsefne's been away." He led Aflane towards an ivory door let into the side of the middle deck. "I'll show you below first."

The cabin they entered held two bunks and was more luxuriously furnished than any cabin Arflane had seen. There were heavy chests, furs, a table of whalebone and chairs of skins slung on bone frames. A door led off this into a narrow companionway.

"These are the cabins of the captain and any guests he happens to have with him," Petchnyoff explained, pointing out doors as they passed them. "The cabin we came through was mine. I share it with the third officer, Kristoff Hinsen. He's on duty, but he wants to meet you."

Petchnyoff showed Arflane the vast holds of the ship. They seemed to go on forever. Arflane began to think that he was lost in a maze the size of a city, the ship was so big. The crew's quarters were clean and spacious. They were under-occupied since only a skeleton crew was aboard, primarily to keep the ship looking at her best and ready to sail at the whim of her owner-captain. Most of the ship's ports were of the original thick, unbreakable glass. As he went by one, Arflane noticed that it was darker outside and that snow was falling in great sheets on to the ice, limiting visibility to a few yards.

Arflane could not help being impressed by the capacity of the ship and envied Petchnyoff his command. If Brershill had one vessel like this, he thought, the city would put her to good use and soon regain her status. Perhaps he should be thankful that the Friesgaltians did not make better use of her, otherwise they might have captured an even bigger proportion of the trade.

They climbed up eventually to the poop deck. It was occupied by an old man who appeared not to notice them. He was staring intently at the dimly-seen wheel that was positioned below on the middle deck. It had been lashed fast so that the runners which it steered would not shift and strain the ship's moorings. Though the old man's eyes were focused on the wheel he seemed to be contemplating some inner thought. He turned as they joined him at the rail. His beard was white and he wore his coarse fur hood up, shadowing his eyes. He had his jerkin tightly laced and there were mittens on his hands. Snow had settled on his shoulders; the snow was still heavy, darkening the air and drifting through the rigging to heap itself on the decks. Arflane heard it pattering on the canvas high above.

"This is our third officer, Kristoff Hinsen," Petchnyoff said, slapping the old man's arm. "Meet the Lord Rorsefne's saviour, Kristoff."

Kristoff regarded Arflane thoughtfully. He had a face like an old snow-kite, with knowing beady black eyes and a hooked nose.

"You're Captain Arflane. You commanded *The North Wind*, eh?"

"I'm surprised you should know that," Arflane replied. "I left her five years ago."

"Aye. Remember a ship you nosed into an icebreak south of here? *The Tanya Ulsenn*?"

Arflane laughed. "I do. We were racing for a whale herd that had been sighted. The others dropped out until there was only us and *The Tanya*. It was a profitable trip once we'd put *The Tanya* into the icebreak. Were you aboard her?"

"I was the captain. I lost my commission through your trick."

Arflane had acted according to the accepted code of the ice sailors, but he studied Kristoff's face for signs of resentment. There seemed to be none.

"They were better times for me," said Arflane.

"And for me," Kristoff said. He chuckled. "So our victories and defeats come to the same thing in the end. You've no ship to captain now—and I'm third officer aboard a fancy hussy who lies in bed all day."

"She should sail," Arflane said, looking around him. "She's worth ten of any other ship."

"The day this old whore sails on a working trip—that's the day the world will end!" Kristoff kicked at the deck in disgust. "I tried your tactic once you know, Captain Arflane, when I was second officer aboard *The Heurfrast*. The captain was hurt —tangled up in a harpoon line of all things—and I was in command. You know that old hunter, *The Heurfrast*?"

Arflane nodded.

"Well, she's hard to handle until you get the feel of her and then she's easy. It was a year or so later and we were racing two brigs from Abersgalt. One overturned in our path and we had to go round her, which gave the other a good start on us. We managed to get up behind her and then we saw this icebreak ahead. I decided to try nosing her in."

"What happened?" Arflane asked, smiling.

"We *both* went in—I didn't have your sense of timing. For that, they pensioned me off on this petrified cow-whale. I realise now that your trick was even harder than I thought."

"I was lucky," Arflane said.

"But you'd used that tactic before—and since. You were a good captain. We Friesgaltians don't usually admit there are any better sailors than our own."

"Thanks," said Arflane, unable to resist the old man's flattery and beginning to feel more comfortable now that he was in the company of men of his own trade. "You nearly pulled yourself out of my trap, I remember."

"Nearly," Hinsen sighed. "The sailing isn't what it was, Captain Arflane."

Arflane grunted agreement.

Petchnyoff smiled and pulled up his hood against the weather. The snow fell so thickly that it was impossible to make out more than the faint outlines of the nearer ships.

Standing there in relaxed silence, Arflane fancied that they could be the only three men in all the world; for everything was still beneath the falling snow that muffled any sound.

"We'll see less of this weather as time goes on," said Petchnyoff thankfully. "Snow comes only once in ten or fifteen days now. My father remembers it falling so often it seemed to last the whole summer. And the winds were harsher in the winter, too."

Hinsen dusted snow off his jerkin. "You're right, lad. The world has changed since I was young—she's warming up. In a few generations we'll be skipping about on the surface naked." He laughed at his own joke.

Arflane felt uneasy. He did not want to spoil the pleasant mood, but he had to speak. "Not talk the Ice Mother should hear, friends," he said awkwardly. "Besides, what you say is untrue. The climate alters a little one way or another from year to year, but over a lifetime it grows steadily colder. That must be so. The world is dying."

"So our ancestors thought and symbolised their ideas in the creed of the Ice Mother," Petchnyoff said, smiling. "But what if there were no Ice Mother? Suppose the sun were getting hotter and the world changing back to what it was before the ice came? What if the idea were true that this is only one of several ages when the ice has covered the world? Certain old books say as much, captain."

"I would call that blasphemous nonsense," Arflane said sharply. "You know yourself that those books contain many strange notions which we know to be false. The only book I believe is the Book of the Ice Mother. She came from the centre of the universe, bringing cleansing ice; one day her purpose will be fulfilled and all will be ice, all will be purified. Read what you will into that, say that the Ice Mother does not exist—that her story only represents the truth—but you must admit that even some of the old books said the same, that all heat must disappear."

Hinsen glanced at him sardonically. "There are signs that the old ideas are false," he murmured. "Followers of the Ice Mother say 'All must grow cold'; but you know that we have scholars in Friesgalt who make it their business to measure the weather. We got our power through their knowledge. The scholars say the level of the ice has dropped a few degrees in the last two or three years, and one day the sun will burn yellow-hot again and it will melt the ice away. They say that the sun is hotter already and the beasts move south, anticipating the change. They smell a new sort of life, Arflane. Life like the weed-plants we find in the warm ponds, but growing on land out of stuff that is like little bits of crumbled rock—out of earth. They believe that these must already exist somewhere— that they have always existed, perhaps on islands in the sea . . ."

"There is no *sea*!"

"The scholars think we could not have survived if there were not a sea somewhere, and these plants growing on islands in the sea."

26

"No!" Arflane turned his back on Hinsen.

"You say not? But reason says it is the truth."

"Reason?" Arflane sneered. "Or some twist of mind that passes for reason? There's no true logic in what you say. You only prattle a warped idea you would *rather* believe. Your kind of thinking will bring disaster to us all!"

Hinsen shook his head. "I see this as a fact, Captain Arflane —the ice is softening as we grow soft. Just as the beasts scent the new life, so do we—that is why our ideas are changing. I *desire* no change. I am only sorry, for I could love no other world than the one I know. I'll die in my own world, but what will our descendants miss? The wind, the snow, and the swift ice—the sight of a herd of whales speeding in flight before your fleet, the harpoon's leap, the fight under a red, round sun hanging frozen in the blue sky; the spout of black whale blood, brave as the men who let it . . . Where will all that be when the icelands become dirty, unfirm earth and brittle green? What will men become? All we love and admire will be belittled and then forgotten in that clogged, hot, unhealthy place. What a tangled, untidy world it will be. But it *will* be!"

Arflane slapped the rail, scattering the snow. "You are insane! How can all this change?"

"You could be right," Hinsen replied softly. "But what I see, sane or not, is what I see, straight and definite—inevitable."

"You'd deny every rule of nature?" Arflane asked mockingly. "Even a fool must admit that nothing becomes hot of its own accord after it has become cold. See what is about you, not what you *think* is here! I understand your reasoning. But it is soft reasoning, wishful reasoning. Death, Kristoff Hinsen, *death* is all that is inevitable! Once there was this dirt, this green, this life—I accept that. But it died. Does a man die, become cold and then suddenly grow warm again, springing up saying 'I died, but now I live!'? Can't you see how your logic deceives you? Whether the Ice Mother is real or only a symbol of what is real, she must be honoured. Lose sight of that, as you in Friesgalt have done, and our people will die sooner than they need. You think me a superstitious barbarian, I know, for holding the views I hold—but there is good sense in what I say."

"I envy you for being able to stay so certain," Kristoff Hinsen said calmly.

"And I pity you for your unnecessary sorrow!"

Embarrassed, Petchnyoff took Arflane's arm. "Can I show you the rest of the ship, captain?"

"Thank you," said Arflane brusquely, "but I have seen all I want. She is a good ship. Don't let her rot, also."

His face troubled, Hinsen started to say something; but Arflane turned away. He left the poop and made his way to

27

the lower deck, clambered over the side, climbed down the ladder and marched back towards the underground city, his boots crunching in the snow.

CHAPTER FOUR

THE SHIPSMASHER HOSTEL

After his visit to the ice schooner Konrad Arflane became increasingly impatient with his wait in Friesgalt. He had still had no word from the Ulsenns about the old man's condition and he was disturbed by the atmosphere he found in the city. He had come to no decision regarding his own affairs; but he resolved to try to get a berth, even as a petty officer for the time being, on the next Brershill ship that came in.

He took to haunting the fringes of the great dock, avoiding contact with all the ships and in particular the *Ice Spirit*, and looking out for a Brershill craft.

On the fourth morning of his wait a three-masted barque was sighted. She was gliding in under full sail, flying a Brershill flag and travelling faster than was wise for a vessel so close to the dock. Arflane smiled as she came nearer, recognising her as the *Tender Maiden*, a whaler skippered by his old friend Captain Jarhan Brenn. She seemed to be sailing straight for the part of the dock where ships were thickest, and the men working there began to scatter in panic, doubtless fearing that she was out of control. When she was only a short distance from the dock she turned smoothly and rapidly in a narrow arc, reefed sails and slid towards the far end of the line where other whaling vessels were already moored. Arflane began to run across the ice, his ridged boots giving him good purchase.

Panting, he reached the *Tender Maiden* just as she was throwing down her anchor ropes to the mooring hands who stood by with their spikes and mallets.

Arflane grinned a little as he seized the bone spikes and heavy iron mallet from a surprised mooring hand and began driving a spike into the ice. He reached out for a nearby line and tautened it, lashing it fast to the spike. The ship stirred for a moment, resisting the lines, and then was still.

From above him on the deck he heard someone laughing. Looking up, he saw that the ship's captain, Jarhan Brenn, was standing at the rail.

"Arflane! Are you down to working as a mooring hand? Where's your ship?"

Arflane shrugged and spread his hands ironically, then grabbed hold of the mooring line and began to swing himself up it until he was able to grasp the rail and climb over it to stand beside his old friend.

"No ship," he told Brenn. "She was given up to honour a bad debt of the owner's. Sold to a Friesgalt merchant."

Brenn nodded sympathetically. "Not the last, I'd guess. You should have stayed at the whaling. There's always work for us whalers, whatever happens. And you didn't even marry the woman in the end." He chuckled.

Brenn was referring to a time, six years since, when Arflane had taken a trading command as a favour to a girl he had wished to marry. It was only after he had done this that he had realised that he wanted no part of a girl who could demand such terms. By then it had been too late to get his command of the whaler back.

He smiled ruefully at Brenn and shrugged again. "With my poor luck, Brenn, I doubt I'd have sighted a whale in all these six years."

His friend was a short, stocky man, with a round, ruddy face and a fringe beard. He was dressed in heavy black fur, but his head and hands were bare. His greying hair was cropped close, for a whaler, but his rough, strong hands showed the callouses that only a harpoon could make. Brenn was respected as a skipper in both the South Ice and North Ice hunting fields. Currently, by the look of his rig, he was hunting the North Ice.

"Poor luck isn't yours alone," Brenn grunted in disgust. "Our holds are just about empty. Two calves and an old cow are all we have aboard. We ran out of provisions and plan to trade our cargo for more supplies, then we'll try the South Ice and hope the hunting's better. Whales are getting hard to find in the north."

Brenn was unusual in that he hunted both south and north. Most whaling men preferred one type of field or the other (for their characteristics were very different) but Brenn did not mind.

"Aren't all the hunting fields poor this season?" Arflane asked. "I heard that even seal and bear are scarcer, and no walrus have been seen for two seasons."

Brenn pursed his lips. "The patch will pass, with the Ice Mother's help." He slapped Arflane's arm and began to move down the deck to supervise the unloading of the cargo from the central hold. The ship stank of whale blood and blubber. "Look at our catch," he said, as Arflane followed him. "There was no need for flenching. We just hauled 'em in and stowed 'em whole." Flenching was the whaling man's term for cutting up the whale. This was normally done on the ice, and then the pieces were winched aboard for stowing. If there had been no need to do this, then the catch must be small indeed.

Balancing himself by gripping ratline, Arflane peered into the hold. It was dark, but he could make out the stiff bodies of two small calves and a cow-whale which did not look much bigger. He shook his head in sympathy. There was hardly enough there to re-provision the ship for the long haul to the South Ice. Brenn must be in a gloomier mood than he seemed.

Brenn shouted orders and his hands began to lower themselves into the hold as derricks were swung across and tackles dropped. The whaling men worked slowly and were plainly depressed. They had every reason to be in poor spirits, since the proceeds of a catch were always divided up at the end of a hunting voyage, and every man's share depended on the number and size of the whales caught. Brenn must have asked his crew to forgo its share in this small catch in the hope that the South Ice would yield a better one. Whaling men normally came into a dock with plenty of credit and they liked to spend it. Whalers with no credit were surly and quick tempered. Arflane realised that Brenn would be aware of this and must be worrying how he would be able to control his crew during its stay in Friesgalt.

"Where are you berthing?" he asked quietly, watching as the first of the calves was swung up out of the hold. The dead calf had the marks of four or five harpoons in its hide. Its four great flippers, front and back, waved as it turned in the tackle. Like all young land-whales, there was only sparse hair on its body. Land-whales normally grew their full covering of wiry hair at maturity, after three years. As it was, this calf was twelve feet long and must weigh only a few tons.

Brenn sighed. "Well, I've good credit at the Shipsmasher hostel. I always pay in a certain amount of my profit there every time we dock in Friesgalt. My men will be looked after all right, for a few days at least, and by that time we should be ready to sail again. It depends on the sort of bargain I can make with the merchants—and how soon I can make it. I'll be out looking for the best offer tomorrow."

The Shipsmasher, named like all whaling men's hostels after a famous whale, was not the best hostel in Friesgalt. It had claims, in fact, for being the worst. It was a 'top-deck' hostel on the third level from the top, cut from ice and not from rock. Arflane realised that this was a bad time to ask his friend for a berth. Brenn must be cutting all possible corners to provision and re-equip his ship on the gamble that the South Ice would yield a better catch.

The derricks creaked as the calf was swung towards the side.

"We're getting 'em out as soon as possible," Brenn said. "There's a chance that someone will want the catch right away. The faster the better."

Brenn shouted to his first officer, a tall, thin man by the name of Olaf Bergsenn. "Take over Olaf, I'm going to the Shipsmasher. Bring the men there when you're finished. You know who to put on watch."

Bergsenn's lugubrious face did not change expression as he

nodded once and moved along the stained deck to supervise the unloading.

A gangplank had been lowered and Arflane and Brenn walked down it in short, jerky steps, watched by a knot of gloomy harpooners who lounged, harpoons across their shoulders, near the mainmast. It was a tradition that only the captain could leave the ship before the cargo had been unloaded.

When they got to the city wall, the guard recognised Arflane and let him and Brenn through. They began to descend the ramp. The ice of the ramp and the wall beside it was ingrained with powdered rock that had itself worn so that it now resembled stone. The rope rail on the other side of the ramp also showed signs of constant wear. On the far wall of the crevasse, for some distance down, Arflane could see people moving up and down the ramps, or working on the ledges. At almost every level the chasm was criss-crossed by rope bridges, and some way up the crevasse, above their heads now, was the single permanent bridge which was only used when especially needed.

As they stumbled down the ramps towards the third level Brenn smiled once or twice at Arflane, but was silent. Arflane wondered if he were intruding and asked his friend if he would like him to leave him at the Shipsmasher, but Brenn shook his head.

"I wouldn't miss a chance of seeing you, Arflane. Let me talk to Flatch, then we'll have a barrel of beer and I'll tell you all my troubles and listen to yours."

There were three whaling hostels on the third level. They walked past the first two—the King Herdarda and the Killer Pers—and came to the Shipsmasher. Like the other two, the Shipsmasher had a huge whale jawbone for a doorway and a small whale skull hanging as a sign outside.

They opened the battered door and walked straight in to the hostel's main room.

It was dark, large and high-roofed, though it gave the impression of being cramped. Its walls were covered with crudely tanned whale hides. Faulty lighting strips flickered at odd places on ceiling and walls and the place smelled strongly of ale, whalemeat and human sweat. Crude pictures of whales, whaling men and whaling ships were hung on the hides, as were harpoons, lances and the three-foot broadbladed cutlasses, similar to the one Arflane wore, that were used mainly for flenching. Some of the harpoons had been twisted into fantastic shapes telling of the death-struggles of particular whales. None of these whaling tools were crossed, for the whalemen regarded it as unlucky to cross harpoons or flenching cutlasses.

Groups of whaling men lounged at the closely-packed tables, sitting on hard benches and drinking a beer that was brewed from one of the many kinds of weed found in the warm ponds.

31

This ale was extremely bitter and few but whaling men would drink it.

Arflane and Brenn walked through the clusters of tables up to the small counter. Behind it, in a cubby hole, sat a shadowy figure who rose as they approached.

Flatch, the owner of the Shipsmasher, had been a whaling man years before. He was taller than Arflane but almost unbelievably obese, with a great belly and enormously fat arm and leg. He had only one eye, one ear, one arm and one leg, as if a huge knife had been used to sheer off everything down one side of him. He had lost these various organs and limbs in an encounter with the whale called Shipsmasher, a huge bull that he had been the first to harpoon. The whale had been killed, but Flatch had been unable to carry on whaling and had bought the hostel out of his share of the proceeds. As a tribute to his kill he had named the hostel after it. As recompense he had used the whale's ivory to replace his arm and leg, and a triangle of its hide was used as a patch for his missing eye.

Flatch's remaining eye peered through the layers of fat surrounding it and he raised his whalebone arm in greeting.

"Captain Arflane. Captain Brenn." His voice was high and unpleasant, but at the same time barely audible, as if it was forced to travel up through all the fat around his throat. His many chins moved slightly as he spoke, but it was impossible to tell if he greeted them with any particular feeling.

"Good morning, Flatch," Brenn said cordially. "You'll remember the beer and provisions I've supplied you with all these past seasons?"

"I do, Captain Brenn."

"I've need of the credit for a few days. My men must be fed, boozed and whored here until I'm ready to sail for the South Ice. I've had bad luck in the north. I ask you only fair return for what I've invested, no more."

Flatch parted his fat lips and his jowls moved up and down. "You'll get it, Captain Brenn. Your help saw me through a bad time for two seasons. Your men will be looked after."

Brenn grinned, as if in relief. He seemed to have been expecting an argument. "I'll want a room for myself," he said. He turned to Arflane. "Where are you staying, Arflane?"

"I have a room in a hostel some levels down," Konrad Arflane told him.

"How many in your crew, captain?" Flatch asked.

Brenn told him, and answered the few other questions Flatch asked him. He began to relax more, glancing around the hostel's main room, looking at some of the pictures on the walls.

As he was finishing with Flatch a man got up from a nearby table and took several steps towards them before stopping and confronting them.

He cradled a long, heavy harpoon in one massive arm and

the other hand was on his hip. His face, even in the poor, flickering light, could be seen to be red, mottled and ravaged by wind, sun and frostbite. It was a near-fleshless head and the bones jutted like the ribs of a ship. His nose was long and narrow, like the inverted prow of a clipper, and there was a deep scar under his right eye and another on his left cheek. His hair was black, piled and plaited on his head in a kind of coiled pyramid that broke at the top into two stiff pieces resembling the fins of a whale or seal. This strange hairstyle was held in place by clotted blubber and its smell was strong. His furs were of fine quality, but matted with whale blood and blubber, smelling rancidly; the jacket was open to the neck, revealing a whale-tooth necklace. From both ear lobes were suspended pieces of flat, carved ivory. He wore boots of soft leather, drawn up to the knee and fastened against his fur breeches by means of bone pins. Around his waist was a broad belt, from which hung a scabbarded cutlass and a large pouch. He seemed a savage, even amongst whaling men, but he had a powerful presence, partially due to his narrow eyes, which were cold, glinting blue.

"You're sailing to the South Ice, did I hear you say, skipper?" His voice was deep and harsh. "To the south?"

"Aye." Brenn looked the man up and down. "And I'm fully crewed—or as fully crewed as I can afford."

The huge man nodded and moved his tongue inside his mouth before spitting into a spittoon near the counter. The spittoon had been made from a whale's cranium. "I'm not asking for a berth, skipper. I'm my own man. Captains ask me to sail with them, not the other way about. I'm Urquart."

Arflane had already recognised the man, but Brenn by some fluke could never have seen him. Brenn's expression changed. "Urquart—Long Lance Urquart. I'm honoured to meet you." Urquart was known as the greatest harpooner in the history of the icelands. He was rumoured to have killed more than twenty bull whales single-handed.

Urquart moved his head slightly, as if acknowledging Brenn's compliment. "Aye." He spat again and looked broodingly at the cranium spittoon. "I'm a South Ice man myself. You hunt the North Ice mainly, I hear."

"Mainly," Brenn agreed, "but I know the South Ice well enough." His tone was puzzled, though he was too polite, or too over-awed, to ask Urquart directly why he had addressed him.

Urquart leaned on his harpoon, clutching it with both big, bony hands and sucking in his lips. The harpoon was ten feet long, and its many barbs were six inches or more across, curving down for nearly two feet of its length, with a big metal ring fixed beneath them where tackle was tied.

"There's a great many North Ice men have turned to the

South Ice this season as well as last," said Urquart. "They've found few fish, Captain Brenn."

Whaling men—particularly harpooners—invariably called whales 'fish' in a spirit of studied disdain for the huge mammals.

"You mean the hunting's poor there, too." Brenn's face clouded.

"Not as poor as on the North Ice, from what I hear," Urquart said slowly. "But I only tell you because you seem about to take a risk. I've seen many skippers—good ones like yourself —do the same. I speak friendly, Captain Brenn. The luck is bad, both north and south. A decent herd's not been sighted all season. The fish are moving south, beyond our range. Our ships follow them further and further. Soon it'll not be possible to provision for long enough voyages." Urquart paused, and then he added, "The fish are leaving."

"Why tell me this?" Brenn said, half-angry with Urquart in his disappointment.

"Because you're Konrad Arflane's friend," Urquart said without looking at Arflane, who had never met him in his life before, had only seen him at a distance.

Arflane was astonished. "You don't know me, man . . ."

"I know your actions," Urquart murmured, then drew in a deep breath as if the talking had winded him. He turned slowly on his heel and walked with a long, loping stride towards the door, ducked his head beneath the top of the frame and was gone.

Brenn snorted and shifted his feet. He slapped his leg several times and then frowned at Arflane. "What was he talking about?"

Arflane leaned back against the counter. " I don't know, Brenn. But if Urquart warned you that the fishing is poor on the South Ice, you should heed that."

Brenn laughed briefly and bitterly. "I can't afford to heed it, Arflane. I'll just pray all night to the Ice Mother and hope she gives me better luck. It's all I can do, man!" His voice had risen almost to a shout.

Flatch had reseated himself in his cubby-hole behind the counter, but he rose, looking like some monstrous beast himself, and glanced enquiringly with his single eye as Brenn faced him again and ordered whale steaks with seka weed and a barrel of beer to be brought to them at their table.

Later, after Brenn's men had come in and been cheered by the discovery that Flatch was willing to provide them with everything they needed, Arflane and Brenn sat opposite each other at a side table with the beer barrel against the wall. Every so often they would turn the spiggot and replenish their cups. The cups were unbreakable, fashioned of some ancient plastic substance. The beer did not, as they had hoped, improve their spirits, although Brenn managed to look confident enough whenever any of his men addressed him through the shadowy gloom of the hostel room.

The beer had in fact succeeded in turning Brenn in on himself and he was uncommunicative, constantly twisting his head round to look at the door, which had now been closed. Arflane knew that Brenn was expecting no one.

At last he leaned over the table and said, "Urquart seemed a gloomy individual, Brenn—perhaps even mad. He sees the bad luck of everything. I've been here for some days, and I've seen the catches unloaded. They're smaller than usual certainly, but not that small. We've both had as poor catches and they've done us no harm in the long term. It happened to me for several seasons running and then I had plenty of luck for another three. The owners were worried, but . . ."

Brenn looked up from his cup. "There you have it, Arflane. I'm my own master now. The *Tender Maiden's* mine. I bought her two seasons back." Again he laughed bitterly. "I thought I was doing a sensible thing seeing that so many of us have had our ships sold over our heads in past years. It looks as if I'll be selling my own craft over my own head at this rate, or hiring out to some Friesgaltian merchant. I'll have no choice. And there's my crew—willing to gamble with me. Do I tell them Urquart's news? They've wives and children, as I have. Shall I tell them?"

"It would do no good," Arflane said quietly.

"And where are the fish going?" Brenn continued. He put his cup down heavily. "What's happening to the herds?"

"Urquart said they're going south. Perhaps the clever man will be the one who learns how to follow them—how to live off what provisions he can find on the ice. There are more warm ponds to the south—possibly a means of tracking the herds could be devised . . ."

"Will that help me this season?"

"I don't know," Arflane admitted. He was thinking now about his conversation aboard the *Ice Spirit* and he began to feel even more depressed.

Flatch's whores came down to the main room of the hostel. Flatch had done nothing by halves. There was a girl for every man, including Arflane and Brenn. Katarina, Flatch's youngest daughter, a girl of eighteen, approached them, holding the hand of another girl who was as dark and pretty as Flatch's daughter was fair and plain. Katarina introduced the other girl as Maji.

Arflane attempted to sound jovial. "Here," he said to Brenn, "here's someone to cheer you up."

Leaning back, with the drunken, dark haired girl Maji

cuddled against his chest, Brenn roared with laughter at his own joke. The girl giggled. On the other side of the table, Arflane smiled and stroked Katarina's hair. She was a warm hearted girl and able instinctively to make men relax. Maji winked up at Brenn. The women had succeeded, where Arflane had failed, in restoring Brenn's natural optimism.

It was very late. The air was stale and hot and the hostel room was noisy with the drunken voices of the whalers. Through the poor, flickering light Arflane could see their fur-clad silhouettes reeling from table to table or sitting slumped on the benches. Brenn's crew was not the only one in the Ship-smasher. There were men from two other ships there; a Fries-galtian North Ice whaler and another North Icer from Abers-galt. If South Ice men had been there there might have been trouble, but these crews seemed to be mingling well with Brenn's men. Out of the press of bulky bodies rose the long lances of the harpooners, swaying like slender masts in a high wind, their barbed tips casting distorted shadows in the shud-dering light from the faulty strips. There were thumps as men fell or knocked over barrels. There was the smell of spilled, bitter beer which ran over the tables and swamped the floor. Arflane heard the giggles of the girls and the harsh laughter of the men and, though the temperature was too warm for his own comfort, he felt himself begin to relax now that he was in the company of men that he understood. Off-ship, crews had more or less equal status with the officers, and this contributed to the free and easy atmosphere in the Shipsmasher.

Arflane poured himself another cup of beer as Brenn began a fresh story.

The outer door opened suddenly and cold air blew in, making Arflane shiver, though he was grateful for it. Silence fell as the men turned. The door slammed shut and a man of medium height, swathed in a heavy sealskin cloak, began to walk between the tables.

He was not a whaling man.

That could be judged from the cut of his cloak, the way he walked, the texture of his skin. His hair was short and dark, cut in a fringe over his eyes and scarcely reaching to the nape of his neck. There was a gold bracelet curving up his right fore-arm and a silver ring on the second finger of his right hand. He moved casually, but somewhat deliberately, and had a slight, ironic smile on his lips. He was handsome and fairly young. He nodded a greeting to the men who still stared at him suspiciously.

One heavily built harpooner opened his mouth and laughed at the young man, and others began to laugh, too. The young man raised his eyebrows and put his head on one side, looking at them coolly.

"I'm seeking Captain Arflane." His voice was melodious and aristocratic, with a Friesgalt accent. "I heard he was here."

"I'm Arflane. What do you want?" Konrad Arflane looked with some hostility at the young man.

"I'm Manfred Rorsefne. May I join you?"

Arflane shrugged and Rorsefne came and sat on the bench next to Katarina Flatch.

"Have a drink," said Arflane, pushing his full cup towards Rorsefne. He realised, as he made the movement, that he was quite drunk. This realisation made him pause and rub his forehead. When he looked up at Manfred Rorsefne, he was glowering.

Rorsefne shook his head. "No thank you, captain. I'm not in a drinking mood. I wanted to speak with you alone if that is possible."

Suddenly petulant, Arflane said, "It is not. I'm enjoying the company of my friends. What is a Rorsefne doing in a top-deck hostel anyway?"

"Looking for you, obviously." Manfred Rorsefne sighed theatrically. "And looking for you at this hour because it is important. However," he began to rise, "I will come to your hostel in the morning. I am sorry for intruding, captain." He glanced at Katarina Flatch a trifle cynically.

As Rorsefne made his way towards the door, one of the men thrust a harpoon shaft in front of his legs and he tripped and stumbled. He tried to recover his balance, but another shaft took him in the back and sent him sprawling. He fell as the whalers laughed raucously.

Arflane watched expressionlessly. Even an aristocrat was not safe in a whaling hostel if he had no connection with whaling. Manfred Rorsefne was simply paying for his folly.

The big harpooner who had first laughed at Rorsefne now stood up and grabbed the young man by the collar of his cloak. The cloak came away and the harpooner staggered back, laughing drunkenly. Another joined him, a stocky, red-headed man, and reached down to grab Rorsefne's jacket. But Rorsefne rolled over to face the man, his smile still ironic, and tried to get to his feet.

Brenn leaned forward to see what was going on. He glanced at Arflane. "D'you want me to stop them?"

Arflane shook his head. "It's his own fault. He's a fool for coming here."

"I've never heard of an intrusion like it," Brenn agreed, settling back.

Rorsefne was now on his feet, reaching past the red-headed whaleman towards the sealskin cloak held by the big harpooner. "I'll thank you for my cloak," he said, his tone light, but shaking slightly.

"That's our payment for your entertainment," grinned the harpooner. "You can go now."

Rorsefne's eyes were hooded as he folded his arms across his chest. Arflane admired him for taking a stand.

"It would seem," said Rorsefne quietly, "that I have given you more entertainment than you have given me." His voice was now firm.

Arflane got up on impulse and squeezed past Flatch's daughter to stand to the left of the harpooner. Arflane was so drunk that he had to lean for a moment against the edge of a table.

"Give him the cloak, lad," he said, his voice slurring. "And let's get on with our drinking. The boy's not worth our trouble."

The big harpooner ignored Arflane and continued to grin at the young aristocrat, dangling the rich cloak in one hand, teasing him. Arflane lurched forward and grabbed the cloak out of the man's hand. The harpooner turned, grunting, and hit Arflane across the face. Brenn stood up from his corner, shouting at his man, but the harpooner ignored him and bent to pick up the cloak from where it had fallen. Perhaps encouraged by Arflane's action, Manfred Rorsefne also stooped forward towards the cloak. The red-headed whaleman hit him. Rorsefne reeled and then struck back.

Arflane, sobered somewhat by the blow, took hold of the harpooner by the shoulder, swung him round, and punched him in the face. Brenn came scrambling over the table, shouting incoherently and trying to stop the fight before it went too far. He attempted to pull Arflane and the harpooner apart.

The Friesgalt whalemen were now yelling angrily, siding, perhaps for the sake of the fight, with Manfred Rorsefne who was wrestling with the red-headed whaler.

The fight became confused. Screaming girls gathered their skirts about them and made for the back room of the hostel. Harpoons were used like quarter-staves to batter at heads and bodies.

Arflane saw Brenn go down with a blow on the head and tried to reach his friend. Every whaleman in the hostel seemed to be against him. He struck out in all directions but was soon overcome by their numbers. Even as he fell to the floor, still fighting, he felt the cold air come through the door again and wondered who had entered.

Then a great roaring voice, like the noise of the north wind at its height, sounded over the din of the fight. Arflane felt the whaleman's hands leave him and got up, wiping blood from his eyes. His ears were ringing as the voice he had heard roared again.

"Fish, you cave-bound fools! Fish, I tell you! Fish, you dog-hunters! Fish, you beer-swillers! Fish to take the rust off your lances! A herd of a hundred or more, not fifty miles distant at sou'-sou'-west!"

Blinking through the blood, which came from a shallow cut on his forehead, Arflane saw that the speaker was the man he and Brenn had encountered earlier—Long Lance Urquart.

Urquart had one arm curled around his great harpoon and the other around the shoulders of a half-grown boy who looked both excited and embarrassed. The lad wore a single plait, coated with whale grease, and a white bearskin coat that showed by its richness that he was a whaling hand, probably a cabin boy.

"Tell them, Stefan," Urquart said, more softly now that he could be heard.

The boy spoke in a stutter, pointing back through the still open doorway into the night. "Our ship passed them coming in at dusk. We were loaded up and could not stop, for we had to make Friesgalt by nightfall. But we saw them. Heading from north to south, on a line roughly twenty degrees west. A big herd. My father—our skipper—says there hasn't been a bigger in twenty seasons."

Arflane bent to help Brenn who was staggering to his feet, clutching his head.

"Did you hear that, Brenn?"

"I did." Brenn smiled in spite of his bruised, swollen lips. "The Ice Mother's good to us."

"There's enough out there for every ship in the dock," Urquart continued, "and more besides. They're travelling fast, from what the lad's father says, but good sailing should catch 'em."

Arflane looked around the room, trying to find Manfred Rorsefne. He saw him leaning against a wall, a flenching cutlass, that had obviously been one of the wall's ornaments, clutched in his right hand. He still wore his ironic smile. Arflane looked at him thoughtfully.

Urquart, also, turned his attention from the men and looked surprised when he saw Rorsefne there. The expression passed quickly and his gaunt features became frozen again. He took his arm from the boy's shoulders and shifted his harpoon to cradle it in his other arm. He walked towards Manfred Rorsefne and took the cutlass from him.

"Thanks," said Rorsefne grinning, "it was becoming heavy."

"What were you doing in this place?" Urquart asked brusquely. Arflane was surprised by his familiarity with the youth.

Rorsefne nodded his head in Arflane's direction. "I came to give a message to Captain Arflane, but he was busy with his friends. Some others decided I should give them some entertainment since I was here. Captain Arflane and I seemed agreed that they had had enough..."

Urquart's narrow, blue eyes turned to look carefully at Arflane. "You helped him, captain?"

Arflane let his face show his disgust. "He was a fool to come alone to a place like this. If you know him take him home, Urquart."

The men were beginning to leave the hostel, pulling their hoods about their heads, picking up their harpoons as they hurried back to their ships, knowing that their skippers would want to sail with the first light.

Brenn clapped Arflane on the shoulder. "I must go. We've enough provisions for a short haul. It was good to see you, Arflane."

In the company of two of his harpooners, Brenn left the hostel. Save for Urquart, Rorsefne and Arflane, the place was now empty.

Flatch came stumping down between the overturned tables, his gross body swaying from side to side. He was followed by three of his daughters who began to clean up the mess. They appeared to take it for granted. Flatch watched them work and did not approach the three men.

Urquart's strangely arranged hair threw a huge shadow on the far wall, by the door. Arflane had not noticed before how closely it resembled the tail of a land-whale.

"So you helped another Rorsefne," Urquart murmured, "though once again you had no need to."

Arflane rubbed his damaged forehead. "I was drunk. I didn't interfere for his sake."

"It was a good fight, however," Manfred Rorsefne said lightly. "I did not realise I could fight so well."

"They were playing." Arflane's tone was weary and contemptuous.

Gravely, Urquart nodded in agreement. He shifted his grip on his harpoon and looked directly at Rorsefne. "They were playing with you," he repeated.

"Then it was a good game, cousin," Rorsefne said, looking up into Urquart's bleak eyes. "Eh?" The Long Lance's tall, gaunt figure was immobile, the features composed. His eyes looked towards the door. Arflane wondered why Rorsefne called Urquart 'cousin', for it was unlikely that there was a true blood-link between the aristocrat and the savage harpooner.

"I will escort you both back to the deeper levels," said Urquart slowly.

"What's the danger now?" Manfred Rorsefne asked him. "None. We'll go alone, cousin, and then perhaps I'll be able to deliver my message to Captain Arflane after all."

Urquart shrugged, turned and left the hostel without a word.

Manfred grinned at Arflane who merely scowled in return.

"A moody man, cousin Long Lance. Now, captain, would you be willing to listen while I tell you what I came to say?"

Arflane spat into the whale cranium nearby. "It can do no harm," he said.

As they walked carefully down the sloping ramps to the lower levels, avoiding the drunken whalers who staggered past them on their way upwards, Manfred Rorsefne said nothing and Arflane was too bored and tired to ask him directly what his message was. The effects of the beer had worn off, and the pains in his bruised body were beginning to make themselves felt. The shadowy figures of the whalers, hurrying back to their ships through the dim light, could be seen both in front of them and behind them. Occasionally a man shouted, but for the most part the whalers moved in comparative silence, though the constant shuffle of their ridged boots on the causeways echoed around the crevasse. Here and there a man clung to the swaying guard ropes, having staggered too close to the edge. It was not unusual for drunken sailors to lose their footing and fall to the mysterious bottom of the gorge.

Only when Arflane stopped at the entrance to his hostel and the last of the whalers had gone by did Rorsefne speak.

"My uncle's better. He seems eager to see you."

"Your uncle?"

"Pyotr Rorsefne. He is better."

"When does he want to see me?"

"Now, if it's convenient."

"I'm too tired. Your fight . . ."

"I apologise, but I had no intention of involving you . . ."

"You should not have gone to the Shipsmasher. You knew that."

"True. The mistake was mine, captain. In fact if cousin Long Lance had not brought his good news, I could have your death on my conscience now . . ."

"Don't be stupid," Arflane said disdainfully. "Why d'you call Urquart your cousin?"

"It embarrasses him. It's a family secret. I'm not supposed to tell anyone that Urquart is my uncle's natural son. Are you coming to our quarters? You could sleep there, if you're so tired, and see my uncle first thing in the morning."

Arflane shrugged and followed Manfred Rorsefne down the ramp. He was half-asleep and half-drunk and the memory which kept recurring as he walked was not that of Pyotr Rorsefne, but of his daugher.

CHAPTER FIVE

THE RORSEFNE HOUSEHOLD

Waking in a bed that was too soft and too hot, Konrad Arflane looked dazedly about the small room. It was lined with rich wall-hangings of painted canvas depicting famous Rorsefne ships on their voyages and hunts. Here a four-masted schooner was attacked by gigantic land whales, there a whale was slain by a captain with poised harpoon; elsewhere ships floundered in ice breaks or approached cities across the panorama of the ice; old wars were fought, old victories glorified; valiant Rorsefne men were at all times in the forefront, usually managing to bear the Rorsefne flag. Action and violence were on all sides.

There was a trace of humour in Arflane's expression as he stared round at the paintings. He sat up, pushing the furs away from his naked body. His clothes lay on a bench against the wall nearest the door. He swung his legs to the floor and stood up, walking across the carpet of fur to where a wash-stand had been prepared for him. As he washed, dousing himself in cold water, he realised that his memory of how he had arrived here was vague. He must have been very drunk to have agreed to Manfred Rorsefne's suggestion that he stay the night. He could not understand how he had come to accept the invitation. As he dressed, pulling on the tight undergarments of soft leather and struggling into his jacket and trousers, he wondered if he would see Ulrica Ulsenn that day.

Someone knocked and then Manfred Rorsefne entered, wearing a fur cloak dyed in red and blue squares. He smiled quizzically at Arflane.

"Well captain? Are you feeling any ill-effects?"

"I was drunk, I suppose," Arflane said resentfully, as if blaming the young man. "Do we see old Rorsefne now?"

"Breakfast first, I think." Manfred led him into a wide passage that was also covered in dark, painted wall hangings. They passed through a door at the end and entered a large room in the centre of which was a square table made of beautifully carved whale ivory. On the table were several loaves of a kind of bread made from warm-pond weed, dishes of whale, seal and bear meat, a full tureen containing a stew, and a large jug of *hess*, which had a taste similar to tea.

Already seated at the table was Ulrica Ulsenn, wearing a simple dress of black and red leather. She glanced up as Arflane entered, gave him a shy smile and looked down at her plate.

"Good morning," Arflane said gruffly.

42

"Good morning." Her voice was almost inaudible. Manfred Rorsefne pulled back the chair next to hers.

"Would you care to sit here, captain?"

Uneasily, Arflane went to sit down. As he pulled his chair in to the table, his knee brushed hers. They both recoiled at once. On the opposite side of the table Manfred Rorsefne was helping himself to seal-meat and bread. He glanced humorously at his cousin and Arflane. Two female servants came into the room. They were dressed in long brown dresses, with the Rorsefne insignia on the sleeves.

One of them remained in the background; the other stepped forward and curtsied. Ulrica Ulsenn smiled at her. "Some more *hess*, please, Mirayn."

The girl took the half-empty jug from the table. "Is everything else in order, my lady?"

"Yes, thank you." Ulrica glanced at Arflane. "Is there anything you lack, captain?"

Arflane shook his head.

As the servants were leaving, Janek Ulsenn pushed in past them. He saw Arflane beside his wife and nodded brusquely, then sat down and began to serve himself from the dishes.

There was an unmistakable atmosphere of tension in the room. Arflane and Ulrica Ulsenn avoided looking at each other. Janek Ulsenn glowered, but did not lift his eyes from his food; Manfred Rorsefne looked amusedly at all of them, adding, it would seem deliberately, to their discomfort.

"I hear a big herd's been sighted," Janek Ulsenn said at last, addressing Manfred and ignoring his wife and Arflane.

"I was one of the first to hear the news," Manfred smiled. "Wasn't I, Captain Arflane?"

Arflane made a noise through his nose and continued to eat. He was embarrassingly aware of Ulrica Ulsenn's presence so close to him.

"Are we sending a ship?" Manfred asked Janek Ulsenn. "We ought to. There's plenty of fish for all, by the sound of it. We ought to go ourselves—we could take the two-mast schooner and enjoy the hunt for as long as it lasted."

Ulrica seemed to welcome the suggestion. "A splendid idea, Manfred. Father's better, so he won't need me. I'll come, too." Her eyes sparkled. "I haven't seen a hunt for three seasons!"

Janek Ulsenn rubbed his nose and frowned. "I've no time to spare for a foolhardy pleasure voyage."

"We could be back within a day." Manfred's tone was eager. "We'll go, Ulrica, if Janek hasn't the spirit for it. Captain Arflane can take command ..."

Arflane scowled. "Lord Ulsenn chose the right word—foolhardy. A yacht—with a woman on board—whale-hunting! I'd take no such responsibility. I'd advise you to forget

43

the idea. All it would need would be for one bull to turn and your boat would be smashed in seconds."

"Don't be dull, captain," Manfred admonished. "Ulrica will come, anyway. Won't you, Ulrica?"

Ulrica Ulsenn shrugged slightly. "If Janek has no objection."

"I have," Ulsenn muttered.

"You are right to advise her against a trip like that," Arflane said. He was unwilling to join forces with Ulsenn, but in this case he knew it was his duty. There was a good chance that a yacht would be destroyed in the hunt.

Ulsenn straightened up, his eyes resentful. "But if you wish to go, Ulrica," he said firmly, staring hard at Arflane, "you may do so."

Arflane shifted his own gaze so that he looked directly into Ulsenn's eyes. "In which case, I feel that you must have an experienced man in command. I'll skipper the craft."

"You must come too, cousin Janek," Manfred put in banteringly. "You have a duty to our people. They will respect you the more if they see that you are willing to face danger."

"I do not care what they think," Ulsenn said, glaring at Manfred Rorsefne. "I am not afraid of danger. I am busy. Someone has to run your father's affairs while he is ill!"

"One day is all you would lose." Manfred was plainly taunting the man.

Ulsenn paused, evidently torn between decisions. He got up from the table, his breakfast unfinished.

"I'll consider it," he said as he left the room.

Ulrica Ulsenn rose.

"You deliberately upset him, Manfred. You have offended him and embarrassed Captain Arflane. You must apologise."

Manfred made a mock bow to Arflane. "I am sorry, captain."

Arflane looked thoughtfully up into Ulrica Ulsenn's beautiful face. She flushed and left the room in the direction her husband had taken.

As the door closed, Manfred burst into laughter. "Forgive me, captain. Janek is so pompous and Ulrica hates him as much as I do. But Ulrica is so *loyal*!"

"A rare quality," Arflane said dryly.

"Oh, indeed!" Manfred got up from the table. "Now. We'll go to see the only one of them who is worth any loyalty."

Heads of bear, walrus, whale and wolf decorated the skin-covered walls of the large bedroom. At the far end was the high, wide bed and in it, propped against folded furs, lay Pyotr Rorsefne. His bandaged hands lay on the bed covers; apart from some faint scars on his face, these were the only sign that he had been so close to death. His face was red and healthy, his eyes bright, and his movements alert as he turned his head to look towards Arflane and Manfred Rorsefne. His great mane of grey hair was combed and fell to his shoulders. He now had a heavy moustache and beard; both were nearly snow white. His body, what Arflane could see of it, had filled out and it was hard to believe that such a recovery could have been possible. Arflane credited the miracle to the old man's natural vitality and love of life, rather than to any care he had received. Momentarily, he wondered why Rorsefne was still in bed.

"Hello, Arflane. I recognise you, you see!" His voice was rich and vibrant, with all trace of weakness gone. "I'm well again—or as well as I'll ever be. Forgive this manner of meeting, but those milksops think I won't be able to get my balance. Lost the feet—but the rest I kept."

Arflane nodded, responding against his will to the old man's friendliness.

Manfred brought up a chair from a corner of the room.

"Sit down," Pyotr Rorsefne said. "We'll talk. You can leave us now, Manfred."

Arflane seated himself beside the bed and Manfred, reluctantly it seemed, left the room.

"You and I thwarted the Ice Mother," Rorsefne smiled, looking closely at Arflane. "What do you feel about that, captain?"

"A man has a right to try to preserve his life for as long as possible," Arflane replied. "The Ice Mother surely does not resent having to wait a little longer."

"It used to be thought that no man should interfere in another man's life—or his death. It used to be said that if a man was about to be taken by the Ice Mother then it was no one's right to thwart her. That was the old philosophy."

"I know. Perhaps I'm as soft as some of the others I've condemned while I've been here."

"You've condemned us, have you?"

"I see a turning away from the Ice Mother. I see disaster resulting from that, sir."

"You hold with the old ideas, not the new ones. You do not believe the ice is melting?"

"I do not, sir."

A small table stood beside the bed. On it was a large chart box, writing materials, a jug of *hess* and a cup. Pyotr Rorsefne reached toward the cup. Arflane forestalled him, poured some *hess* from the jug, and handed him the drink. Rorsefne grunted his thanks. His expression was thoughtful and calculating as he looked into Arflane's face.

Konrad Arflane stared back, boldly enough. This man was one he believed he could understand. Unlike the rest of his family, he did not make Arflane feel uncomfortable.

"I own many ships," Rorsefne murmured.

"I know. Many more than actually sail."

"Something else you disapprove of, captain? The big clippers not at work. Yet you're aware, I'm sure, that if I set them to hunting and trading, we should reduce all your other cities to poverty within a decade."

"You're generous." Arflane found it surprising that Rorsefne should boast about his charity; it did not seem to fit with the rest of his character.

"I'm wise." Rorsefne gesticulated with one bandaged hand. "Friesgalt needs the competition as much as your city and its like need the trade. Already we're too fat, soft, complacent. You agree, I think."

Arflane nodded.

"It's the way of things," Rorsefne sighed. "Once a city becomes so powerful, it begins to decline. It lacks stimulus. We are reaching the point, here on the plateau of the eight cities, where we have nothing left to spur us on. What's more, the game is leaving. I see death for all in not too short a time, Arflane."

Arflane shrugged. "It's the Ice Mother's will. It must happen sooner or later. I'm not sure that I follow all your reasoning, but I do know that the softer people become the less chance they have of survival . . ."

"If the natural conditions are softer, then the people can afford to become so," Rorsefne said quietly. "And our scientists tell us that the level of the ice is dropping, that the weather is improving, season by season."

"I once saw a great line of ice-cliffs on the horizon," Arflane interrupted. "I was astonished. There'd never been cliffs there before—particularly ones that stood on their peaks, with their bases in the clouds. I began to doubt all I knew about the world. I went home and told them what I had seen. They laughed at me. They said that what I had seen was an illusion —something to do with light—and that if I went to look the next day the cliffs would be gone. I went the next day. The cliffs were gone. I knew then that I could not always trust my senses, but that I could trust what I knew to be right within me. I know that the ice is not melting. I know that your scientists have been deceived, as I was, by illusions."

Rorsefne sighed. "I would like to agree with you, Arflane . . ."

"But you do not. I have had this argument already."

"No, I meant it. I want to agree with you. It is simply that I need proof, one way or the other."

"Proof surrounds you. The natural course is towards utter coldness and death. The sun must die and the wind must blow us into the night."

"I've read that there were other ages when ice covered the

46

world and then disappeared." Rorsefne straightened his back and leaned forward. "What of those?"

"They were only the beginning. Two or three times, the Ice Mother was driven back. But she was stronger, and had patience. You know the answers. They are in the creed."

"The scientists say that again her power is waning."

"That cannot be. Her total domination of all matter is inevitable."

"You quote the creed. Have you no doubts?"

Arflane got up from his seat. "None."

"I envy you."

"That, too, has already been said to me. There is nothing to envy. Perhaps it is better to believe in an illusion."

"I cannot believe in it, Arflane." Rorsefne leant forward his bandaged hands reaching for Arflane's arm. "Wait. I told you I needed proof. I know, I think, where that proof may be found."

"Where?"

"Where I went with my ship and my crew. Where I returned from. A city—many months travel from here, to the distant north. New York. Have you heard of it?"

Arflane laughed. "A myth. I spoke of illusions . . ,"

"I've seen it—from a distance, true, but there was no doubting its existence. My men saw it. We were short of provisions and under attack from barbarians. We were forced to turn before we could get closer. I planned to go back with a fleet. I saw New York, where the Ice Ghosts have their court. The city of the Ice Mother. A city of marvels. I saw its buildings rising tier upon tier into the sky."

"I know the tale. The city was drowned by water and then frozen, preserved complete beneath the ice. An impossible legend. I may believe in the doctrines of the Ice Mother, my lord, but I am not so superstitious . . ."

"It is true. I have seen New York. Its towers thrust upwards from a gleaming field of smooth ice. There is no telling how deep they go. Perhaps the Ice Mother's court is there, perhaps that part is a myth . . . But if the city has been preserved, then its knowledge has been preserved too. One way or the other, Arflane, the proof I spoke of is in New York."

Arflane was perplexed, wondering if the old man's fever were still with him.

Rorsefne seemed to guess his thoughts. He laughed, tapping the chart box. "I'm sane, captain. Everything is in here. With a good ship—better than the one I took—New York can be reached and the truth discovered."

Arflane sat down again. "How was the first ship wrecked?"

Rorsefne sighed. "A series of misfortunes—ice-breaks, shifting cliffs, land whale attacks, the attacks of the barbarians. Finally, ascending to the plateau up the Great North Course,

47

the ship could stand no more and fell apart, killing most of us. The rest set off to walk to Friesgalt, the boats being crushed, hoping we should meet a ship. We did not. Soon, only I remained alive."

"So bad luck was the cause of the wreck?"

"Essentially. A better ship would not suffer such luck."

"You know this city's location?"

"More—I have the whole course plotted."

"How did you know where to go?"

"It wasn't difficult. I read the old books, compared the locations they gave."

"And now you want to take a fleet there?"

"No." Rorsefne sank back on the furs. "I would be a hindrance on such a voyage. I went secretly the first time, because I wanted no rumours spreading to disturb the people. At a time of stress, such news could destroy the stability of our entire society. I think it best to keep the city a secret until one ship has been to New York and discovered what knowledge the city actually does hold. I intend to send the *Ice Spirit.*"

"She's the best ship in the eight cities."

"They say a ship's as good as her master," Rorsefne murmured. His strength was beginning to fail him, it appeared. "I know of no better master than yourself, Captain Arflane. I trust you—and your reputation is good."

Arflane did not refuse immediately, as he had expected he would. He had half anticipated the old man's suggestion, but he was not sure that Rorsefne was completely sane. Perhaps he too had seen a mirage of some kind, or a line of mountains that had looked like a city frim a distance. Yet the idea of New York, the thought of discovering the mythical palace of the Ice Mother and of verifying his own instinctive knowledge of the inevitability of the ice's rule, appealed to him and excited his imagination. He had, after all, nothing to keep him on the plateau; the quest was a noble one, almost a holy one. To go north toward the home of the Ice Mother, to sail, like the mariners of ancient times, on a great voyage of many months, seeking knowledge that might change the world, suited his essentially romantic nature. What was more he would command the finest ship in the world, sailing across unknown seas of ice, discovering new races of men if Rorsefne's talk of barbarians were true. New York, the fabled city, whose tall towers jutted from a plain of smooth ice . . . What if after all it did not exist? He would sail on and on, farther and farther north, while everything else travelled south.

Rorsefne's eyes were half-closed now. His appearance of health had been deceptive; plainly, he had exhausted himself.

Arflane got up for the second time.

"I have agreed—against my better judgment—to captain a

yacht in which your family intend to follow a whale hunt today."

Rorsefne smiled weakly. "Ulrica's idea?"

"Manfred's. He has somehow committed Lord Janek Ulsenn, your daughter and myself to the scheme. Your daughter supported Manfred. As head of the family you should . . ."

"It is not your affair, captain. I know you speak from good will, but Manfred and Ulrica know what is right for them. Rorsefne stock breeds best encountering danger—it needs to seek it out." Rorsefne paused, studying Arflane's face again, frowning a little curiously. "I should not have thought it like you to offer unasked for advice, captain . . ."

"It is not my way, normally." Arflane himself was now perplexed. "I don't know why I mentioned this. I apologise." He was not acting in a normal fashion at all, he realised. What was causing the change?

For a moment he saw the whole Rorsefne family as representing danger for him, but the danger was nebulous. He felt a faint stirring of panic and rubbed his bearded chin rapidly. Looking down into Rorsefne's face, he saw that the man was smiling very slightly. The smile seemed sympathetic.

"Is Janek going, did you say?" Rorsefne asked suddenly, breaking the mood.

"It seems so."

Rorsefne laughed quietly. "I wonder how he was convinced. No matter. With luck he'll be the one killed and she'll find herself a man to marry, though they're scarce enough. You'll skipper the yacht?"

"I said I would, though I don't know why. I am doing many things that I would not do elsewhere. I am in something of a quandary, Lord Rorsefne."

"Don't worry," Rorsefne chuckled. "You're simply not adjusted to our way of doing things."

"Your nephew puzzles me. Somehow he manages to talk me into agreeing with him, when everything I feel disagrees with him. He is a subtle young man."

"He has his own kind of strength," Rorsefne said affectionately. "Do not under-estimate Manfred, captain. He appears weak, both in character and in physique, but he likes to give that appearance."

"You make him seem very mysterious," Arflane said half jokingly.

"He is more complicated than us, I think," Rorsefne replied. "He represents something new—possibly just a new generation. You dislike him, I can see. You may come to like him as much as you like my daughter."

"Now you are being mysterious, sir. I expressed no liking for anyone in particular."

Rorsefne ignored this remark. "See me after the hunt," he

said in his failing voice. "I'll show you the charts. You can tell me then if you accept the commission."

"Very well. Good-bye, sir."

Leaving the room, Arflane realised that he had been drawn irrevocably into the affairs of the Rorsefne household and that, ever since he had saved the man's life, his fate had been linked with theirs. They had somehow seduced him; made him their man. He knew that he would take the command offered by Pyotr Rorsefne just as he had taken the command of the yacht offered by Manfred Rorsefne. Without appearing to have lost any of his integrity, he was no longer his own master. Pyotr Rorsefne's strength of character. Ulrica Ulsenn's beauty and grace, Manfred Rorsefne's subtlety, even Janek Ulsenn's belligerence, had combined to trap him. Disturbed, Arflane walked back toward the breakfast room.

CHAPTER SIX

THE WHALE HUNT

Divided from the main fleet by a low wall of ice blocks, the yacht, slim-prowed and handsome, lay in her anchor lines in the private Rorsefne yard.

Tramping across the ice in the cold morning, with the sky a smoky yellow, broken by streaks of orange and a dark pink that the ice reflected, Arflane followed Manfred Rorsefne as he made his way towards the yacht through the still soft layer of snow. Behind Arflane came Janek and Ulrica Ulsenn, sitting on a small, ornate sleigh drawn by servants. Man and wife sat side by side, swathed in rich furs, their hands buried in huge muffs, their faces almost wholly hidden by their hoods.

The yacht had already been crewed, and the men were preparing to sail. A bulky, spring operated harpoon gun, rather like a giant crossbow, had been loaded and set up in the bow. The big, savage harpoon with its half-score of tapering barbs jutted out over the bowsprit, a virgin's vision of a phallus.

Arflane smiled as he looked at the heavy harpoon. It seemed too big for the slender yacht that carried it. It dominated the boat—a fore-and-aft rigged schooner—it drew all attention to itself. It was a fine, cruel harpoon.

He followed Manfred up the gangplank and was surprised to see Urquart standing there, watching them from sharp, sardonic eyes, his own harpoon cradled as always in his left arm, his gaunt features and tall body immobile until he turned his back on them suddenly and walked aft up the deck towards the wheelhouse.

Janek Ulsenn, his lips pursed and his expression one of

thinly disguised anxiety, was helping his wife on board. Arflane thought that perhaps she should be helping her husband.

A ship's officer in white and grey fur came along the deck towards the new arrivals. He addressed Manfred Rorsefne, though protocol demanded that he address the senior member of the family, Janek Ulsenn.

"We're ready to sail, sir. Will you be taking command?"

Manfred shook his head slowly and smiled, stepping aside so that he no longer stood between Arflane and the officer.

"This is Captain Arflane. He will be master on this trip. He has all powers of captain."

The officer, a stocky man in his thirties with a black, rimed beard, nodded to Arflane in recognition. "I know of you, sir. Proud to sail with you. Can I show you the ship before we loose lines?"

"Thanks." Arflane left the rest of the party and accompanied the officer towards the wheelhouse. "What's your name?"

"Haeber, sir. First officer. We have a second officer, a bosun and the usual small complement. Not a bad crew, sir."

"Used to whale hunting?"

A shadow passed across Haeber's face. He said quietly: "No, sir."

"Any of the men whaling hands?"

"Very few, sir. We have Mr. Urquart aboard, as you know, but he's a harpooner of course."

"Then your men will have to learn quickly, won't they?"

"I suppose so, sir." Haeber's tone was carefully noncommittal. For a moment it was in Arflane's mind to echo Haeber's doubt; then he spoke briskly.

"If your crew's as good as you say, Mr. Haeber, then we'll have no trouble on the hunt. I know whales. Make sure you listen carefully to every order I give and there'll be no great problems."

"Aye, aye, sir." Haeber's voice became more confident.

The yacht was small and neat. She was a fine craft of her class, but Arflane could see at once that his suspicions as to her usefulness as a whaler were justified. She would be fast—faster than the ordinary whaling vessels—but she had no strength to her. She was a brittle boat. Her runners and struts were too thin for heavy work and her hull was liable to crack on collision with an outcrop of ice, another ship, or a fully-grown whale.

Arflane decided he would take the wheel himself. This would give the crew confidence, for his helmsmanship was well known and highly regarded. But first he would let one of the officers take the ship on to the open ice while he got the feel of her. Her sails were ready for letting out and men stood by the anchor capstans along both sides of the deck.

After testing the wheel, Arflane took the megaphone Haeber handed him and climbed the companionway to the bridge above the wheelhouse.

Ahead he could see the distant outlines of ships sailing under full canvas towards the South Ice. The professional whalers were well ahead and Arflane was satisfied that at least the yacht would not get in their way before the main hunting began and the whale herd scattered. It was always at this time that the greatest confusion arose, with danger of collision as the ships set off after their individual prey. The yacht should come in after the whalers had divided and be able to select a small whale to chase—preferably some half-grown calf. Arflane sighed, annoyed at having to hunt such unmanly prey just for the sport of the aristocrats who were now traipsing along the deck towards the bridge. They were plainly planning to join him and, since the craft was theirs, they had a right to be on the bridge so long as they did not interefere with the captain's efficient command of the ship.

Arflane lifted the megaphone.

"All hands to their posts!"

The few crewmen who were not at their posts hastened to them. The others tensed, ready to obey Arflane's orders.

"Cast off all anchors!"

As one, the anchor men let go the anchor lines and the ship began to slide towards the gap in the ice wall. Her runners scraped and bumped rhythmically as she gained speed down the slight incline and passed between the ice blocks, making for the open ice.

"Ready the mains'l!"

The men in the yards of the mainmast placed their hands on their halyards.

"Let go the mains'l!"

The sail cracked open, its boom swinging as it filled out. The boat's speed doubled almost at once. At regular intervals Arflane ordered more sail on and soon the yacht was gliding over the ice under full canvas. Air slapped Arflane's face, making it tingle with cold. He breathed in deeply, savouring the sharp chill of it in his nostrils and lungs, clearing the stale city air from his system. He gripped the bridge rail as the boat rode the faint undulations of the ice, carving her way through the thin layer of snow, crossing the black scars left by the runners of the ships who had gone ahead of her.

The sun was almost at zenith, a dull, deep red in the torn sky. Clouds swept before them, their colours changing gradually from pale yellow to white against the clear blue of the sky; the colour of the ice changed to match the clouds, now pure white and sparkling. The other ships were hull down below the distant horizon. Save for the slight sounds that the ship made, the creak of yards and the bump of the runners, there was silence.

Tossed by the tearing skids, a fine spray of snow rose on both sides of the boat as she plunged towards the South Ice.

Arflane was conscious of the three members of the Friesgalt ruling family standing behind him. He did not turn. Instead he looked curiously at the figure who could be seen leaning in the bow by the harpoon gun, his gloved fingers gripping a line, his bizarre, strangely-dressed hair streaming behind him, his lance cradled in the crook of his arm. Urquart, either from pride or from a wish for privacy, had spoken to no one since he had come aboard. Indeed, he had boarded the craft of his own accord and his right to be there had not been questioned as yet.

"Will we catch the whalers, captain?" Manfred Rorsefne spoke as quietly as ever; there was no need to raise his voice in the near-tangible silence of the icelands.

Arflane shook his head. "No chance."

He knew in fact there was every chance of catching the professional whalers; but he had no intention of doing so and fouling their hunting. As soon as they were well under way he planned to take in sail on some pretext and cut his speed.

An hour later the excuse occurred to him. They were leaving the clean ice and entering a region sparsely occupied by ridges of ice standing alone and fashioned into strange shapes by the action of the wind. He deliberately allowed the boat to pass close by one of these, to emphasise the danger of hitting it.

When they were past the spur, he half-turned to Rorsefne, who was standing behind him. "I'm cutting speed until we're through the ridges. If I don't, there's every chance of our hitting one and breaking up—then we'll never see the whale herd."

Rorsefne gave him a cynical smile, doubtless guessing the real reason for the decision, but made no comment.

Sail was taken in, under Arflane's instructions, and the boat's speed decreased by almost half. The atmosphere on board became less tense. Urquart, still in his self-appointed place in the bow, turned to glance up at the bridge. Then as if he had satisfied himself on some point, he shrugged slightly and turned back to look out towards the horizon.

The Ulsenns were sitting on a bench under the awning behind Arflane. Manfred Rorsefne leaned on the rail, staring up at the streamers of clouds above them.

The ridges they were now passing were carved into impossible shapes by the elements.

Some were like half-finished bridges, curving over the ice and ending suddenly in jagged outline. Others were squat, a mixture of rounded surfaces and sharp angles; and still others were tall and slender, like gigantic harpoons stuck butt-foremost into the ice. Most of them were in clumps set far enough apart to afford easy passage for the yacht as she glided on her course, but every so often Haeber at the wheel would steer a turn or two to one side or another to avoid a ridge.

The ice under the runners was rougher than it had been, for this ground was not travelled as much as the smoother terrain surrounding the cities. The boat's motion was still easy, but the undulation was more marked than before.

In spite of the lack of canvas, the yacht continued to make good speed, sails swelling with the steady following wind.

Knowing there was as yet little for him to do, Arflane agreed to Rorsefne's suggestion that they go below and eat. He left Haeber in charge of the bridge and the bosun at the wheel.

The cabins below were surprisingly large, since no space was used for carrying cargo of any kind other than ordinary supplies. The main cabin was as luxuriously furnished, by Arflane's standards, as the *Ice Spirit*'s had been, with chairs of canvas stretched on bone frames, an ivory table and ivory shelves and lockers lining the bulkhead. The floor was carpeted in the tawny summer coat of the wolf (a beast becoming increasingly rare) and the ports were large, letting in a great deal more light than was usual in a boat of her size.

The four of them sat around the carved ivory table while the cook served their midday meal of broth made from the meat of the snow kite, seal steaks and a mess of the lichen that grew on the surface of the ice in certain parts of the plateau. There was hardly any conversation during the meal, which suited Arflane. He sat at one end of the table, while Ulrica Ulsenn sat at the other. Janek Ulsenn and Manfred Rorsefne sat on his right and left. Occasionally Arflane would look up from his food at the same time as Ulrica Ulsenn and their eyes would meet. For him, it was another uncomfortable meal.

By the early afternoon the boat was nearing the region where the whales had been sighted. Arflane, glad to be away from the company of the Ulsenns and Manfred Rorsefne, took over the wheel from the bosun.

The masts of some of the whalers were now visible in the distance. The whaling fleet had not, it appeared, divided yet. All the ships seemed to be following much the same course, which meant that the whales were still out of sight.

As they drew nearer, Arflane saw the masts of the ships begin to separate; it could only mean that the herd had been sighted. The whalers were spreading out, each ship chasing its individual quarry.

Arflane blew into the bridge speaking tube. Manfred Rorsefne answered.

"The herd's been spotted," Arflane told him. "It's splitting up. The big ones will be what the whalers are after. I suppose we'll find a little whale for ourselves."

"How long to go, captain?" Rorsefne's voice now held a trace of excitement.

"About an hour." Arflane answered tersely, and replaced the stopper of the speaking tube.

On the horizon to starboard was a great cliff of ice rising hundreds of feet into the deep purple of the sky. To port were small sharp ridges of ice running parallel to the cliffs. The yacht was sailing between them now towards the slaughtering grounds where ships could be discerned already engaged in hunting down and killing the great beasts.

Standing on the bridge, Arflane prepared to go down and take the wheel again as he saw the prey that the yacht would hunt: a few bewildered calves about half a mile ahead of them, almost directly in line with the boat's present course. Rorsefne and the Ulsenns came up to the rail, craning their necks as they stared at the quarry.

They were soon passing close enough to be able to see individual ships at work.

With both hands firmly on the wheel and Haeber beside him with his megaphone ready to relay orders, Arflane guided the boat surely on her course, often steering in a wide arc to avoid the working ships.

Dark red whale blood ran over the churned whiteness of the ice; small boats, with harpooners ready in their bows, sped after the huge mammals or elsewhere were hauled at breakneck pace in the wake of skewered leviathans, towed by taut harpoon lines wound around the small capstans in the bows. One boat passed quite close, seeming hardly to touch the ground as it bounced over the ice, drawn by a pain-enraged cow who was four times the length and twice the height of the boat itself. She was opening and shutting her massive, tooth-filled jaws as she moved, using front and back flippers to push herself at almost unbelievable speed away from the source of her agony. The boat's runners, sprung on a matrix of bone, came close to breaking as she was hurled into the air and crashed down again. Her crew were sweating and clinging grimly to her sides to avoid being flung out; those who could doused the running lines with water to stop them burning. The cow's hide, scarred, ripped and bleeding from the wounds of a dozen harpoons, was a brown-grey colour and covered in wiry hair. Like most of her kind, it did not occur to her to turn on the boat which she could have snapped in two in an instant with her fifteen-foot jaws.

She was soon past, and beginning to falter as Arflane watched.

In another place a bull had been turned over onto his back

55

and was waving his massive flippers feebly in his death throes. Around him, several boatloads of hunters had disembarked on to the ice and were warily approaching with lances and flenching cutlasses at the ready. The men were dwarfed by the monster who lay dying on his back, his mouth opening and shutting, gasping for breath.

Beyond, Arflane saw a cow writhing and shuddering as her blood spouted from a score of wounds.

The yacht was almost on the calves now.

Arflane's eyes were attracted by a movement to starboard. A huge bull whale was rushing across the ice directly in the path of the yacht, towing a longboat behind him. A collision was imminent.

Desperately, he swung his wheel hard over. The yacht's runners squealed as she began to turn, narrowly missing the snorting whale, but still in danger of fouling the boat's lines and wrecking them both. Arflane leaned with all his strength on the wheel and barely succeeded in steering the yacht on to a parallel course. Now he could see the occupants of the boat. Standing by the prow, a harpoon ready in one hand, the other gripping the side, was Captain Brenn. His face was twisted in hatred for the beast as it dragged his longboat after it. The whale, startled by the sudden appearance of the yacht, now turned round until its tiny eyes glimpsed Brenn's boat. Instantly it rushed down on Brenn and his crew. Arflane heard the captain scream as the huge jaws opened to their full extent and crunched over the longboat.

A great cry went up from the whalers as the bull shook the broken boat. Arflane saw his friend flung to the ice and attempt to crawl away, but now the whale saw him and its jaws opened again, closing on Brenn's body.

For a moment the whaling captain's legs kicked, then they too disappeared. Arflane had automatically turned the wheel again, to go to the rescue of his friend, but it was too late.

As they bore down on the towering bulk of the bull, he saw that Urquart was no longer at the bow. Manfred Rorsefne stood in his place, swinging the great harpoon gun into line.

Arflane grabbed his megaphone and yelled through it.

"Rorsefne! Fool! Don't shoot it!"

The other evidently heard him, waved a one-handed acknowledgement, then bent back over the gun.

Arflane tried to turn the boat's runners in time, but it was too late. There was a thudding concussion that ran all along the boat as the massive harpoon left the gun and, its line racing behind it, buried itself deep in the whale's side.

The monster rose on its hind flippers, its front limbs waving. A high screaming sound came from its open jaws and its shadow completely covered the yacht. The boat lurched forward, dragged by the harpoon line, its forward runners rising off the ice. Then the line came free. Rorsefne had not secured it properly. The boat thudded down.

The bull lowered his bulk to the ice and began to move rapidly towards the yacht, its jaws snapping. Arflane managed to turn again; the jaws missing the prow, but the gigantic body smashed against the starboard side. The yacht rocked, nearly toppled, then righted herself.

Manfred Rorsefne was fumbling with the gun, trying to load another harpoon. Then the starboard runners, strained beyond endurance by the jolt they had taken, cracked and broke. The yacht collapsed on to her starboard side, the deck sloping at a steep angle. Arflane was sent flying against the bulkhead as the yacht skidded sideways across the ice, colliding with the rear quarters of the whale as it turned to attack.

Arflane reached out and grabbed the rail of the companionway, began with great difficulty to crawl up to the bridge. His only thoughts now were for the safety of Ulrica Ulsenn.

As he clambered up, he stared into the terrified face of Janek Ulsenn. He swung aside to let the man push past him. When he reached the bridge, he saw Ulrica lying crumpled against the rail.

Arflane slithered across the sloping deck, and crouched to turn her over. She was not dead, but there was a livid bruise on her forehead.

Arflane paused, staring at the beautiful face; then he swung her across his shoulder and began to fight his way back to the companionway as the whale bellowed and returned to the attack.

When he reached the deck the crewmen were clambering desperately over the port rail, dropping to the ice and running for their lives. Manfred Rorsefne, Urquart and Haeber were nowhere to be seen; but Arflane made out the figure of Janek Ulsenn being helped away from the wrecked boat by two of the crew.

Climbing across the sloping deck by means of the tangle of rigging, Arflane had almost reached the rail when the whale crashed down on the boat's bow. He fell backwards against the wheelhouse, seeing the vast bulk of the creature's head a few feet away from him.

He lost his hold on Ulrica and she rolled away from him towards the stern. He crawled after her, grabbing at the trailing fabric of her long skirt. Again the boat listed, this time towards the bow; he barely managed to stop himself being catapulted into the gaping jaws by clinging to the mainmast shrouds. Supporting the woman with one arm, he glanced around for a means of escape.

As the whale's head turned, the cold, pain-glazed eyes of the monster regarding him, he grabbed the starboard rail and flung himself and the girl toward and over it, careless of any consideration other than escaping the beast for a few moments.

They fell heavily to the snow. He dragged himself upright, once again got Ulrica Ulsenn over his shoulder and began to stumble away, his boots sliding on the ice beneath the thin covering of snow. Ahead of him lay a harpoon that must have been shaken from the ship. He paused to pick it up, then staggered on. Behind him the whale snorted; he heard the thump of its flippers, felt them shaking the ground as the beast lumbered in pursuit.

He turned, saw the creature bearing down on him, threw Ulrica's body as far away from him as possible and poised the harpoon. His only chance was to strike one of the eyes and pierce the brain, killing the beast before it killed him; then he might save Ulrica.

He flung the harpoon at the whale's glaring right eye. The barbs struck true, pierced, but did not reach the brain. The whale stopped in its tracks, turning as it attempted to shake the lance from its blinded eye.

Then the left eye saw Arflane.

The creature paused, snorting and squealing in a curiously high-pitched tone.

Then, before it could come at him again, Arflane saw a movement to his right. The whale saw it too and moved its head, opening its jaws.

Urquart with his huge harpoon held in one hand, came running at the beast; hurled himself without stopping at its body, his fingers grasping its hair.

The whale reared again, but could not dislodge the harpooner. Urquart began relentlessly to climb up on to its back. The whale, instinctively aware that once it rolled over and exposed its belly it would be lost, bucked and threshed, but could not rid itself of the small creature that had now reached its back and, on hands and knees, was moving up to its head.

The whale saw Arflane again and snorted.

Cautiously, it pushed itself forward on its flippers, forgetting its burden. Arflane was transfixed, watching in fascination as Urquart slowly rose to a standing position, planting his feet firmly on the whale's back and raising his harpoon in both hands.

The whale quivered, as if anticipating its death. Then Urquart's muscles strained as, with all his strength, he drove the mighty harpoon deep into the creature's vertebrae, dragged it clear and plunged it in again.

A great column of blood gouted from the whale's back, obscuring all sight of Urquart and spattering down on Arflane. He turned towards Ulrica Ulsenn as she stirred and moaned.

The hot black blood rained down her too, drenching them both.

She stood up dazedly and opened her arms, her golden eyes looking deep into Arflane's.

He stepped forward and embraced her, holding her tightly against his blood-slippery body while behind them the monster screamed, shuddered and died. For minutes its pungent, salty blood gushed out in huge spurts, drenching them, but they were hardly aware of it.

Arflane held the woman to him. Her hands clutched at his back as she shivered and whimpered. She had begun to weep.

He stood there holding her for several minutes at the very least, his own eyes tightly shut, before he became aware of the presence of others.

He opened his eyes and looked about him.

Urquart lounged nearby, his body relaxed, his eyes hooded, his face as sternly set as ever. Near him was Manfred Rorsefne. The young man's left arm hung limply at his side and his face was white with pain, but when he spoke it was in the same light, insouciant tone he always used.

"Forgive me this interruption, captain. But I think we are about to see the noble Lord Janek . . ."

Reluctantly Arflane released Ulrica; she wiped blood from her face and looked about her vaguely. For a second she held his arm, then released it as she recognised her cousin.

Arflane turned and saw the dead bulk of the monster towering over them only a few feet away. Rounding it, aided by two of his men, came Janek Ulsen. He had broken at least one leg, probably both.

"Haeber is dead," Manfred said. "And half the crew."

"We all deserve to be dead," grunted Arflane. "I knew that boat was too brittle—and you were a fool to use the harpoon. It might have avoided us if you hadn't provoked it."

"And then we should have missed the excitement!" Rorsefne exclaimed. "Don't be ungrateful, captain."

Janek Ulsenn looked at his wife and saw something in her expression that made him frown. He glanced at Arflane questioningly. Manfred Rorsefne stepped forward and gave Ulsenn a mock salute.

"Your wife is still in one piece, Janek, if that's what concerns you. Doubtless you're curious as to her fate after you left her on the bridge . . ."

Arflane looked at Rorsefne. "How did you know he did that?"

Manfred smiled. "I, captain, climbed the rigging. I had a splendid view. I saw everything. No one saw me." He turned his attention back to Janek Ulsenn. "Ulrica's life was saved by Captain Arflane and later, when he killed the whale, by Cousin Urquart. Will you thank them, my lord?"

Janek Ulsenn said: "I have broken both my legs."

Ulrica Ulsenn spoke for the first time. Her voice was as vibrant as ever though a little distant, as if she had not entirely recovered from her shock.

"Thank you, Captain Arflane. I am very grateful. You seem to make it your business, saving Rorsefnes." She smiled weakly and looked round at Urquart. "Thank you, Long Lance. You are a brave man. You are both brave."

The glance she then turned on her husband was one of pure contempt. His own expression, already drawn by the pain from his broken legs, became increasingly tense. He spoke sharply. "There is a ship which will take us back." He motioned with his head. "It is over there. We will go to it, Ulrica."

When Ulrica obediently followed her departing husband as he was helped away by his men, Arflane made to step forward; but Manfred Rorsefne's hand gripped his shoulder.

"She is his wife," Manfred said softly and quite seriously.

Arflane tried to shake off the young man's grip. In a lighter tone Manfred added: "Surely you, of all people, respect our old laws and customs most, Captain Arflane?"

Arflane spat on the ice.

CHAPTER SEVEN

THE FUNERAL ON THE ICE

Lord Pyotr Rorsefne had died in their absence; two days later his funeral took place.

Also to be buried that day were Brenn of the *Tender Maiden* and Haeber, first officer of the ice yacht. There were three separate funerals being held beyond the city, but only Rorsefne's was splendid.

Looking across the white ice, with its surface snow whipped into eddying movement by the frigid wind, Arflane could see all three burial parties. He reflected that it was the Rorsefnes who had killed his old friend Brenn and Haeber, too; their jaunt to the whaling grounds had caused both deaths. But he could not feel much bitterness.

On his distant left and right were the black sledges bearing the plain coffins of Brenn and Haeber, while ahead of him moved the funeral procession of Pyotr Rorsefne, of which he was part, coming behind the relatives and before the servants and other mourners. His face was solemn, but Arflane felt very little emotion at all, although initially he had been shocked to learn of Rorsefne's death.

Wearing the black sealskin mourning cloak, stitched with the red insignia of the Rorsefne clan, Arflane sat in a sleigh drawn by wolves with black-dyed coats. He held the reins himself. Also in the heavy black cloaks Manfred Rorsefne and the dead man's daughter, Ulrica, sat together on another sleigh drawn by black wolves, and behind them were miscellaneous members of the Rorsefne and Ulsenn families. Janek Ulsenn was too ill to attend. At the head of the procession, moving slowly, was the black funeral sleigh, with its high prow and stern, bearing the ornate ivory coffin in which lay the dead lord.

Ponderously, the dark procession crossed the ice. Above it, heavy white clouds gathered and the sun was obscured. Light snow was falling.

At length the burial pit came into sight. It had been carved from the ice and gleaming blocks of ice stood piled to one side. Near this pile stood a large loading boom which had been used to haul up the blocks. The boom with its struts and hanging tackle looked like a gallows, silhouetted against the cold sky.

The air was very quiet, save for the slow scrape of the runners and the faint moan of the wind.

A motionless figure stood near the piled ice blocks. It was Urquart, face set as usual, bearing his long lance as usual, come to witness his father's burial. Snow had settled on his piled hair and his shoulders, increasing his resemblance to a member of the Ice Mother's hierarchy.

As they came nearer Arflane was able to hear the creak of the loading beam as it swung in the wind, he saw that Urquart's face was not quite without expression. There was a peculiar look of disappointment there, as well as a trace of anger.

The procession gradually came to a halt near the black hole in the ice. Snow pattered on the coffin and the wind caught their cloaks and ripped the hood from Ulrica Ulsenn's head. Arflane glimpsed her tear-streaked face as she pulled the fabric back into place. Manfred Rorsefne, his broken arm in a sling beneath his cloak, turned to nod at Arflane. They got down from their sleighs and, with four of the male relatives, approached the coffin.

Manfred, helped by a boy of about fifteen, cut loose the black wolves and handed their harness to two servants who stood ready. Then, three men on either side, they pushed the heavy sleigh to the pit.

It balanced on the edge for a moment, as if in reluctance, then slid over and fell into the darkness. They heard it crash at the bottom; then they walked to the pile of ice blocks to thrown them into the pit and seal it. But Urquart had already taken the first block in both hands, his harpoon for once lying on the ice where he had placed it. He lifted the block high and flung it down with great force, his lips drawn back from his teeth, his eyes full of fire. He paused, looking into the pit, wiping his hands on his greasy coat, then, picking up his harpoon, he walked away from the pit as Arflane and the others began to push the rest of the blocks towards it.

It took an hour to fill the pit and erect the flag bearing the Rorsefne arms. The flag fluttered in the wind. Gathered around it now were the mourners, their heads bowed as Manfred

Rorsefne used his good hand to climb clumsily to the top of the heaped ice to begin the funeral oration.

"The Ice Mother's son returns to her cold womb," he began in the traditional way. "As she gave him life, she takes it; but he will exist now for eternity in the halls of ice where the Mother holds court. Imperishable, she rules the world. Imperishable are those who join her now. Imperishable she will make the world one thing, without age or movement; without desire or frustration; without anger or joy; perfect and whole and silent. Let us join her soon."

He had spoken well and clearly, with some emotion.

Arflane dropped to one knee and repeated the final sentence. "Let us join her soon."

Behind him, responding with less fervour, the others followed his example, muttering the words where he had spoken them boldly.

CHAPTER EIGHT

RORSEFNE'S WILL

Arflane, possibly more than anyone, sensed the guilt that Ulrica Ulsenn felt over her father's death. Very little guilt, or indeed grief now, showed on her features but her manner was at once remote and tense. It was at her instigation, as well as Manfred's, that the disastrous expedition had set off on the very day that her father had died.

Arflane realised that she was not to blame for thinking him almost completely recovered; in fact there seemed no logical reason why he should have weakened so rapidly. It appeared that his heart, always considered healthy, had given out soon after he had dictated a will which was to be read later that afternoon to Arflane and the close relatives. Pyotr Rorsefne had died at about the same time that the whale had attacked and destroyed the yacht, a few hours after he had spoken to Arflane of New York.

Sitting stiffly upright in a chair, hands clasped in her lap, Ulrica Ulsenn waited with Arflane, Manfred Rorsefne and her husband, who lay on a raised stretcher, in the ante-room adjoining what had been her father's study. The room was small, its walls crowded with hunting trophies from Pyotr Rorsefne's youth. Arflane found unpleasant the musty smell that came from the heads of the beasts.

The door of the study opened and Strom, the wizened old man who had been Pyotr Rorsefne's general retainer, beckoned them wordlessly into the room.

Arflane and Manfred Rorsefne stooped to pick up Ulsenn's stretcher and followed Ulrica Ulsenn into the study.

The study was reminiscent of a ship's cabin, though the light came from dim lighting strips instead of portholes. Its walls were lined from floor to ceiling with lockers. A large desk of yellow ivory stood in the centre; on it rested a single sheet of thin plastic. The sheet was large and covered in brown writing, as if it had been inscribed in blood. It curled at the ends; evidently it had been unrolled only recently.

The old man took Manfred Rorsefne to the desk and sat him down in front of the paper; then he left the room.

Manfred sighed and tapped his fingers on the desk as he read the will. Normally Janek Ulsenn should have fulfilled this function, but the fever which had followed his accident had left him weak and only now was he pushing himself into a sitting position so that he could look over the top of the desk and regard his wife's cousin through baleful, disturbed eyes.

"What does it say?" he asked, weakly but impatiently.

"Little that we did not expect," Manfred told him, still reading. There was a slight smile on his lips now.

"Why's this man here?" Ulsenn motioned with his hand towards Arflane.

"He is mentioned in the will, cousin."

Arflane glanced over Ulsenn's head at Ulrica, but she refused to look in his direction.

"Read it out," said Ulsenn, sinking back on to one arm. "Read it out, Manfred."

Manfred shrugged and began to read.

"'The Will of Pyotr Rorsefne, Chief Ship Lord of Friesgalt'," he began. "'The Rorsefne is dead. The Ulsenn rules'," he glanced sardonically at the reclining figure. "'Save all my fortune and estates and ships, which I hereby will to be divided equally between my daughter and my nephew. I hereby present the command of my schooner the *Ice Spirit*, to Captain Konrad Arflane of Brershill, so that he may take her to New York on the course charted on the maps I also leave to him. If Captain Arflane should find the city of New York and live to return to Friesgalt, he shall become whole owner of the *Ice Spirit*, and any cargo she may then carry. To benefit from my will, my daughter Ulrica and my nephew Manfred must accompany Captain Arflane upon his voyage. Captain Arflane shall have complete power over all who sail with him. Pyotr Rorsefne of Friesgalt.'"

Ulsenn was raising himself to a sitting position again. He glowered at Arflane. "The old man was full of fever. He was insane. Forget this condition. Dismiss Captain Arflane, divide the property as the will stipulates. Would you embark upon another crazy voyage so soon after the first? Be warned; the first voyage anticipates the second, should you take it!"

"By the Ice Mother, cousin, how superstitious you have

become," Manfred Rorsefne murmured. "You know very well that should we ignore one part of the will, then the other becomes invalid. And think how you would benefit if we did perish! Your wife's share and mine would make you the most powerful man ever to have ruled in all the Eight Cities."

"I care nothing for the wealth. I am wealthy enough. It is my wife I wish to protect!"

Again Manfred Rorsefne smiled cynically and reminiscently, plainly remembering Ulsenn's desertion of his wife aboard the yacht. Ulsenn scowled at him then relapsed, gasping, onto his pillows.

Stony-faced, Ulrica rose. "He had best be taken to his bed," she said.

Arflane and Manfred picked up the stretcher between them. Ulrica led the way through dark passages to Ulsenn's bedroom, where servants took him and helped him into the large bed. His face was white with pain and he was almost fainting, but he continued to mutter about the stupidity of the old man's will.

"I wonder if he will decide to accompany us when we sail," Manfred said as they left. He smiled ironically. "Probably he will find his health and his duties as the new lord will keep him in the crevasse."

The three of them walked back to one of the main living rooms. It was furnished with brightly painted wall hangings and chairs and couches of wood and fibreglass frames padded and covered in animal skins. Arflane threw himself on to one of the couches and Ulrica sat opposite him, her eyes downcast. Only her long-fingered hands moved slightly in her lap.

Manfred did not sit.

"I must go to proclaim my uncle's will—or rather most of it," he said. He had to go to the top of the crevasse city and use a megaphone to repeat the words of the will to all the citizens. Friesgalt was mourning Pyotr Rorsefne's death in the traditional way. All work had ceased and the citizens had retired to their cavern homes for the three days of mourning.

When Manfred left Ulrica did not, as Arflane had expected, make some excuse to follow. Instead she ordered a servant to bring them some hot *hess*. "You will have some, captain?" she asked faintly.

Arflane nodded, looking at her curiously. She got up and moved about the room for a moment, pretending to inspect scenes on the wall hangings; they must have been more than familiar to her.

Arflane said at length, "You should not feel that you did any wrong, Lady Ulsenn."

She turned, raising her eyebrows. "Wrong? What do you mean?"

"You did not desert your father. We all thought he was completely recovered. He said so himself. You are not guilty."

"Thank you," she said. She bowed her head, a trace of irony in her tone. "I was not aware that I felt guilt."

"I'm sorry that I should have thought so," he said.

When she next looked at him, it was with a more candid expression as she studied his face. Gradually a look of despair and quiet agony came into her eyes.

He rose awkwardly and went towards her, taking her hands in his, holding them firmly.

"You are strong, Captain Arflane," she murmured. "I am weak."

"Not so," he said heavily. "Not so, ma'am."

She gently removed her hands from his and went to sit on a couch. The servant returned, placed the *hess* on a small table near the couch and left again. She reached forward and poured a goblet of the stuff, handing it up to him. He took it, standing over her with his legs slightly apart, looking down at her sympathetically.

"I was thinking that there is much of your father in you," he said. "The strength is there."

"You did not know my father well," she reminded him quietly.

"Well enough, I think. You forget that I saw him when he thought he was alone and dying. It was what I felt was in him, then, that I see in you now. I would not have saved his life if I had not seen that quality."

She gave a great sigh and her golden eyes glistened with tears. "Perhaps you were wrong," she said.

He sat beside her on the couch, shaking his head. "All the strength of the family went into you for this generation. Your weakness is probably his, too."

"What weakness?"

"A wild imagination. It took him to New York—or so he said—and it took you on the whale hunt."

She smiled gratefully, her features softening as she looked directly at him. "If you are trying to comfort me, captain, I think you are succeeding."

"I'd comfort you more if you'd give me the chance." He had not meant to speak. He had not meant to take her hands again as he did; but she did not resist and though her expression became serious and thoughtful, she did not seem offended.

Now Arflane breathed rapidly, remembering when he had embraced her on the ice; and her breasts were rising and falling also. She flushed, but still she let him grip her hands.

"I love you," said Arflane, almost miserably.

Then she burst into tears, took her hands away, and flung herself against him. He held her tightly while she wept, stroking her long, fine hair, kissing her forehead, caressing her shoulders. He felt the tears in his own eyes as he responded to her grief. Only barely aware of what he did next, he picked her up in his arms and carried her from the room. The passages were deserted as he took her towards her bedroom where he still believed he intended to lie her on the bed and let her sleep. He kicked open the door—it was across the corridor from Ulsenn's—and kicked it shut behind him when he had entered.

The room was furnished with chairs, lockers and dressing table of softly tinted ivory. White furs were heaped on the wide bed and also lined the walls.

He stooped and placed her on the bed, but he did not straighten up.

Now he knew that, in spite of the dreadful guilt he felt, he could do nothing to control his actions. He kissed her mouth. Her arms went around his neck as she responded, and he lowered his massive body on to hers, feeling the warmth and the contours of her flesh through the fabric of the dress; feeling her writhe and tremble beneath him like a delicate, frightened bird. With one hand he pushed the dress higher and she tried to stop him, clinging to his hand and moaning; but he continued, savagely now, to push his hand through the folds of her clothing until he found her flesh and his goal.

Then she shuddered under his touch and whimpered that she was a virgin, that she had never allowed Janek to consummate their marriage. This did not stop him. Fiercely he took her, reddening the white fur with her blood; and then they lay panting side by side, to turn eventually again to each other, as they were to turn several times through that night.

CHAPTER NINE

ULRICA ULSENN'S CONSCIENCE

Early in the morning, looking down on her as she slept with her face just visible above the furs and her black hair spread out on the pillow, Arflane felt remorse. No remorse, he knew, would be sufficient to make him part with Ulrica now, but he had broken the law he respected; the law he regarded as just and vital to the existence of his world. This morning he saw himself as a hypocrite, as a deceiver, and as a thief. While he was reconciled to these new rôles, the fact that he had assumed them depressed him; and he was further depressed by the knowledge that he had taken advantage of the woman's vulnerability at a time when her own guilt and grief had combined to weaken her moral strangth.

Arflane did not regret his actions. He considered regret a useless emotion. What was done was done, and now he must decide what to do next.

He sighed as he clothed himself, unwilling to leave her but aware of what the law would do to her if she were discovered as an adulteress. At worst, she would be exposed on the ice to die. At the very least both he and she would be ostracised in all the Eight Cities; this in itself was effectually a lingering death sentence.

She opened her eyes and smiled at him sweetly; then the smile faltered.

"I'm leaving," he whispered. "We'll talk later."

She sat up in the bed, the furs falling away from her breasts. He bent forward to kiss her, gently pulling her arms from his neck as she tried to embrace him.

"What are you going to do?" she asked.

"I don't know. I'd thought of going away—to Brershill."

"Janek would break your city apart to find us. Many would die."

"I know. Would he divorce you?"

"He owns me because I have the highest rank of any woman in Friesgalt; because I am beautiful and well mannered and rich." She shrugged. "He is not particularly interested in demanding his rights. He would divorce me because I refused to entertain his guests, not because I refused to make love to him."

"Then what can we do? I have no intention of deceiving him for any longer than I must protect you. I doubt in any case if I would be able to deceive him for long."

She nodded. "I doubt it, also." She smiled up at him again. "But if you took me away, where could we go?"

He shook his head. "I don't know. To New York, perhaps. Remember the will?"

"Yes—New York."

"We will talk later today, when we have an opportunity," he said. "I must go before the servants come."

It had not occurred to either of them to question the fact that she was Janek Ulsenn's property, no matter how little he deserved her; but now, as he made to leave, she grasped his arm and spoke earnestly.

"I am yours," she said. "I am rightfully yours, despite my marriage vows. Remember that."

He muttered something and went to the door, opening it cautiously and slipping out into the corridor.

From Ulsenn's room, as Arflane passed it, there came a groan of pain as the new Lord of Friesgalt turned in his bed and twisted his useless legs.

At breakfast, they were as shy as ever of exchanging glances. They sat at opposite ends of the table, with Manfred Rorsefne between them. His arm was still strapped in splints to his chest, but he appeared to be in as light-hearted a mood as ever.

"I gather my uncle already told you he wanted you to command the *Ice Spirit* and take her to New York?" he said to Arflane.

Arflane nodded.

"And did you agree?" Manfred asked.

"I half agreed," Arflane replied, pretending a greater interest in his meal than he felt, resentful of Manfred's presence in the room.

"What do you say now?"

"I'll skipper the ship," Arflane said. "She'll take time to crew and provision. She may need to be refitted. Also I'll want a careful look at those charts."

"I'll get them for you," Manfred promised. He glanced sideways at Ulrica. "How do you feel about the proposed voyage, cousin?"

She flushed. "It was my father's wish," she said flatly.

"Good." Manfred sat back in his chair, evidently in no hurry to leave. Arflane resisted the temptation to frown.

He tried to prolong the meal, hoping that Manfred would lose patience, but finally he was forced to let the servants take away his plate. Manfred made light conversation, seemingly oblivious of Arflane's reluctance to talk to him. At length, evidently unable to bear this, Ulrica got up from the table and left the room. Arflane controlled his desire to follow her immediately.

Almost as soon as she had gone, Manfred Rorsefne pushed back his chair and stood up. "Wait here, captain. I'll bring the charts."

Arflane wondered if Manfred guessed anything of what had happened during the night. He was almost sure that, if he did guess, the young man would say nothing to Janek Ulsenn, whom he despised. Yet three days before on the ice Manfred had restrained him from following Ulrica and had seemed resolved to make sure that Arflane would not interfere between Ulsenn and his wife. Arflane found the young man an enigma. At some times he seemed cynical and contemptuous of tradition; at others he seemed only anxious to preserve it.

Rorsefne returned with the maps tucked under his good arm. Arflane took them from him and spread them out on the table that had now been cleared of the remains of the meal.

The largest chart was drawn to the smallest scale, showing an area of several thousand miles. Superimposed on it in outline were what Arflane recognised as the buried continents of North and South America. Old Pyotr Rorsefne must have gone to considerable trouble with his charts, if this were his work. Clearly marked was the plateau occupying what had once been the Matto Grosso territory and where the Eight Cities now lay; also clearly marked, about two-thirds up the eastern coastline of the northern continent, was New York. From the

Matto Grosso to New York a line had been drawn. In Rorsefne's hand-writing were the words "Direct Course (Impossible)". A dotted line showed another route that roughly followed the ancient land masses, angling approximately N.W. by N. before swinging gradually to E. by N. This marked "Likely Course". Here and there it had been corrected in a different coloured ink; it was obvious that these were the changes made on the actual voyage, but there were only a few scribbled indications of what the ship had been avoiding. There were several references to ice-breaks, flaming mountains, barbarian cities, but no details of their precise positions.

"These charts were amended from memory," Manfred said. "The log and the original charts were lost in the wreck."

"Couldn't we look for the wreck?" Arflane asked.

"We could—but it would hardly be worth it. The ship broke up completely. Anything like the log or the charts would have been destroyed or buried by now."

Arflane spread the other charts out. They were of little help, merely giving a clearer idea of the region a few hundred miles beyond the plateau.

Arflane spoke rather petulantly. "All we know is where to look when we get there," he said. "And we know that it's possible to get there. We can follow this course and hope for the best—but I'd expected more detailed information. I wonder if the old man really did find New York?"

"We'll know in a few months, with any luck," Manfred said smiling.

"I'm still unhappy with the charts." Arflane began to roll up the big chart. "To risk men's lives, not to mention a woman's—on a voyage like that is only what we expect. But to risk them totally . . ."

"We'll have a better ship, a better crew—and a better captain than my uncle took." Manfred spoke reassuringly.

Arflane rolled up the other charts. "I'll pick every member of my crew myself. I'll check every inch of rigging and every ounce of provisions we take aboard. It will be at least two weeks before we're ready to sail."

Manfred was about to speak when the door opened. Four servants walked in carrying Janek Ulsenn's stretcher. The new ruler of Friesgalt seemed in better health than he had been on the previous evening. He sat up in the stretcher.

"There you are, Manfred. Have you seen Strom this morning?"

Strom was Pyotr Rorsefne's old general retainer. Manfred shook his head. "I was in my uncle's quarters earlier. I didn't see him."

Ulsenn signalled abruptly for the servants to lower the stretcher to the floor. They did so carefully.

"Why were you in those quarters? They are mine now, you know." Ulsenn's haughty voice rose.

Manfred indicated the rolled charts on the table.

"I had to get these to show Captain Arflane. They are the chart we need to plan the *Ice Spirit*'s voyage."

"You mean to follow the letter of the will, then?" Janek Ulsenn said acidly. "I still object to the venture. Pyotr Rorsefne was mad when he wrote the will, he has made a common foreign sailor one of his heirs! He might just as well have left his wealth to Urquart, who is, after all, his kin. I could declare the will void . . ."

Manfred pursed his lips and shook his head slowly. "You could not, cousin. Not the will of the old Lord. I have declared it publicly. Everyone will know if you do not adhere to its instructions . . ."

A thought occurred to Arflane. "You told the whole crevasse about New York? The old man didn't want the knowledge made general——"

"I didn't mention New York by name, but only as a 'distant city below the plateau'," Manfred assured him.

Ulsenn smiled. "Then there you are. You merely sail to the most distant of the Eight Cities . . ."

Manfred sneered very slightly. "Below the plateau? Besides, if it were one of the Eight that the will referred to, then it would have been making what was virtually a declaration of war. Your pain clouds your intelligence, cousin."

Ulsenn coughed and glared up at Manfred. "You are impertinent, Manfred. I am Lord now. I could order you both put to death . . ."

"With no trial? These are really empty threats, cousin. Would the people accept such an action?"

In spite of the great personal authority of the Chief Ship Lord the real power still rested in the hands of the mass of citizens, who had been known in the past to depose an unwelcome or tyrannical owner of the title. Ulsenn knew that he could not afford to take drastic action against any member of the much respected Rorsefne family. As it was, his own standing in the city was comparatively slight. He had risen to the title by marriage, not by direct blood line or by winning it by some other means. If he were to imprison Manfred or someone whom Manfred protected Ulsenn might easily find himself with a civil war on his hands, and he knew just what the result of such a war would be.

Ulsenn, therefore, remained silent.

"It is Pyotr Rorsefne's *will*, cousin," Manfred reminded him firmly. "Whatever you may feel about it, Captain Arflane commands the *Ice Spirit*. Don't worry. Ulrica and I will go along to represent the family."

Ulsenn darted a sharp, enigmatic look at Arflane. He sig-

70

nalled for his servants to pick up the stretcher. "If Ulrica goes —I will go!" The servants carried him from the room.

Arflane realised that Manfred Rorsefne was looking with amused interest at his face. The young man must have read the expression there. Arflane had not been prepared for Ulsenn's declaration. He had been confident that Ulsenn would have been too involved with his new power, too ill and too cowardly to join the expedition. He had been confident in his anticipation of Ulrica's company on the proposed voyage. Now he could anticipate nothing.

Manfred laughed.

"Cheer up, captain. Janek won't bother us on the voyage. He's an accountant, a stay-at-home merchant who knows nothing of sailing. He could not interfere if he wished to. He won't help us find the Ice Mother's lair—but he won't hinder us, either."

Although Manfred's reassurance seemed genuine, Arflane still could not tell if the young man had actually guessed the real reason for his disappointment. For that matter, he wondered if Janek Ulsenn had guessed what had happened in his wife's bedroom that night. The look he had given Arflane seemed to indicate that he suspected something, though it seemed impossible that he could know what had actually taken place.

Arflane was disturbed by the turn of events. He wanted to see Ulrica at once and talk to her about what had happened. He had a sudden feeling of deep apprehension.

"When will you begin inspecting the ship and picking the crew, captain?" Manfred was asking him.

"Tomorrow," Arflane told him ungraciously. "I'll see you before I get out there."

He made a curt farewell gesture with his hand and left the room. He began to walk through the low corridors, searching for Ulrica.

He found her in the main livingroom, where on the previous night, he had first caressed her. She rose hurriedly when he entered. She was pale; she held her body rigidly, her hands gripped tightly together at her waist. She had bound up her hair, drawing it back tightly from her face. She was wearing the black dress of fine sealskin which she had worn the day before at the funeral. Arflane closed the door, but she moved towards it, attempting to pass him. He barred the way with one arm and tried to look into her eyes, but she averted her head.

"Ulrica, what is it?" The sense of foreboding was now even stronger. "What is it? Did you hear that your husband intends to come with us on the voyage? Is that why . . .?"

She looked at him coolly and he dropped his arm away from the door.

"I am sorry, Captain Arflane," she said formally. "But it

71

would be best if you forgot what passed between us. We were both in unusual states of mind. I realise now that it is my duty to remain faithful to my——"

Her whole manner was artificially polite.

"Ulrica!" He gripped her shoulders tightly. "Did he tell you to say this? Has he threatened you ...?"

She shook her head. "Let me go, captain."

"Ulrica ..." His voice had broken. He spoke weakly, dropping his hands from her shoulders. "Ulrica, why ...?"

"I seem to remember you speaking quite passionately in favour of the old traditions," she said. "More than once I've heard you say that to let slip our code will mean our perishing as a people. You mentioned that you admired my father's strength of mind and that you saw the same quality in me. Perhaps you did, captain. I intend to stay faithful to my husband."

"You aren't saying what you mean. I can tell that. You love me. This mood is just a reaction—because things seem too complicated now. You told me that you were rightfully mine. You *meant* what you said this morning." He hated the tone of desperation in his own voice, but he could not control it.

"I mean what I am saying now, captain; and if you respect the old way of life, then you will respect my request that you see as little of me as possible from now on."

"No!" He roared in anger and lurched towards her. She stepped back, face frozen and eyes cold. He reached out to touch her and then slowly withdrew his hands and stepped aside to let her pass.

She opened the door. He understood now that it was no outside event that had caused this change in her, but her own conscience. He could not argue with her decision. Morally, it was right. There was nothing he could do; there was no hope he could hold. He watched her walk slowly away from him down the corridor. Then he slammed the door, his face twisted in an expression of agonised despair. There was a snapping sound and the door swung back. He had broken its lock. It would no longer close properly.

He hurried to his room and began to bundle his belongings together. He would make sure that he obeyed her request. He would not see her again, at least until the ship was ready to sail. He would go out to the *Ice Spirit* at once and begin his work.

He slung the sack over his shoulders and hurried through the winding corridors to the outer entrance. Bloody thoughts were in his mind and he wanted to get into the open, hoping that the clean air of the surface would blow them away.

As he reached the outer door, he met Manfred Rorsefne in the hall. The young man looked amused.

"Where are you off to, captain?"

Arflane glared at him, wanting to strangle the supercilious expression from Rorsefne's face.

"I see you're leaving, captain. Off to the *Ice Spirit* so soon? I thought you were going tomorrow ..."

"Today," Arflane growled. He recovered some of his self-assurance. "Today. I'll get started at once. I'll sleep on board until we sail. It will be best ..."

"Perhaps it will," Rorsefne agreed, speaking half to himself as he watched the big, red-bearded sailor stride rapidly from the house.

CHAPTER TEN

KONRAD ARFLANE'S MOOD

Of the newly discovered facts about his own character that obsessed Konrad Arflane, the most startling was that he had never suspected himself capable of renouncing all his principles in order to possess another man's wife. He also found it difficult to equate with his own idea of himself the knowledge that, having been stopped from seeing the woman, he should not become reconciled, or indeed grateful.

He was far from being either. He slept badly, his attention turned constantly to thoughts of Ulrica Ulsenn. He waited without hope for her to come to him and when she did not he was angry. He stalked about the big ship, bawling out the men over quibbling details, dismissing hands he had hired the day before, muttering offensively to his officers in front of the men, demanding that he should be made aware of all problems aboard, then swearing furiously when some unnecessary matter was brought to him.

He had had the reputation of being a particularly good skipper; stern and remote, but fair. The whaling hands, whom he preferred for his crewmen, had been eager to sign with the *Ice Spirit*, in spite of the mysterious voyage she was to make. Now many were regretting it.

Arflane had appointed three officers—or rather he had let two appointments stand and had signed on Long Lance Urquart as third officer, below Petchnyoff and old Kristoff Hinsen. Urquart seemed oblivious to Arflane's irrational moods, but the two other men were puzzled and upset by the change in their new skipper. Whenever Urquart was not in their quarters —which was often—they would take the opportunity to discuss the problem. Both had liked Arflane when they had first met him. Petchnyoff had had a high regard for his integrity and strength of will; Kristoff Hinsen felt a more intimate relationship with him, based on memories of the days when they had been rival skippers. Neither was capable of analysing the cause of the change in Arflane's temperament; yet so much did they trust their earlier impressions of him that they were prepared for a while to put up with his moods in the hope that, once under way, he would become once more the man they had first encountered. Petchnyoff's patience as the days passed became increasingly strained and he began to think of resigning his command, but Hinsen persuaded him to wait a little longer.

The huge vessel was being fitted with completely new canvas and rigging. Arflane personally inspected every pin, every knot, and every line. He climbed over the ship inch by inch, checking the set of the yards, the tension of the rigging, the snugness of the hatch covers, the feel of the bulkheads, until he was satisfied. He tested the wheel time after time, turning the runners this way and that to get to know their exact responses. Normally the steering runners and their turntable were immovably locked in relation with each other. On the foredeck though, immediately above the great gland of the steering pin, was housed the emergency bolt, with a heavy mallet secured beside it. Dropping the bolt would release the skids, allowing them to turn in towards each other, creating in effect a huge ploughshare that dug into the ice, bringing the vessel to a squealing and frequently destructive halt. Arflane tested this apparatus for hours. He also dropped the heavy anchors once or twice. These were on either side of the ship, beneath her bilges. They consisted of two heavy blades. Above them, through guides let into the hull, rods reached to the upper deck. Pins driven through the rods kept the blades clear of ice; beside each stanchion mallets were kept ready to knock the pegs clear in case of danger or emergency. The heavy anchors were seldom used, and never by a good skipper; contact with racing ice would wear them rapidly away, and replacements were now nearly unobtainable.

At first men and officers had called out cheerfully to him as he went about the ship; but they soon learned to avoid him, and the superstitious whaling hands began to speak of curses and of a foredoomed voyage; yet very few disembarked of their own accord.

Arflane would watch moodily from the bridge as bale after bale, barrel after barrel of provisions were swung aboard, packing every inch of available space. With each fresh ton that was taken into the holds, he would again test the wheel and the heavy anchors to see how the *Ice Spirit* responded.

One day on deck Arflane saw Petchnyoff inspecting the work of a sailor who had been one of a party securing the mainmast ratlines. He strode up to the pair and pulled at the lines, checking the knots. One of them was not as firm as it could be.

"Call that a knot, do you, Mr. Petchnyoff?" he said offen-

74

sively. "I thought you were supposed to be inspecting this work!"

"I am, sir."

"I'd like to be able to trust my officers," Arflane said with a sneer. "Try to see that I can in future."

He marched off along the deck. Petchnyoff slammed a belaying pin he had been holding down on to the deck, narrowly missing the surprised hand.

That evening, Petchnyoff had got half his kit packed before Hinsen could convince him to stay on board.

The weeks went by. There were four floggings for minor offences. It was as if Arflane were deliberately trying to get his crew to leave him before the ship set sail. Yet many of the men were fascinated by him and the fact that Urquart had thrown in his lot with Arflane must have had something to do with the whaling hands staying.

Manfred Rorsefne would occasionally come aboard to confer with Arflane. Originally Arflane had said that it would take a fortnight to ready the ship, but he had put off the sailing date further and further on one excuse and another, telling Rorsefne that he was still not happy that everything had been done that could be done, reminding him that a voyage of this kind demanded a ship that was as perfect as possible.

"True, but we'll miss the summer at this rate," Manfred Rorsefne reminded him gently. Arflane scowled in reply, saying he could sail in any weather. His carefulness on one hand, and his apparent recklessness on the other, did little to reassure Rorsefne; but he said nothing.

Finally there was absolutely no more to be done aboard the ice schooner. She was in superb trim; all her ivory was polished and shining, her decks were scrubbed and freshly boned. Her four masts gleamed with white, furled canvas; her rigging was straight and taut; the boats, swinging in davits fashioned from the jawbones of whales, hung true and firm; every pin was in place and every piece of gear was where it should be. The barbaric whale skulls at her prow glared towards the north as if defying all the dangers that might be awaiting them. The *Ice Spirit* was ready to sail.

Still reluctant to send for his passengers, Arflane stood in silence on the bridge and looked at the ship. For a moment it occurred to him that he could take her out now, leaving the Ulsenns and Manfred Rorsefne behind. The ice ahead was obscured by clouds of snow that were lifted by the wind and sent drifting across the bow; the sky was grey and heavy. Gripping the rail in his gauntleted hands, Arflane knew it would not be difficult to slip out to the open ice in weather like this.

75

He sighed and turned to Kristoff Hinsen who stood beside him.

"Send a man to the Rorsefne place, Mr. Hinsen. Tell them if the wind holds we'll sail tomorrow morning."

"Aye aye, sir." Hinsen paused, his weather-beaten features creased in doubt. "Tomorrow morning, sir?"

Arflane turned his brooding eyes on Hinsen. "I said tomorrow. That's the message, Mr. Hinsen."

"Aye aye, sir." Hinsen left the bridge hurriedly.

Arflane knew why Hinsen queried his orders. The weather was bad and obviously getting worse. By morning they would have a heavy snow storm; visibility would be poor, the men would find it difficult to set the canvas. But Arflane had made up his mind; he looked away, back towards the bow.

Two hours later he saw a covered sleigh being drawn across the ice from the city. Tawny wolves pulled it, their paws slipping on the ice.

A strong gust of wind blew suddenly from the west and buffeted the side of the ship so that it moved slightly to starboard in its mooring cables. Arflane did not need to order the cables checked. Several hands instantly ran to see to them. It was a larger crew than he normally liked to handle, but he had to admit, even in his poor temper, that their discipline was very good.

The wolves came to an untidy stop close to the ship's side. Arflane cursed and swung down from the bridge, moving to the rail and leaning over it. The driver had brought the carriage in too close for his own safety.

"Get that thing back!" Arflane yelled. "Get beyond the mooring pegs. Don't you know better than to come so close to a ship of this size while there's a heavy wind blowing? If we slip one cable you'll be crushed."

A muffled head poked itself from the carriage window. "We are here, Captain Arflane. Manfred Rorsefne and the Ulsenns."

"Tell your driver to get back! He ought to——" A fresh gust of wind slammed against the ship's side and sent it skidding several feet closer to the carriage until the slack of the mooring cables in the other side was taken up. The driver looked startled and whipped his wolves into a steep turn. They strained in their harness and loped across the ice with the carriage in tow.

Arflane smiled unpleasantly.

With a wind as erratic as this few captains would allow their ships out of their moorings, but he intended to sail anyway. It might be dangerous, but it would seem worse to Ulsenn and his relatives.

Manfred Rorsefne and the Ulsenns had got out of the carriage and were standing uncertainly, looking up at the ship, searching for Arflane.

Arflane turned away from them and went back to the bridge.

Fydur, the ship's bosun, saluted him as he began to climb the companionway. "Shall I send out a party to take the passengers aboard, sir?"

Arflane shook his head. "Let them make their own way on board," he told the bosun. "You can lower a gangplank if you like."

A little later he watched Janek Ulsenn being helped up the gangplank and along the deck. He saw Ulrica, completely swathed in her furs, moving beside her husband. Once she looked up at the bridge and he caught a glimpse of her eyes—the only part of her face not hidden by her hood. Manfred strolled along after them, waving cheerfully up at Arflane, but he was forced to clutch at a line as the ship moved again in her moorings.

Within a quarter of an hour he had joined Arflane on the bridge.

"I've seen my cousin and her husband into their respective cabins, captain," he said. "I'm settled in myself. At last we're ready, eh?"

Arflane grunted and moved down the rail to starboard, plainly trying to avoid the young man. Manfred seemed unaware of this; he followed, slapping his gloved hands together and looking about him. "You certainly know your ships, captain. I thought the *Spirit* was as neat as she could be until you took over. We should have little trouble on the voyage, I'm sure."

Arflane looked round at Rorsefne.

"We should have no trouble at all," he said grimly. "I hope you'll remind your relatives that I'm in sole command of this ship from the moment she sails. I'm empowered to take any measures I think fit to ensure the smooth running of the vessel . . ."

"All this is unnecessary, captain," Rorsefne smiled. "We accept that, of course. That is the law of the ice. No need for details; you are the skipper, we do as you tell us to do."

Arflane grunted. "Are you certain Janek Ulsenn understands that?"

"I'm sure he does. He'll do nothing to offend you—save perhaps scowl at you a little. Besides, his legs are still bothering him. He's not entirely fit; I doubt if he'll be seen above deck for a while." Manfred paused and then stepped much closer to Arflane. "Captain—you haven't seemed yourself since you took this command. Is something wrong? Are you disturbed by the idea of the voyage? It occurred to me that you might think there was—um—sacrilege involved."

Arflane shook his head, looking full into Manfred Rorsefne's face. "You know I don't think that."

Rorsefne appeared to be disconcerted for a moment. He pursed his lips. "It's no wish of mine to intrude on your personal . . ."

"Thank you."

"It would seem to me that the safety of the ship depends almost wholly upon yourself. If you are in poor spirits, captain, perhaps it would be better to delay the voyage longer?"

The wind was whining through the top trees. Automatically, Arflane looked up to make sure that the yards were firm. "I'm not in poor spirits," he said distantly.

"I think I could help . . ."

Arflane raised the megaphone to his lips and bawled at Hinsen as he crossed the quarter deck.

"Mr. Hinsen! Get some men into the mizzen to'g'l'nt yards and secure that flapping canvas!"

Manfred Rorsefne said nothing more. He left the bridge.

Arflane folded his arms across his chest, his features set in a scowl.

CHAPTER ELEVEN

UNDER SAIL

At dawn the next morning a blizzard blew in a great white sheet across the city and the forest of ships, heaping snow on the decks of the *Ice Spirit* till the schooner strained at her anchor lines. Sky and land were indistinguishable and only occasionally were the masts of the other vessels to be seen, outlined in black against the sweeping wall of snow. The temperature had fallen below zero. Ice had formed on the rigging and in the folds of the sails. Particles of ice, whipped by the wind, flew in the air like bullets; it was almost impossible to move against the blustering pressure of the storm. Loose canvas flapped like the broken flippers of seals; the wind shrilled and moaned through the tall masts and boats swung and creaked in their davits.

As a muffled tolling proclaimed two bells in the morning watch, Konrad Arflane, wearing a bandage over his mouth and nose and a snow visor over his eyes, stepped from his cabin below the bridge. Through a mist of driving snow he made his way forward to the bow and peered ahead; it was impossible to see anything in the swirling wall of whiteness. He returned to his cabin, passing Petchnyoff, the officer of the watch, without a word.

Petchnyoff stared after his skipper as the door of the cabin closed. There was a strange, resentful look in the first officer's eyes.

By six thirty in the morning, as the bell rang five, the driving snow had eased and weak sunshine was filtering through the clouds. Hinsen stood beside Arflane on the bridge, a megaphone in his hand. The crew were climbing into the shrouds, their thickly-clad bodies moving slowly up the ratlines. On the deck by the mainmast stood Urquart, his head covered by a tall hood, in charge of the men in the yards. The anchor men stood by their mooring lines watching the bridge and ready to let go.

Arflane glanced at Hinsen. "All ready, Mr. Hinsen?"

Hinsen nodded.

Aware that Rorsefne and the Ulsenns were still sleeping below, Arflane said, "Let go the anchor lines."

"Let go the anchor lines!" Hinsen's voice boomed over the ship and the men sprang to release the cables. The taut lines whipped away and the schooner lurched forward.

"Set upper and lower fore to'g'l'nts."

The order was repeated and obeyed.

"Set stays'ls."

The staysails blossomed out.

"Set upper and lower main to'g'l'nts and upper tops'l."

The sails billowed and swelled as they caught the wind, curving like the wings of monstrous birds, pulling the ship gradually away. Snow sprayed as the runners sliced through the surface and the schooner began to move from the port, passing the still anchored ships near her, dipping her bowsprit as she descended a slight incline in the ice, surging as she felt the rise on the other side. Kites squawked, swooping and circling excitedly around the top trees where the grandiose standard of the Rorsefne stood straight in the breeze. In her wake the ship left deep twin scars in the churned snow and ice. A huge, graceful creature, making her stately way out of port in the early morning under only a fraction of her sail, the ice in the rigging melting and falling off like a shower of diamonds, the *Ice Spirit* left Friesgalt behind and moved north beneath the lowering sky.

"All plain sail, Mr. Hinsen."

Sheet by sheet the sails were set until the ship sped over the ice under full canvas. Hinsen glanced at Arflane questioningly; it was unusual to set so much canvas while leaving port. But then he noticed Arflane's face as the ship began to gain speed. The captain was relaxing visibly. His expression was softening, there seemed to be a trace of a smile on his lips and his eyes were beginning to brighten.

Arflane breathed heavily and pushed back his visor, exhilarated by the wind on his face, the rolling of the deck beneath his feet. For the first time since Ulrica Ulsenn had rejected him he felt a lifting of the weight that had descended on him. He half smiled at Hinsen. "She's a real ship, Mr. Hinsen."

Old Kristoff, overjoyed at the change in his master, grinned broadly, more in relief than in agreement. "Aye, sir. She can move."

Arflane stretched his body as the ship lunged forward over the seemingly endless plateau of ice, piercing the thinning curtain of snow. Below him on the decks, and above in the rigging, sailors moved like dark ghosts through the drifting whiteness, working under the calm, fixed eye of Long Lance Urquart as he strode up and down the deck, his harpoon resting in its usual place in the crook of his arm. Sometimes Urquart would jump up into the lower shrouds to help a man in difficulties with a piece of tackle. The cold and the snow, combined with the need to wear particularly thick gloves, made it difficult for even the whalemen to work, though they were better used to the conditions than merchant sailors.

Arflane had hardly spoken to Urquart since the man had come aboard to sign on. Arflane had been happy to accept the harpooner, offering him the berth of third officer. It had vaguely occurred to him to wonder why Urquart should want to sail with him, since the tall harpooner could have no idea of where the ship was bound; but his own obsessions had driven the question out of his head. Now, as he relaxed, he glanced curiously at Urquart. The man caught his eye as he turned from giving instructions to a sailor. He nodded gravely to Arflane.

Arflane had instinctively trusted Urquart's ability to command, knowing that the harpooner had great prestige amongst the whalers; he had no doubts about his decision, but now he wondered again why Urquart had joined the ship. He had come, uninvited, on the whale hunt. That was understandable maybe; but there was no logical reason why a professional harpooner should wish to sail on a mysterious voyage of exploration. Perhaps Urquart felt protective towards his dead father's daughter and nephew, had decided to come with them to be sure of their safety on the trip; the image of the Long Lance at old Rorsefne's graveside suddenly came back to Arflane. Perhaps though Urquart felt friendship towards him personally. After all, only Urquart had seemed instinctively to respect Arflane's troubled state of mind over the past weeks and to understand his need for solitude. Of all the ship's complement, Arflane felt comradeship only towards Urquart, who was still a stranger to him. Hinsen he liked and admired, but since their original disagreement on the *Ice Spirit* over two months earlier, he had not been able to feel quite the same warmth towards him as he might have done otherwise.

Arflane leaned on the rail, watching the men at work. The ship was in no real danger until she had to descend the plateau and they would not reach the edge for several days sailing at full speed; he gave himself the pleasure of forgetting everything but the motion of the ship beneath him, the sight of the snow-spray spurting from the runners, the long streamers of clouds above him breaking up now and letting through the early morning sunlight and glimpses of a pale red and yellow sky that had begun to be reflected by the ice.

There was an old saying amongst sailors that a ship beneath a man was as good as a woman, and Arflane began to feel that he could agree. Once the schooner had got under way, his mood had lifted. He was still concerned about Ulrica; but he did not feel the same despair, the same hatred for all humanity that had possessed him while the ship was being readied for the voyage. He began to feel guilty, now that he thought back, that he had been so ill-mannered towards his officers and so irrational in his dealings with the crew. Manfred Rorsefne had been concerned that his mood would continue. Arflane had rejected the idea that he was in any kind of abnormal mood, but now he realised the truth of Rorsefne's statement of the night before; he would have been in no state to command the ship if his temper had not changed. It puzzled him that mere physical sensation, like the ship's passage over the ice, could so alter a man's mental attitudes within the space of an hour. Admittedly in the past he had always been restless and ill-tempered when not on board ship, but he had never gone so far as to behave unfairly towards the men serving under him. His self-possession was his pride. He had lost it; now he had found it again.

Perhaps he did not realise at that point that it would take only a glimpse or two of Ulrica Ulsenn to make him once more lose that self-possession in a different way. Even when he looked round to see Janek Ulsenn being helped up to the bridge by Petchnyoff, his spirits were unimpaired; he smiled at Ulsenn in sardonic good humour.

"Well, we're under way, Lord Ulsenn. Hope we didn't wake you."

Petchnyoff looked surprised. He had become so used to the skipper's surly manner that any sign of joviality was bound to set him aback.

"You did wake us," Ulsenn began, but Arflane interrupted him to address Petchnyoff.

"You took the middle watch and half the morning watch, I believe, Mr. Petchnyoff."

Petchnyoff nodded. "Yes, sir."

"I would have thought it would have suited you to be in your bunk by now," Arflane said as pleasantly as he could. He did not want an officer who was going to be half-asleep when his watch came round again.

Petchnyoff shrugged. "I'd planned to get some rest in, sir, after I'd eaten. Then I met Lord Ulsenn coming out of his cabin . . ."

Arflane gestured with his hand. "I see. You'd better go to your bunk now, Mr. Petchnyoff."

"Aye aye, sir."

Petchnyoff backed down the companionway and disappeared. Ulsenn was left alone. Arflane had deliberately ignored him and Ulsenn was aware of it; he stared balefully at Arflane.

"You may have complete command of this ship, captain, but it would seem to me that you could show courtesy both to your officers and your passengers. Petchnyoff has told me how you have behaved since you took charge. Your boorishness is a watchword in all Friesgalt. Because you have been given a responsibility that elevates you above your fellows, it is no excuse for taking the opportunity to . . ."

Arflane sighed. "I have made sure that the ship is in the best possible order, if that's what Petchnyoff means," he commented reasonably. He was surprised that Petchnyoff should show such disloyalty; but perhaps the man's ties were, after all, closer to the ruling class of Friesgalt than to a foreign skipper. His own surliness over the past weeks must in any case have helped turn Petchnyoff against him. He shrugged. If the first officer was offended then he could remain so, as long as he performed his duties efficiently.

Ulsenn had seen the slight shrug and misinterpreted it. "You are not aware of what your men are saying about you, captain?"

Arflane leaned casually with his back against the rail, pretending an interest with the racing ice to starboard. "The men always grumble about the skipper. It's the extent of their grumbling and how it affects their work that's the thing to worry about. I've hired whaling men for this voyage, Lord Ulsenn—wild whaling men. I'd expect them to complain."

"They're saying that you carry a curse," Ulsenn murmured, looking cunningly at Arflane.

Arflane laughed. "They're a superstitious lot. It gives them satisfaction to believe in curses. They wouldn't follow a skipper unless they could colour his character in some way. It appeals to their sense of drama. Calm down, Lord Ulsenn. Go back to your cabin and rest your legs."

Ulsenn's lean face twitched in anger. "You are an impertinent boor, captain!"

"I am also adamant, Lord Ulsenn. I'm in full command of this expedition and any attempt to oust my authority will be dealt with in the normal manner." Arflane relished the opportunity to threaten the man. "Have the goodness to leave the bridge!"

"What if the officers and crew aren't satisfied with your command? What if they feel you are mishandling the ship?" Ulsenn leant forward, his voice high-pitched.

Having so recently regained his own self-control, Arflane felt a somewhat ignoble enjoyment in witnessing Ulsenn losing his. He smiled again. "Calm yourself, my lord. There is an accepted procedure they may take if they are dissatisfied with my command. They could mutiny, which would be unwise; or they could vote for a temporary command and appeal to me to relinquish my post. In which case they must abandon the expedition, return immediately to a friendly city and make a formal report." Arflane gestured impatiently. "Really, sir, you must accept my command once and for all. Our journey will be a long one and conflicts of this kind are best avoided."

"You have produced the conflict, captain."

Arflane shrugged in contempt and did not bother to reply.

"I reserve the right to countermand your orders if I feel they are not in keeping with the best interests of this expedition," Ulsenn continued.

"And I reserve the right, sir, to hang you if you try. I'll have to warn the crew that they're to accept only my orders. That would embarrass you, I think."

Ulsenn snorted. "You're aware, surely, that most of your crew, including your officers, are Friesgaltians? *I* am the man they will listen to before they take such orders from—a foreign—"

"Possibly," Arflane said equably. "In which case, my rights as commander of this ship entitle me, as I believe I've pointed out, to punish any attempt to usurp my authority, whether in word or deed."

"You know your rights, captain," Ulsenn retaliated with attempted sarcasm, "but they are artificial. Mine are the rights of blood—to command the men of Friesgalt."

Beside Arflane, Hinsen chuckled. The sound was totally un-expected; both men turned to stare. Hinsen looked away, covering his mouth a trifle ostentatiously with one gloved hand.

The interruption had, however, produced its effect. Ulsenn was completely deflated. Arflane moved forward and took his arm, helping him towards the companionway.

"Possibly all our rights are artificial, Lord Ulsenn, but mine are designed to keep discipline on a ship and make sure that it is run as smoothly as possible."

Ulsenn began to clamber down the companionway. Arflane motioned Hinsen forward to help him; but, when the older man attempted to take his arm, Ulsenn shook him off and made something of a show of controlling his pain as he limped unaided across the deck.

Hinsen grinned at Arflane. The captain pursed his lips in disapproval. The sky was lightening now, turning to a bright, pale blue that reflected in the flat ice to either side, as the last shreds of clouds disappeared.

The ship moved smoothly, sharply outlined against a mirror amalgam of sky and sea. Looking forward Arflane saw the men relaxing, gathering in knots and groups on the deck. Through them, moving purposefully, Urquart was shouldering his way towards the bridge.

CHAPTER TWELVE

OVER THE EDGE

Vaguely surprised, Arflane watched the harpooner climb to the poop. Perhaps Urquart sensed that his mood had changed now and that he would be ready to see him. The harpooner nodded curtly to Hinsen and presented himself before Arflane, stamping the butt of his great weapon down on the deck and leaning on it broodingly. He pushed back the hood of his coat, revealing his heap of matted black hair. The clear blue eyes regarded Arflane steadily; the gaunt, red face was as immobile as ever. From him came a faint stink of whale blood and blubber.

"Well, sir." His voice was harsh but low. "We are under way." There was a note of expectancy in his tone.

"You want to know where we're bound Mr. Urquart?" Arflane said on impulse. "We're bound for New York."

Hinsen, standing behind Urquart, raised his eyebrows in surprise. "New York!"

"This is confidential," Arflane warned him. "I don't propose to tell the men just yet. Only the officers."

Over Urquart's grim features there spread a slow smile. When he spun his lance and drove it point first into the deck it seemed to be a gesture of approval. The smile quickly disappeared, but the blue eyes were brighter. "So we sail to the Ice Mother, captain." He did not question the existence of the mythical city; quite plainly he believed firmly in its reality. But Hinsen's old, rugged face bore a look of heavy scepticism.

"Why do we sail to New York, sir? Or is the voyage simply to discover if such a place does exist?"

Arflane, more absorbed in studying Urquart's reaction, answered abstractedly. "The Lord Pyotr Rorsefne discovered the city, but was forced to turn back before he could explore it. We have charts. I think the city exists."

"And the Ice Mother's in residence?" Hinsen could not avoid the hint of irony in his question.

"We'll know that when we get there, Mr. Hinsen." For a moment Arflane turned his full attention to his second officer.

"She'll be there," Urquart said with conviction.

Arflane looked curiously at the tall harpooner, then addressed Kristoff Hinsen again. "Remember, Mr. Hinsen, I've told you this in confidence."

"Aye, sir." Hinsen paused. Then he said tactfully, "I'll take a tour about the ship, sir, if Mr. Urquart wants a word with you. Better have someone keeping an eye on the men."

"Quite right, Mr. Hinsen. Thank you."

When Hinsen had left the bridge, the two men stood there in silence for a while, neither feeling the need to speak. Urquart wrested his harpoon from the deck and walked towards the rail. Arflane joined him.

"Happy with the voyage, Mr. Urquart?" he asked at length.

"Yes, sir."

"You really think we'll find the Ice Mother?"

"Don't you, captain?"

Arflane gestured uncertainly. "Three months ago, Mr. Urquart—three months ago I would have said yes, there would be evidence in New York to support the doctrine. Now . . ." He paused helplessly. "They say that the scientists have disproved the doctrine. The Ice Mother is dying."

Urquart shifted his weight. "Then she'll need our help, sir. Maybe that's why we're sailing. Maybe it's fate. Maybe she's calling for us."

"Maybe." Arflane sounded doubtful.

"I think so, captain. Pyotr Rorsefne was her messenger, you see. He was sent to you—that's why you found him on the ice—and when he had delivered his message to us, he died. Don't you see, sir?"

"It could be true," Arflane agreed.

Urquart's mysticism was disconcerting, even to Arflane. He looked directly at the harpooner and saw the fanaticism in the face, the utter conviction in the eyes. Not so long ago he had had a similar conviction. He shook his head sadly.

"I am not the man I was, Mr. Urquart."

"No, sir." Urquart seemed to share Arflane's sadness. "But you'll find yourself on this voyage. You'll recover your faith, sir."

Offended for the moment by the intimacy of Urquart's remark, Arflane drew back. "Perhaps I don't need that faith any more, Mr. Urquart."

"Perhaps you need it most of all now, captain."

Arflane's anger passed. "I wonder what has happened to me," he said thoughtfully. "Three months ago . . ."

"Three months ago you had not met the Rorsefne family, captain." Urquart spoke grimly, but with a certain sympathy. "You've become infected with their weakness."

"I understood you to feel a certain loyalty—a certain protective responsibility to the family," Arflane said in surprise. He realised that this understanding had been conjecture on his part, but he had been convinced that he was right.

"I want them kept alive, if that's what you mean," Urquart said non-committally.

"I'm not sure I understand you . . ." Arflane began, but was cut short by Urquart turning away from him and looking distantly towards the horizon.

The silence became uncomfortable and Arflane felt disturbed by the loss of Urquart's confidence. The half-savage harpooner did not elaborate on his remark, but eventually turned back to look at Arflane, his expression softening by a degree.

"It's the Ice Mother's will," he said. "You needed to use the family so that you could get the ship. Avoid our passengers all you can from now on, captain. They are weak. Even the old man was too indulgent, and he was better than any that still live . . ."

"You say it was the Ice Mother," Arflane replied gloomily. "But I think it was a different kind of force, just as mysterious, that involved me with the family."

"Think what you like," Urquart said impatiently, "but I know what is true. I know your destiny. Avoid the Rorsefne family."

"What of Lord Ulsenn?"

"Ulsenn is nothing." Urquart sneered.

Impressed by Urquart's warning, Arflane was careful to say nothing more of the Rorsefne family. He had already noted how much involved with the three people he had become. Yet surely, he thought, there were certain strengths in all of them. They were not as soft as Urquart thought. Even Ulsenn, though a physical coward, had his own kind of integrity if it was only a belief in his absolute right to rule. It was true that his association with the family had caused him to forsake many of his old convictions, yet surely that was his weakness, not theirs? Urquart doubtless blamed their influence. Perhaps he was right.

He sighed and dusted at the rail with his gloved hand. "I hope we find the Ice Mother," he said eventually. "I need to be reassured, Mr. Urquart."

"She'll be there, captain. Soon you'll know it, too." Urquart reached out and gripped Arflane's shoulder. Arflane was startled, but he did not resent the gesture. The harpooner peered into his face. The blue eyes were alight with the certainty of his own ideas. He shook his harpoon. "This is true," he said passionately. He pointed out to the ice. "That is true." He dropped his arm. "Find your strength again, captain. You'll need it on this voyage."

The harpooner clambered down from the bridge and disappeared, leaving Arflane feeling at the same time uneasy and more optimistic than he had felt for many months.

From that time on, Urquart would frequently appear on the bridge. He would say little; would simply stand by the rail or lean against the wheelhouse, as if by his presence he sought to transmit his own strength of will to Arflane. He was at once both silent mentor and support to the captain as the ship moved rapidly towards the edge of the plateau.

A few days later Manfred Rorsefne and Arflane stood in Arflane's cabin consulting the charts spread on the table before them.

"We'll reach the edge tomorrow," Rorsefne indicated the chart of the plateau (the only detailed map they had). "The descent should be difficult, eh, captain?"

Arflane shook his head. "Not necessarily. By the look of it, there's a clear run down at this point." He put a finger on the chart. "The Great North Course, your uncle called it."

"Where he was wrecked?" Rorsefne pulled a face.

"Where he was wrecked." Arflane nodded. "If we steer a course North East by North by three quarters North we should reach this spot where the incline is fairly smooth and gradual and no hills in our way. The ice only gets rough at the bottom and we should have lost enough momentum by then to be able to cross without much difficulty. I can take her down, I think."

Rorsefne smiled. "You seem to have recovered your old self-confidence, captain."

Arflane resented the suggestion. "We'd best set the course," he said coldly.

As they left his cabin and came out on deck they almost bumped into Janek and Ulrica Ulsenn. She was helping him towards the entrance to the gangway, that led to their quarters. Rorsefne bowed and grinned at them, but Arflane scowled. It was the first time since the voyage began that he had come so close to the woman. She avoided his glance, murmuring a greeting as she passed. Ulsenn, however, directed a poisonous glare at Arflane.

His legs very slightly weak, Arflane clambered up the companionway to the bridge. Urquart was standing there, nursing his harpoon and looking to starboard. He nodded to Arflane as the two men entered the wheelhouse.

The helmsman saluted Arflane as they came in. The heavy wheel moved very slightly and the man corrected it.

Arflane went over to the big, crude compass. The chronometer next to it was centuries old and failing, but the equipment was still sufficient to steer a fairly accurate course. Arflane unrolled the chart and spread it on the table next to the compass, making a few calculations, then he nodded to himself, satisfied that he had been right.

"We'd better have an extra man on that wheel," he decided. He put his head round the door of the wheelhouse and spoke to Urquart. "Mr. Urquart—we need another hand on the wheel. Will you get a man up here?"

Urquart moved towards the companionway.

"And put a couple more hands aloft, Mr. Urquart," Arflane called. "We need plenty of look-outs. The edge's coming up."

Arflane went back to the wheel and took it over from the helmsman. He gripped the spokes in both hands, letting the wheel turn a little of its own accord as its chains felt the great pull of the runners. Then, his eye on the compass, he turned the *Ice Spirit* several points to starboard.

When he was satisfied that they were established on their new course, he handed the wheel back to the helmsman as the second man came in.

"You've got an easy berth for a while, sailor," Arflane told the new man. "I want you to stand by to help with the wheel if it becomes necessary."

Rorsefne followed Arflane out on to the bridge again. He looked towards the quarter deck and saw Urquart speaking to a small group of hands. He pointed towards the harpooner. "Urquart seems to have attached himself to you, too, captain. He must regard you as one of the family." There was no sarcasm in his voice, but Arflane glanced at him suspiciously.

"I'm not so sure of that."

The young man laughed. "Janek certainly isn't, that's certain. Did you see how he glared at you as we went by? I don't know why he came on this trip at all. He hates sailing. He has responsibilities in Friesgalt. Maybe it was to protect Ulrica from the attentions of a lot of hairy sailors!"

Again Arflane felt uncomfortable, not sure how to interpret Rorsefne's words. "She's safe enough on this ship," he growled.

"I'm sure she is," Manfred agreed. "But Janek doesn't know that. He treats her jealously. She might be a whole storehouse full of canvas, the value he puts on her!"

Arflane shrugged.

Manfred lounged against the rail, staring vacantly up into the shrouds where one of the look-outs appointed by Urquart was already climbing towards the crow's nest in the mainmast royals.

"I suppose this will be our last day on safe ice," he said. "It's been too uneventful for me so far, this voyage. I'm looking forward to some excitement when we reach the edge."

Arflane smiled grimly. "I doubt if you'll be disappointed."

The sky was still clear, blue and cloudless. The ice scintillated with the mirrored glare of the sun and the white, straining sails of the ship seemed to shimmer, reflecting in turn the brilliance of the ice. The runners could be heard faintly, bumping over the slightly uneven terrain, and sometimes a yard creaked above them. The mainmast look-out had reached his post and was settling himself into the crow's nest.

Rorsefne grinned. "I hope I won't be. And neither will you, I suspect. I thought you enjoyed a little adventure yourself. This kind of voyage can't be much pleasure for you, either."

The next day, the edge came into sight. It seemed that the horizon had drawn nearer, or had been cut off short, and Arflane, who had only passed close to the edge once in his life, felt himself shiver as he looked ahead.

The slope was actually fairly gradual, but from where he was positioned it looked as if the ground ended and that the ship would plunge to destruction. It was as if he had come to the end of the world. In a sense he had; the world beyond the edge was completely unknown to him. Now he felt a peculiar kind of fear as the prow dipped and the ship began her descent.

On the bridge, Arflane put a megaphone to his lips.

"Get some grappling lines over the side. Mr. Petchnyoff," he shouted to his first officer on the quarter deck. "Jump to it!"

Petchnyoff hurried towards the lower deck to get a party together, Arflane watched as they began to throw out the grappling lines. The barbed prongs would slow their progress since all but the minimum sail had been taken in.

The grapples bit into the ice with a harsh shrieking and the ship began to lose speed. Then she began to wobble dangerously.

Hinsen was shouting from the wheelhouse. "Sir!"

Arflane strode into the wheelhouse. "What is it, Mr. Hinsen?"

The two hands at the wheel were sweating, clinging to the wheel as they desperately tried to keep the *Ice Spirit* on course.

"The runners keep turning, sir," Hinsen said in alarm. "Just a little this way and that, but we're having difficulty holding them. We could go over at this rate. They're catching in the channels in the ice, sir."

Arflane positioned himself between the two hands and took hold of the wheel. He realised at once what Hinsen meant. The runners were moving along shallow, iron-hard grooves in the ice caused by the gradual descent of ice flows over the centuries. There was a real danger of the ship turning side-on, toppling over on the slope.

"We'll need two more hands on this," Arflane said. "Find two of the best helmsmen we've got, Mr. Hinsen—and make sure they've got muscles!"

Kristoff Hinsen hurried from the wheelhouse while Arflane and the hands hung on to the wheel, steering as best they could.

The ship had begun to bump noticeably now and her whole deck was vibrating.

Hinsen brought the two sailors back with him and they took over. Even with the extra hands the ship still continued to bump and veer dangerously on the slope, threatening to go completely out of control. Arflane looked to the bow. The bottom of the incline was out of sight. The slope seemed to go on forever.

"Stay in charge here, Mr. Hinsen," Arflane said. "I'll go forward and see if I can make out what kind of ice is lying ahead of us."

Arflane left the bridge and made his way along the shivering deck until he reached the forecastle. The ice ahead seemed the same as the kind they were on at the moment. The ship bumped, veered, and then swung back on course again. The angle of the incline seemed to have increased and the deck sloped forward noticeably. As he turned back, Arflane saw Ulrica Ulsenn standing quite close to him. Janek Ulsenn was a little further behind her, clinging to the port rail, his eyes wide with alarm.

"Nothing to worry about, ma'am," Arflane said as he approached her. "We'll get her out of this somehow."

Janek Ulsenn had looked up and was calling his wife to him. With a hint of misery in her eyes, she looked back at her husband, gathered up her skirts and moved away from Arflane across the swaying deck.

It was the first time he had seen any emotion at all in her face since they had parted. He felt a certain amount of surprise. His concern for the safety of the ship had made him forget his feelings for her and he had spoken to her as he might have spoken to reassure any passenger.

He was tempted to follow her then, but the ship lurched suddenly off course again and seemed in danger of sliding sideways.

Arflane ran rapidly back towards the bridge, clambered up and dashed into the wheelhouse. Hinsen and the four sailors were wrestling with the wheel, their faces streaming with sweat and their muscles straining. Arflane grabbed a spoke and joined them as they tried to get the ship back on course.

"We're travelling too damned slowly," he grunted. "If we could make better speed there might be a chance of bouncing over the channels or even slicing through them."

The ship lurched again and they grappled with the wheel. Arflane gritted his teeth as they forced the wheel to turn.

"Drop the bolts, sir!" Hinsen begged him. "Drop the heavy anchors!"

Arflane scowled at him. A captain never dropped the heavy anchors unless the situation was insoluble.

90

"What's the point of slowing down, Mr. Hinsen?" he said acidly. "It's extra speed we need—not less."

"Stop the ship altogether, sir—knock out the emergency bolt as well. It's our only chance. This must be what happened to Lord Rorsefne's ship when it was wrecked."

Arflane spat on the deck. "Heavy anchors—emergency bolts —we're as likely to be wrecked using them as not! No, Mr. Hinsen—we'll go down under full canvas!"

Hinsen almost lost control of the wheel again in his astonishment. He stared unbelievingly at his skipper.

"Full canvas, sir?"

The wheel jumped again and the ship's runners squealed jarringly as she began to lurch sideways. For several moments they strained at the wheel in silence until they had turned her back on to course.

"Two or three more like that we'll lose her," the hand nearest Arflane said with conviction.

"Aye," Arflane grunted, glaring at Hinsen. "Set all sail, Mr. Hinsen."

When Hinsen hesitated once more Arflane impatiently left the wheel, grabbed a megaphone from the wall and went out on to the bridge.

He saw Petchnyoff on the quarter deck. The man looked frightened. There was an atmosphere of silent panic on the ship.

"Mr. Petchnyoff!" Arflane bellowed through the megaphone. "Get the men into the yards! Full canvas!"

The shocked faces of the crew stared back at him. Petchnyoff's face was incredulous. "What was that, sir?"

"Set all sails, Mr. Petchnyoff. We need some speed so we can steer this craft!"

The ship shuddered violently and began to turn again.

"All hands into the shrouds!" Arflane yelled. dropped the megaphone and ran back into the wheelhouse to join the men on the wheel. Hinsen avoided his eye, evidently convinced that the captain was insane.

Through the wheelhouse port, Arflane saw the men scrambling aloft. Once again they barely succeeded in turning the ship back on her course. Everywhere the sails began to crack down and billow out as they caught the wind. The ship began to move even faster down the steepening slope.

Arflane felt a strong sense of satisfaction as the wheel became less hard to handle. It still needed plenty of control, but they were having no great difficulty in holding their course. Now the danger was that they would find an obstruction on the slope and crash into it at full speed.

"Get on to the deck, Mr. Hinsen," he ordered the frightened second officer. "Tell Mr. Urquart to go aloft with a megaphone and keep an eye out ahead!"

The ice on both sides of the ship was now a blur as the ship gathered speed. Arflane glanced through the port and saw Urquart climbing into the lower yards of the foremast.

The huge ship leapt from the surface and came down again hard with her runners creaking, but she had become increasingly easier to handle and there were no immediate obstacles in sight.

Urquart's face was calm as he glanced back at the wheelhouse, but the crew looked very frightened still. Arflane enjoyed their discomfort. He grinned broadly, his exhilaration tinged with some of their panic as he guided the ship down.

For an hour the schooner continued her rapid descent; it seemed that she sped down a slope that had no top and no bottom, for both were completely out of sight. The ship was handling easily, the runners hardly seeming to touch the ice. Arflane decided he could give the wheel to Hinsen. The second officer did not seem to relish the responsibility.

Going forward, Arflane climbed into the rigging to hang in the ratlines beside Urquart.

The harpooner smiled slightly. "You're in a wild mood, skipper," he said approvingly.

Arflane grinned back at him. "I'm just showing those cavebound scuts how to sail a ship, that's all."

Before them, the ice sloped sharply, seeming to stretch on forever. On both sides it raced past, the spray of ice from the runners falling on deck. Once a chip of ice caught Arflane on the mouth, drawing blood, but he hardly felt it.

Soon the slope began to level out and the ice became rougher, but the ship's speed hardly slowed at all. Instead the great craft bounced over the ice, rising and falling as if carried on a series of huge waves.

The sensation added to Arflane's good spirits. He began to relax. The danger was as good as past. Swinging in the ratlines, he hummed a tune, sensing the tension decrease throughout the ship.

Some time later Urquart's voice said quietly: "Captain." Arflane glanced at the man and saw that his eyes had widened. He was pointing ahead.

Arflane peered beyond the low ridges of ice and saw what looked like a greenish black streak cutting across their path in the distance. He could not believe what it was. Urquart spoke the word.

"Crevasse, captain. Looks like a wide one, too. We'll never cross it."

Since the last chart had been made, a crack must have appeared in the surface of the ice at the bottom of the slope. Arflane cursed himself for not having anticipated something like it, for new crevasses were common enough, particularly in terrain like this.

"And we'll never stop in time at this speed." Arflane began to climb down the ratlines to the deck, trying to appear calm, hoping that the men would not see the crevasse. "Even the heavy anchors couldn't stop us—we'd just flip right over and tumble into it wrongside up."

Arflane reached the deck, trying to force himself to take some action when he was full of a deeply apathetic knowledge that there was no action to be taken.

Now the men saw the crevasse as the ship sped closer. A great shout of horror went up from them as they, too, realised there was no chance of stopping.

As Arflane reached the companionway leading to the bridge, Manfred Rorsefne and the Ulsenns hurried on to the deck. Manfred shouted to Arflane as he began to climb the ladder.

"What's happening, captain?"

Arflane laughed bitterly. "Take a look ahead!"

He reached the bridge and ran across to the wheelhouse, taking over the wheel from the ashen faced Hinsen.

"Can you turn her, sir?"

Arflane shook his head.

The ship was almost on the crevasse now. Arflane made no attempt to alter course.

Hinsen was almost weeping with fear. "Please, sir—try to turn her!"

The huge, yawning abyss rushed closer, the deep green ice of its sides flashing in the sunlight.

Arflane felt the wheel swing loose in his grasp; the front runners left firm ground and reached out over the crevasse as the ship hurtled into it.

Arflane sensed a peculiar feeling, almost of relief, as he anticipated the plunge downwards. Then, suddenly, he began to smile. The schooner was travelling at such speed that she might just reach the other side. The far edge of the crevasse was still on the incline, lower than the opposite edge.

Then the schooner had leapt through the air and smashed down on the other side. She rolled, threatening to capsize. Arflane staggered, but managed to cling to the wheel and swing her hard over. She began to slow under her impact, the runners scraping and bumping.

"We're all right, sir!" Hinsen was grinning broadly. "You got us across, sir!"

"Something did, Mr. Hinsen. Here—take the wheel again, will you."

When Hinsen had taken over the wheel, Arflane went slowly out on to the bridge.

Men were picking themselves up from where they had fallen. One man lay still on the deck. Arflane left the bridge and made his way to where the hand was sprawled. He bent down beside him, turning him over. Half the bones in the body were broken. Blood crawled from the mouth. The man opened his eyes and smiled faintly at Arflane.

"I thought I'd had it that time, sir," he said. The eyes closed and the smile faded. The man was dead.

Arflane got up with a sigh, rubbing his forehead. His whole body was aching from handling the wheel. There was a scuffle of movement as the hands moved to the rails to look back at the crevasse, but not one of them spoke.

From the foremast, where he still clung, Urquart was roaring with laughter. The harsh sound echoed through the ship and broke the silence. Some of the men began to cheer and shout, turning away from the rails and waving at Arflane. Stern-faced, the skipper made his way back to the bridge and stood there for a moment while his men continued to cheer. Then he picked up his megaphone from where he had dropped it earlier and put it to his lips.

"All hands back aloft! Take in all sail! Jump to it!"

In spite of their high spirits, the crew leapt readily to obey him and the yards were soon alive with scurrying sailors reefing the sails.

Petchnyoff appeared on the quarter-deck. He looked up at his skipper and gave him a strange, dark look. He wiped his sleeve across his forehead and moved down towards the lower deck.

"Better get those grapples in, Mr. Petchnyoff," Arflane shouted at him. "We're out of danger now."

He looked aft at the disappearing crevasse, congratulating himself on his good fortune. If he had not decided to go down at full speed they would have reached the crevasse and been swallowed by it. The ship must have leapt forty feet.

He went back to the wheel to test it and judge if the runners were in good order. They seemed to be working well, so far as their responses were concerned, but he wanted to satisfy himself that they had sustained no damage of any kind.

As the ship bumped to a gradual halt, all her sail furled, Arflane prepared to go over the side. He climbed down a rope ladder on to the ice. The big runners were scratched and indented in places but were otherwise undamaged. He looked up admiringly at the ship, running his hand along one of her struts. He was convinced that no other vessel could have taken the impact after leaping the crevasse.

Clambering back to the deck, he encountered Janek Ulsenn. The man's lugubrious features were dark with anger. Ulrica stood just behind him, her own face flushed. Beside her, Manfred Rorsefne looked as amusedly insouciant as ever. "Congratulations, captain," he murmured. "Great foresight."

Ulsenn began to bluster. "You are a reckless fool, Arflane! We were almost destroyed, every one of us! The men may think you anticipated that crevasse—but I know you did not. You have lost all their confidence!"

The statement was patently false. Arflane laughed and glanced about the ship.

"The men seem in good spirits to me. Excellent spirits, in fact."

"Mere reaction, now that the danger's past. Wait until they start to think what you nearly did to them!"

"I'm inclined to think, cousin," Manfred said, "that this incident will simply restore their faith in their captain's good luck. The hands place great store on a skipper's luck, you know."

Arflane was looking at Ulrica Ulsenn. She tried to glance away, but then she returned his look and Arflane thought that her expression might be one of admiration; then her eyes became cold and he shivered.

Manfred Rorsefne took Ulrica's arm and helped her back towards the gangway to her cabin, but Ulsenn continued to confront Arflane.

"You will kill us all, Brershillian!" he went on, apparently unaware that Arflane was paying little attention to him. His fear had plainly caused him to forget his humiliation of a few days before. Arflane looked at him calmly.

"I will certainly kill somebody one day," he smiled, and strode towards the foredeck under the admiring eyes of his crew and the enraged glare of Lord Janek Ulsenn.

With the plateau left behind, the ice became rough but easier to negotiate so long as the ship maintained a fair speed. The outline of the plateau was visible behind them for several days, a vast wall of ice rising into the clouds. The air was warmer now and there was less snow. Arflane felt uncomfortable as the heat increased and the air wavered, sometimes seeming to form odd shapes out of nothing. There were glaciers to be seen to all points ahead and, in the heat, Arflane became afraid that they would hit an ice break. Ice breaks occurred where the crust of the ice became thin over an underground river. A ship floundering in an ice break, since it had not been built for any kind of water, often had little chance of getting out and could easily sink.

As the ship moved on, travelling N.W. by N., and nearing the equator, the crew and officers settled into a more orderly routine. Arflane's previous moods were forgotten; his luck was highly respected, and he had become very popular with the men.

Only Petchnyoff surprised Arflane in his refusal to forgive him for his earlier attitude. He spent most of his spare time with Janek Ulsenn; the two men could often be seen walking along the deck together. Their friendliness irritated Arflane to some extent. He felt that in a sense Petchnyoff was betraying him, but it was no business of his what company the young first officer chose, and he performed his duties well enough. Arflane even began to feel a slight sympathy for Ulsenn; he felt he could allow the man one friend on the voyage.

Urquart still had the habit of standing near him on the bridge and the gaunt harpooner had become a comfort to Arflane. They rarely talked, but the sense of comradeship between them had become very strong.

It was even possible for Arflane to see Ulrica Ulsenn without attempting to force some reaction from her, and he had come to tolerate Manfred Rorsefne's sardonic, bantering manner.

It was only the heat that bothered him now. The temperature had risen to several degrees above zero and the crew were working stripped to the waist. Arflane, against his will, had been forced to remove his heavy fur jacket. Urquart, however, had refused to take off any of his clothing and stoically bore his discomfort.

Arflane kept two look-outs permanently on watch for signs of thin ice. At night, he took in all sail and threw out grappling hooks so that the ship drifted very slowly.

The wind was poor and progress was slow enough during the day. From time to time mirages were observed, usually in the form of inverted glaciers, and Arflane had a great deal of difficulty explaining them to the men who superstitiously regarded them as omens that had to be interpreted.

Till one day the wind dropped altogether, and they were becalmed.

CHAPTER THIRTEEN

THE HARPOON

They were becalmed for a week in the heat. The sky and ice glared shimmering copper under the sun. Men sat around in bunches, disconsolately playing simple games, or talking in low, miserable voices. Though stripped of most of their clothes, they still wore their snow visors; from a distance they looked like so many ungainly birds clustered on the deck. The officers kept them as busy as they could, but there was little to do. When Arflane gave a command the men obeyed less readily than before; morale was becoming bad.

Arflane was frustrated and his own temper was starting to fray again. His movements became nervous and his tone brusque.

Walking along the lower deck, he was approached by Fydur,

the ship's bosun, a hairy individual with great black beetling eyebrows.

"Excuse me, sir, sorry to bother you, but any idea how long we'll . . ."

"Ask the Ice Mother, not me." Arflane pushed Fydur to one side, leaving the man sour-faced and angry.

There were no clouds to be seen; there was no sign of the weather changing. Arflane, brooding again on Ulrica Ulsenn, stalked about the ship with his face set in a scowl.

On the bridge one day he looked down and saw Janek Ulsenn and Petchnyoff talking with some animation to Fydur and a group of the hands. By the way in which some of them glanced at the bridge, Arflane could guess the import of the conversation. He glanced questioningly at Urquart, leaning against the wheelhouse; the harpooner shrugged.

"We've got to give them something to do," Arflane muttered. "Or tell them something to improve their spirits. There's the beginnings of a mutiny in that little party, Mr. Urquart."

"Aye, sir." Urquart sounded almost smug.

Arflane frowned, then made up his mind. He called to the second officer, at his post on the quarter deck.

"Get the men together, Mr. Hinsen. I want to talk to them."

"All hands in line!" Hinsen shouted through his megaphone. "All hands before the bridge. Captain talking."

Sullenly the hands began to assemble, many of them scowling openly at Arflane. The little group with Ulsenn and Petchnyoff straggled up and stood behind the main press of men.

"Mr. Petchnyoff. Will you come up here!" Arflane looked sharply at his first officer. "You too please, Mr. Hinsen. Bosun —to your post."

Slowly Petchnyoff obeyed the command and Fydur, with equally poor grace, took up his position facing the men.

When all the officers were behind him on the bridge Arflane cleared his throat and gripped the rail, leaning forward to look down at the crew.

"You're in a bad mood, lads, I can see. The sun's too hot and the wind's too absent. There isn't a damned thing I can do about getting rid of the first or finding the second. We're becalmed and that's all there is to it. I've seen you through one or two bad scrapes already—so maybe you'll help me sweat this one out. Sooner or later the wind will come."

"But *when*, sir?" A hand spoke up; one of those who had been conversing with Ulsenn.

Arflane glanced grimly at Fydur. The bosun pointed a finger at the hand. "Hold your tongue."

Arflane was in no mood to answer the remark directly. He paused, then continued.

"Perhaps we'll get a bit of wind when discipline aboard this ship tightens up. But I can't predict the weather. If some of you are so damned eager to be on the move, then I suggest you get out on to the ice and pull this tub to her destination!'"

Another man muttered something. Fydur silenced him. Arflane leaned down. "What was that, bosun?"

"Man wanted to know just what our destination was, sir," Fydur replied. "I thing a lot of us . . ."

"That's why I called you together," Arflane went on. "We're bound for New York."

Some of the men laughed. To go to New York was a metaphor meaning to die—to join the Ice Mother.

"New York," Arflane repeated, glaring at them. "We've charts that show the city's position. We're going north to New York. Questions?"

"Aye, sir—they say New York doesn't exist on this world, sir. They say it's in the sky—or—somewhere . . ." The tall sailor who spoke had a poor grasp of metaphysics.

"New York's as solid as you and on firm ice," Arflane assured him. "The Lord Pyotr Rorsefne saw it. That was where he came from when I found him. It was in his will that we should go there. You remember the will? It was read out soon after the lord died."

The men nodded, murmuring to one another.

"Does that mean we'll see the Ice Mother's court?" another sailor asked.

"Possibly," Arflane said gravely.

The babble that broke out among the men rose higher and higher. Arflane let them talk for a while. Most of them had received the news dubiously at first, but now some of them were beginning to grin with excitement, their imagination captured.

After a while Arflane told the bosun to quieten them down. As the babble died, and before Arflane could speak, the clear, haughty tones of Janek Ulsenn came over the heads of the sailors. He was leaning against the mizzen mast, toying with a piece of rope. "Perhaps that is why we are becalmed, captain?"

Arflane frowned. "What do you mean by that, Lord Ulsenn?"

"It occurred to me to wonder that the reason we are getting no wind is because the Ice Mother isn't sending us any. She does not want us to visit her in New York!" Ulsenn was deliberately playing on the superstition of the hands. This new idea set them babbling again.

This time Arflane roared at them to stop talking. He glowered at Ulsenn, unable to think of a reply that would satisfy his men.

Urquart stepped forward then and leaned his harpoon against the rail. Still dressed in all his matted furs, his blue eyes cold and steady, he seemed, himself, to be some demi-god of the ice. The men fell silent.

"What do we suffer from?" he called harshly. "From cold impossible to bear? No! We suffer from *heat*! Is that the Ice Mother's weapon? Would she use her enemy to stop us? No! You're fools if you think she's against us. When has the Ice Mother decreed that men should not sail to her in New York? Never! I know the doctrine better than any man aboard. I am the Ice Mother's pledged servant; my faith in her is stronger than anything you could feel. I *know* what the Ice Mother wishes; she wishes us to sail to New York. She wishes us to pay her court so that when we return to the Eight Cities we may silence all who doubt her! Through Captain Arflane she fulfils her will; that's why I sail with him. That's why we all sail with him! It's our destiny."

The harsh, impassioned tones of Urquart brought complete silence to the crew, but they had no apparent effect on Ulsenn.

"You're listening to a madman talk," he called. "And another madman's in command. If we follow these two our only destiny is a lonely death on the ice."

There was a blur of movement, a thud; Urquart's great harpoon flew across the deck over the heads of the sailors to bury itself in the mast, an inch from Ulsenn's head. The man's face went white and he staggered back, eyes wide. He began to splutter something, but Urquart vaulted over the bridge rail to the deck and pushed his way through the crowd to confront the aristocrat.

"You speak glibly of death, Lord Ulsenn," Urquart said savagely. "But you had best speak quietly or perhaps the Ice Mother may see fit to take you to her bosom sooner than you might wish." He began to tug the harpoon from the mast. "It is for the sake of your kind that we sail. Best let a little of your blood tonight, my tame little lord, to console the Ice Mother—lest all your blood be let before this voyage ends."

With tears of rage in his eyes, Ulsenn hurled himself at the massive harpooner. Urquart smiled quietly and picked the man up to throw him, almost gently, to the deck. Ulsenn landed on his face and rolled over, his nose bleeding. He crawled back, away from the smiling giant. The men were laughing now, almost in relief.

Arflane's lips quirked in a half-smile too; then all his humour vanished as Ulrica Ulsenn ran over the deck to her injured husband, knelt beside him and wiped the blood from his face.

Manfred Rorsefne joined them on the bridge.

"Shouldn't you have a little better control over your officers, captain?" he suggested blandly.

Arflane wheeled to face him. "Urquart knows my will," he said.

Hinsen was pointing to the south. "Captain—big clouds coming up aft!"

Within an hour the sails were filled with a wind that also brought chilling sleet, forcing them to huddle back into their furs.

They were soon under way through the grey morning. The crew were Arflane's men again. Ulsenn and his wife had disappeared below and Manfred Rorsefne had joined them; but, for the moment, Arflane insisted that all his officers stay with him on the bridge while he ordered full canvas set and sent the look-outs aloft.

Hinsen and Petchnyoff waited expectantly until he turned his attention back to them. He looked at Petchnyoff sombrely for a time; tension grew between them before he turned away shrugging. "All right, you're dismissed."

With Urquart a silent companion beside him, Arflane laughed quietly as the ship gathered speed.

Two nights later Arflane lay in his bunk unable to sleep. He listened to the slight bumping of the runners over the uneven surface of the ice, the sleet-laden wind in the rigging and the creak of the yards. All the sounds were normal; yet some sixth sense insisted that something was wrong. Eventually he swung from his bunk, climbed into his clothes, buckled on his flenching cutlass and went on deck. He had been ready for trouble of some kind ever since he had watched Petchnyoff, Ulsenn and Fydur talking together. Urquart's oratory would have had little effect on them, he was certain. Fydur might be loyal again, but Ulsenn certainly wasn't; on the few occasions when he had showed himself above decks it had invariably been with Petchnyoff.

Arflane looked up at the sky. It was still overcast and there were few stars visible. The only light came from the moon and the lights that burned dimly in the wheelhouse. He could just make out the silhouettes of the look-outs in the crosstrees high above, the bulky forms of the look-outs forward and aft. He looked back at the wheelhouse. Petchnyoff should be on watch, but he could see no one but the helmsman on the bridge.

He climbed up and strode into the wheelhouse. The helmsman gave him a short nod of recognition. "Sir."

"Where's the officer of the watch, sailor?"

"He went forward, sir, I believe."

Arflane pursed his lips. He had seen no one forward but the man on watch. Idly he walked over to the compass, comparing it with a chart.

They were a full three degrees off course. Arflane looked up sharply at the helmsman. "Three degrees off course, man! Have you been sleeping?"

"No, sir!" The helmsman looked aggrieved. "Mr. Petchnyoff said our course was true, sir."

"Did he?" Arflane's face clouded. "Alter your course, helmsman. Three degrees starboard."

He left the bridge and began to search the ship for Petchnyoff. The man could not be found. Arflane went below to the lower deck where the hands lay in their hammocks. He slapped the shoulder of the nearest man. The sailor grunted and cursed.

"What's up?"

"Captain here. Get on deck with the helmsman. Know any navigation?"

"A bit, sir," the man mumbled as he swung out of his hammock scratching his head.

"Then get above to the bridge. Helmsman'll tell you what to do."

Arflane stamped back through the dark gangways until he reached the passengers' quarters. Janek Ulsenn's cabin faced his wife's. Arflane hesitated and then knocked heavily on Ulsenn's door. There was no reply. He turned the handle. The door was not locked. He went in.

The cabin was empty. Arflane had expected to find Petchnyoff there. The pair must be somewhere else on the ship. No lights shone in any of the other cabins.

His rage increasing with every pace, Arflane returned to the quarter deck, listening carefully for any murmur of conversation which would tell him where the two men were.

A voice from the bridge called to him.

"Any trouble, sir?"

It was Petchnyoff.

"Why did you desert your watch, Mr. Petchnyoff?" Arflane shouted. "Come down here!"

Petchnyoff joined him in a few moments. "Sorry, sir, I——"

"How long were you gone from your post?"

"A little while, sir. I had to relieve myself."

"Come with me to the bridge, Mr. Petchnyoff." Arflane clambered up the companionway and pushed on into the wheelhouse. He stood by the compass as Petchnyoff entered. The two men by the wheel looked curiously at the first officer.

"Why did you tell this man that we were on course when we were three degrees off?" Arflane thundered.

"Three degrees, sir?" Petchnyoff sounded offended. "We weren't off course, sir."

"Weren't we, Mr. Petchnyoff? Would you like to consult the charts?"

Petchnyoff went to the chart table and unrolled one of the maps. His voice sounded triumphant as he said, "What's wrong, sir? This is the course we're following."

Arflane frowned and came over to look at the chart. Peering at it closely he could see where a line had been erased and another one drawn in. He looked at the chart he had consulted earlier. That showed the original course. Why should someone tamper with the charts? And if they did, why make such a small alteration that was bound to be discovered? It could be Ulsenn, making mischief, Arflane supposed. Or even Petchnyoff trying to cause trouble.

"Can you suggest how this chart came to be changed, Mr. Petchnyoff?"

"No, sir. I didn't know it had been. Who could have..."

"Has anyone been here tonight—a passenger, perhaps? Any member of the crew who had no business here?"

"Only Manfred Rorsefne earlier, sir. No one else."

"Were you here the whole time?"

"No, sir. I went to inspect the watch."

Petchnyoff could easily be lying. He was in the best position to alter the chart. There again the helmsman could have been bribed by Manfred Rorsefne to let him look at the charts. There was no way of knowing who might be to blame.

Arflane tapped his gloved fingers on the chart table.

"We'll look into this in the morning, Mr. Petchnyoff."

"Aye, aye, sir."

As he left the wheelhouse, Arflane heard the look-out shouting. The man's voice was thin against the sounds of the wind-blown sleet. The words, however, were quite clear.

"Ice break! Ice break!"

Arflane ran to the rail, trying to peer ahead. An ice break at night was even worse than an ice break in the day. The ship was moving slowly; there might be time to throw out grapples. He shouted up to the bridge. "All hands on deck. All hands on deck, Mr. Petchnyoff!"

Petchnyoff's voice began to bellow through a megaphone, repeating Arflane's orders.

In the darkness, men began to surge about in confusion. Then the whole ship lurched to one side and Arflane was thrown off his feet. He slid forward, grabbing the rail and hauling himself up, struggling for a footing on the sloping deck as men yelled in panic.

Over the sound of their voices, Arflane heard the creaking and cracking as more ice gave way under the weight of the ship. The vessel dipped further to port.

Arflane swore violently as he staggered back towards the wheelhouse. It was too late to drop the heavy anchors; now they might easily help push the ship through the ice.

Around him in the night pieces of ice were tossed high into the air to smash down on the deck. There was a hissing and gurgling of disturbed water, a further creaking as new ice gave way.

Arflane rushed into the wheelhouse, grabbed a megaphone from the wall and ran back to the bridge.

"All hands to the lines! All hands over the starboard side! Ice break! Ice break!"

Elsewhere Petchnyoff shouted specific orders to hands as

they grabbed mooring cables and ran to the side. They knew their drill. They had to get over the rail with the cables and try to drag the ship back off the thin ice by hand. It was the only chance of saving her.

Again the ice creaked and collapsed. Spray gushed; slabs of ice began to groan upwards and press against the vessel's sides. Water began to creep over the deck.

Arflane swung his leg over the bridge rail and leapt down to the deck. The starboard runners were now lifting into the air; the *Ice Spirit* was in imminent danger of capsizing.

Hinsen, half-dressed, appeared beside Arflane. "This is a bad one, sir—we're too deep in by the looks of it. If the ice directly beneath us goes, we don't stand a chance . . ."

Arflane nodded curtly. "Get over the side and help them haul. Is someone looking after the passengers?"

"I think so, sir."

"I'll check. Do your best, Mr. Hinsen."

Arflane slid down towards the door below the bridge, pushing it open and stumbling down the gangway towards the passengers' cabins.

He passed both Manfred Rorsefne's cabin and Ulsenn's. When he reached Ulrica Ulsenn's cabin he kicked the door open and rushed in.

There was no one there.

Arflane wondered grimly whether his passengers had somehow left the ship before the ice break had come.

CHAPTER FOURTEEN

THE ICE BREAK

The monstrous ship lurched heavily again, swinging Arflane backwards into the doorframe of Ulrica Ulsenn's cabin.

Manfred Rorsefne's door opened. The young man was dishevelled and gasping; blood from a head wound ran down his face. He tried to grin at Arflane, staggered into the gangway and fell against the far wall.

"Where are the others?" Arflane yelled above the sound of creaking and shattering ice. Rorsefne shook his head.

Arflane stumbled along the gangway until he could grab the handle of the door to Janek Ulsenn's cabin. The ship listed, this time to port, as he opened the door and saw Ulsenn and his wife lying against the far bulkhead. Ulsenn was whimpering and Ulrica was trying to get him to his feet. "I can't make him move," she said. "What has happened?"

"Ice break," Arflane replied tersely. "The ship's half in the water already. You've all got to get overboard at once. Tell him that." Then he grunted impatiently and grabbed Ulsenn by the front of his jacket, hauling the terrified man over his shoulder. He gestured towards the gangway. "Can you help your cousin, Ulrica—he's hurt."

She nodded and pulled herself to her feet, following him out of the cabin.

Manfred managed to smile at them as they came out, but his face was grey and he was hardly able to stand. Ulrica took his arm.

As they fought their way out to the swaying deck Urquart joined them; the harpooner shouldered his lance and helped Ulrica with Manfred, who seemed close to fainting.

Around them in the black night slabs of ice still rose and fell, crashing on to the deck, but the ship slipped no further into the break.

Arflane led them to the rail, grasped a dangling line and swung himself and his burden down the side, jumping the last few feet to the firm ice. Dimly seen figures milled around; over his head the mooring lines running from the rail strummed in the darkness. Urquart and Ulrica Ulsenn were somehow managing between them to lower Rorsefne down. Arflane waited until they were all together and then jerked the trembling form of Janek Ulsenn from his shoulder and let the man fall to the ice. "Get up," he said curtly. "If you want to live you'll help the men with the lines. Once the ship goes, we're as good as dead."

Janek Ulsenn climbed to his feet; he scowled at Arflane and looked around him angrily until he saw Ulrica and Manfred standing with Urquart. "This man," he said, pointing at Arflane, "this man has once again put our lives in jeopardy by his senseless—"

"Do as he says, Janek," Ulrica said impatiently. "Come. We'll both help with the lines."

She walked off into the darkness. Ulsenn scowled back at Arflane for a second and then followed her. Manfred swayed, looking faintly apologetic. "I'm sorry, captain. I seem . . ."

"Stay out of the way until we've done what we can," Arflane instructed him. "Urquart—let's get on with it."

With the harpooner beside him he pushed through the lines of men heaving on the ropes until he found Hinsen in the process of hammering a mooring spike home.

"What are our chances?" Arflane asked.

"We've stopped the slide, sir. There's firm ice here and we've got a few pegs in. We might do it." The bearded second officer straightened up. He pointed to the next gang who were struggling to keep their purchase on their line. "Excuse me, sir. I must attend to that."

Arflane strode along, inspecting the gangs of sailors as they slipped and slithered on the ice, sometimes dragged forward by the weight of the ship; but now her angle of list was less than forty-five degrees and Arflane saw that there was a reasonable chance of saving the *Ice Spirit*. He stopped to help haul on a line and Urquart moved up to the next team to do the same.

Slowly the ship wallowed upright. The men cheered; then the sound died as the *Ice Spirit*, drawn by the mooring lines, continued to slide towards them under the momentum. The ship began to loom over them.

"Get back!" Arflane cried. "Run for it!"

The crew panicked, skidding and sliding on the ice as they ran. Arflane heard a scream as a man slipped and fell beneath the side-turned runners. Others died in the same way before the ship slowed and bumped to a stop.

Arflane began to walk forward, calling back over his shoulder. "Mr. Urquart, will you attend to the burial of those men?"

"Aye, aye, sir." Urquart's voice replied from the darkness.

Arflane moved round to the port side of the great ship, inspecting the damage. It did not seem to be very bad. One runner was slightly askew, but that could be rectified by a little routine repair work. The ship could easily continue her journey.

"All right," he shouted. "Everybody except the burial gang on board. There's a runner out of kilter and we'll need a working party on it right way. Mr. Hinsen, will you do what's necessary?"

Arflane clambered up a loose mooring line and returned to the poop deck. He took a megaphone from its place in the wheelhouse and shouted through it. "Mr. Petchnyoff. Come up to the bridge, please."

Petchnyoff joined him within a few minutes. He looked enquiringly at Arflane. His deceptively foolish look had increased and, seeing him through the darkness, Arflane thought he had the face of an imbecile. He wondered vaguely if, in fact, Petchnyoff were unstable. If that were the case then it was just possible that the first officer had himself altered the course and for no reason but petty spite and a wish to create trouble for a captain he disliked.

"See that the ship's firmly moored while the men make the repairs, Mr. Petchnyoff."

"Aye, aye, sir." Petchnyoff turned away to obey the order.

"And when that's done, Mr. Petchnyoff, I want all officers and passengers to assemble in my cabin."

Petchnyoff glanced back at him questioningly.

"See to it, please," Arflane said.

"Aye, aye, sir." Petchnyoff left the bridge.

Shortly before dawn the three officers, Petchnyoff, Hinsen and Urquart, together with the Ulsenns and Manfred Rorsefne, stood in Arflane's cabin while the captain sat at his table and studied the charts he had brought with him from the wheelhouse.

Manfred Rorsefne's injury had not been as bad as it had looked; his head was now bandaged and his colour had returned. Ulrica Ulsenn stood apart from her husband who leant against the bulkhead beside Petchnyoff. Urquart and Hinsen stood together, their arms folded across their chests, waiting patiently for their captain to speak.

At length Arflane, who had remained deliberately silent for longer than he needed to, looked up, his expression bleak. "You know why I have these charts here Mr. Petchnyoff," he said. "We've already discussed the matter. But most of you others won't understand." He drew a long breath. "One of the charts was tampered with in the night. The helmsman was misled by it and altered course by a full three points. As a result we landed in the ice break and were almost killed. I don't believe anyone could have known we were heading for the break, so it's plain that the impulse to spoil the chart came from some irresponsible desire to irritate and inconvenience me—or maybe to delay us for some reason I can't guess. Manfred Rorsefne was seen in the wheelhouse and . . ."

"Really, captain!" Manfred's voice was mockingly offended. "I was in the wheelhouse, but I hardly know one point of the compass from another. I certainly could not have been the one."

Arflane nodded. "I didn't say I suspected you, but there's no doubt in my mind that one of you must have made the alteration. No one else has access to the wheelhouse. For that reason I've asked you all here so that the one who did change the chart can tell me. I'll take no disciplinary action in this case. I'm asking this so I can punish the helmsman on duty if he was bribed or threatened into letting the chart be changed. In the interests of all our safety it is up to me to find out who it was."

There was a pause. Then one of them spoke. "It was I. And I did not bribe the helmsman. I altered the chart days ago while it was still in your cabin."

"It was a foolish thing to do," Arflane said wearily. "But I thought it would have been you. Presumably this was when you were trying to get us to turn back."

"I still think we should turn back," Ulsenn said. "Just as I altered the chart, I'll use any means in my power to convince either you or the men of the folly of this venture."

Arflane stood up, his expression suddenly murderous. Then he controlled himself and leant forward over the table, resting his weight on his palms. "If there's any more trouble aboard of that kind, Lord Ulsenn," he said icily, "I will not hold an enquiry. Neither will I ignore it. I will make no attempt to be just. I will simply put you in irons for the rest of the voyage."

Ulsenn shrugged and scratched ostentatiously at the side of his face.

"Very well," Arflane told them. "You may all leave. I expect the officers to pay attention to any suspicious action Lord Janek Ulsenn might make in future, and I want it reported. I'd also appreciate the co-operation of the other passengers. In future I will treat Ulsenn as an irresponsible fool—but he can remain free so long as he doesn't endanger us again."

Angered by the slight, Ulsenn stamped from the cabin and slammed the door in the faces of his wife and Manfred Rorsefne as they attempted to follow him.

Hinsen was smiling as he left, but the faces of Petchnyoff and Urquart were expressionless, doubtless for very different reasons.

CHAPTER FIFTEEN

URQUART'S FEAR

The ship sailed on, with the crew convinced of their skipper's outstanding luck. The weather was good, the wind strong and steady, and they made excellent speed. The ice was clear of glaciers or other obstructions as long as they followed old Rorsefne's chart closely and thus they were able to sail both day and night.

One night, as Arflane stood with Urquart on the bridge, they saw a glow on the horizon that resembled the first signs of dawn. Arflane checked the big old chronometer in the wheelhouse. The time was a few minutes before six bells in the middle watch—three in the morning.

Arflane rejoined Urquart on the bridge. The harpooner's face was troubled. He sniffed the air, turning his head this way and that, his flat bone earrings swinging. Arflane could smell nothing.

"Do you know what it means?" he asked Urquart.

Urquart grunted and rubbed at his chin. As the ship sped closer to the source of the reddish light Arflane himself began to notice a slight difference in the smell of the air, but he could not define it.

Without a word Urquart left the bridge and began to walk forward, hefting his harpoon up and down in his right hand. He seemed unusually nervous.

Within an hour the glow on the horizon filled half the sky and illuminated the ice with blood-red light. It was a bizarre sight; the smell on the breeze had become much stronger; an acrid, musty odour that was entirely unfamiliar to Arflane. He, too, began to feel troubled. The air seemed to be warmer, the whole deck awash with the strange light. Ivory beams, belaying pins, hatch-covers and the whale skulls in the prow all reflected it; the face of the helmsman in the wheelhouse was stained red, as were the features of the men on watch who looked questioningly up at him. Night was virtually turned to day, though overhead the sky was pitch black—blacker than it normally seemed now that it contrasted with the lurid glare ahead.

Hinsen came out on to deck and climbed the companionway to stand beside Arflane. "What is it, sir?" He shuddered violently and moistened his lips.

Arflane ignored him, re-entered the wheelhouse and consulted Rorsefne's map. He had not been using the old man's original, but a clearer copy. Now he unrolled the original and peered at it in the red, shifting light from the horizon. Hinsen joined him, staring over his shoulder at the chart.

"Damn," Arflane murmured. "It's here and we ignored it. The writing's so hard to read. Can you see what it says, Mr. Hinsen?"

Hinsen's lips moved as he tried to make out the tiny printed words that Rorsefne had inscribed in his failing hand before he died. He shook his head and gave a weak smile of apology. "Sorry, sir."

Arflane tapped two fingers on the chart. "We need a scholar for this."

"Manfred Rorsefne, sir? I think he might be something of a scholar."

"Go fetch him please, Mr. Hinsen."

Hinsen nodded and left the wheelhouse. The air bore an unmistakable stink now. Arflane found it hard to breathe, for it carried dust that clogged his mouth and throat.

The light, now tinged with yellow, was unstable. It flickered over the ice and the swiftly-travelling ship. Sometimes part of the schooner was in shadow, sometimes it was illuminated completely. Arflane was reminded of something that had frightened him long ago. He was beginning to guess the meaning of old Rorsefne's script well before Manfred Rorsefne, rubbing at his eyes with one finger, appeared in the wheelhouse.

"It's like a great fire," he said and glanced down at the chart Arflane was trying to show him. Arflane pointed to the word.

"Can you make that out? Can you read your uncle's writing better than us?"

Manfred frowned for a moment and then his face cleared. "Fire mountains," he said. "That's it. Volcanoes was the old word for them. I was right. It is fire." He looked at Arflane with some anxiety, his air of insouciance gone completely.

"Fire . . ." Arflane, too, made no attempt to disguise the horror he felt. Fire, in the mythology of the ice, was the arch enemy of the Ice Mother. Fire was evil. Fire destroyed. It melted the ice. It warmed things that should naturally be cold.

"We'd better throw out the grapples, captain," Hinsen said thickly.

But Arflane was consulting the chart. He shook his head. "We'll be all right, Mr. Hinsen, I hope. This course takes us through the fire mountains as far as I can tell. We don't get close to them at all—not enough to endanger ourselves at any rate. Rorsefne's chart's been good up to now. We'll hold our course."

Hinsen looked at him nervously but said nothing.

Manfred Rorsefne's initial anxiety seemed over. He was looking at the horizon with a certain curiosity. "Flaming mountains," he exclaimed. "What wonders we're finding, captain!"

"I'll be happier when this particular wonder's past," Arflane said with an attempt at humour. He cleared his throat twice, slapped his hand against his leg and paced about the wheelhouse. The helmsman's face caught his attention; it was a parody of fear. Arflane forgot his own nervousness in his laughter at the sight. He slapped the helmsman on the shoulder. "Cheer up, man. We'll sail miles to starboard of the nearest if that chart's accurate!" Rorsefne joined in his laughter and even Hinsen began to smile.

"I'll take the wheel, sir, if you like," Hinsen said. Arflane nodded and tapped the helmsman's arm.

"All right, lad," Arflane told him as Hinsen took over. "You get below. You don't want to be blinded."

He went out on to the bridge, his face tense as he looked towards the horizon.

Soon they could see the individual mountains silhouetted in the distance. Red and yellow flames and rolling black smoke gouted from their craters and luminous crimson lava streamed down their sides; the heat was appalling and the poisoned air stung and clogged their lungs. From time to time a cloud of smoke would drift across the ship, making strange patterns of light and shadow on the decks and sails. The earth shook slightly and across the ice came the distant rumble of the volcanoes.

The scene was so unfamiliar to them that they could hardly believe in its reality; it was like a nightmare landscape. Though the night was turned almost as bright as day and they could see for miles in all directions, the light was lurid and shifted constantly, and when not obscured by the smoke they could make out the dark sky with the stars and the moon clearly visible.

Arflane noticed that the others were sweating as much as he. He looked for Urquart and saw the outline of the harpooner forward, unmistakable with his barbed lance held close to his body. He left the bridge and moved through the weird light towards Urquart, his shadow huge and distorted.

Before he reached the harpooner, he saw him fall to both knees on the deck near the prow. The harpoon was allowed to fall in front of him. Arflane hurried forward and saw, even in that light, that Urquart's face was as pale as the ice. The man was muttering to himself and his body was racked by

109

violent shuddering; his eyes were firmly shut. Perhaps it was the nature of the light, but on his knees Urquart looked impossibly small, as if the fire had melted him. Arflane touched his shoulder, astounded by this change in a man whom he regarded as the soul of courage and self-control.

"Urquart? Are you ill?"

The lids opened, revealing prominent whites and rolling orbs. The savage features, scarred by wind, snow and frost-bite, twitched.

To Arflane the display was almost a betrayal; he had looked to Urquart as his model. He reached out and grasped the man's broad shoulders, shaking him ferociously. "Urquart! Come on, man! Pull yourself out of this!"

The eyes fell shut and the strange muttering continued; Arflane furiously smacked the harpooner across the face with the back of his hand. "Urquart!"

Urquart flinched at the blow but did nothing; then he flung himself face forward on the deck, spreadeagled as if in cringing obeisance to the fire. Arflane turned, wondering why so many emotions in him should be disturbed. He strode rapidly back to the bridge saying nothing to Manfred Rorsefne as he rejoined him. Men were coming out on deck now; they looked both frightened and fascinated as they recognised the source of the light and the stink.

Arflane raised the megaphone to his lips.

"Back to your berths, lads. We're sailing well away from the mountains and we'll be through them by dawn. Back below. I want you fresh for your duties in the morning."

Reluctantly, muttering among themselves, the sailors began to drift back below decks. As the last little knot of men climbed the companionway to their quarters Janek Ulsenn emerged from below the bridge. He glanced quickly at Arflane and then moved along the deck to stand by the mizzen mast. Petchnyoff came out a few seconds later and also began to make his way towards the mizzen. Arflane bawled at him through the megaphone.

"To your berth, Mr. Petchnyoff! It's not your turn on watch. The passengers can do what they want—but you've your duty to remember."

Petchnyoff paused then glared at Arflane defiantly. Arflane motioned with the megaphone. "We don't need your help, thanks. Get back to your cabin."

Petchnyoff now turned towards Ulsenn, as if expecting orders. Ulsenn signed with his hand and in poor grace Petchnyoff went back below. Shortly afterwards Ulsenn followed him. Arflane reflected that they were probably nursing their imagined wrongs together, but as long as there were no more incidents to affect the voyage he did not care what the two men said to each other.

110

A little while later he ordered the watch changed and gave orders to the new look-outs to keep a special eye open for any sign of an ice break or the steam that would indicate one of the small warm lakes fed by underground geysers that would doubtless occur in this region. That done, he decided to get some sleep himself. Hinsen had been roused well before his turn on watch was due to begin, so Manfred Rorsefne agreed to share the morning watch with him.

Before he opened the door of his cabin, Arflane glanced back along the deck. The red, shadowy light played over Urquart's still prone figure as if in a victory dance. Arflane rubbed at his beard, hesitated, then went into his cabin and closed the door firmly behind him. He stripped off his coat and laid it on the lid of his chest, then went to the water-barrel in one corner and poured water into a bowl, washing himself clean of the sweat and dust that covered him. The image of Urquart preyed on his mind; he could not understand why the man should be so affected by the fire mountains. Naturally, since fire was their ancient enemy, they were all disturbed by it, but Urquart's fear was hysterical.

Arflane drew off his boots and leggings and washed the rest of his body. Then he lay down on the wide bunk, finding it difficult to sleep. Finally he fell into a fitful doze, rising as soon as the cook knocked on the door with his breakfast. He ate little, washed again and dressed, then went out on deck, noticing at once that Urquart was no longer there.

The morning was overcast and in the distance the fire mountains could still be seen; in the daylight they did not look so alarming. He saw that the sails had been blackened by the smoke and that the whole deck was smothered in a light, clinging grey ash.

The ship was moving slowly, the runners hampered by the ash that also covered the ice for miles around, but the fire mountains were well behind them. Arflane dragged his body up to the bridge, feeling tired and ill. The men on deck and in the yards were also moving with apparent lethargy. Doubtless they were all suffering from the effects of the fumes they had inhaled the night before.

Petchnyoff met him on the bridge. The first officer was taking his turn on watch and made no attempt to greet him; Arflane ignored him, went into the wheelhouse and took a megaphone from the wall. He returned to the bridge and called to the bosun who was on duty on the middle deck. "Let's get this craft ship-shape, bosun. I want this filth cleaned off every surface and every inch of sail as soon as you like."

Fydur acknowledged Arflane's order with a movement of his hand. "Aye, aye, sir."

"You'd better get the grappling anchors over the side," Arflane continued. "We'll rest in our lines for today while

111

she's cleaned. There must be warm ponds somewhere. We'll send out a party to find them and bring us back some fresh seal-meat."

Fydur brightened up at the prospect of fresh meat. "Aye, aye, sir," he said emphatically.

Since they had been becalmed Fydur seemed to have avoided the company of Ulsenn and Petchnyoff, and Arflane was sure the bosun was no longer in league with them.

At Fydur's instructions the sails were taken in and the grappling anchors heaved over the side so that their sharp barbs dug into the ice, gradually slowing the ship to a stop. Then a party of mooring hands were sent over to drive in the pegs and secure the *Ice Spirit* until she was ready to sail.

As soon as the men were working on cleaning the schooner and volunteers had been called to form an expedition to look for the warm ponds and the seals that would inevitably be there, Arflane went below and knocked on the door of Urquart's small cabin. There was a stirring sound and a heavy thump from within, but no reply.

"Urquart," Arflane said hesitantly. "May I enter? It's Arflane."

Another noise from the cabin and the door was flung open, revealing Urquart standing glaring. The harpooner was stripped to the waist. His long, sinewy arms were covered in tiny tattoos and his muscled torso seemed to be a mass of white scars. But it was the fresh wound, across his upper arm that Arflane noticed. He frowned and pointed to it.

"How did this happen?"

Urquart grunted and stepped backward into the crowded cabin that was little bigger than a cupboard. His chest of belongings filled one bulkhead and the other was occupied by the bunk. Furs were scattered over the bunk and on the floor. Urquart's harpoon stood against the opposite bulkhead, dominating the tiny cabin. A knife lay on top of the chest and beside it was a bowl of blood.

Then Arflane realised the truth; that Urquart had been letting his blood for the Ice Mother. It was a custom that had almost died out in recent generations. When a man had blasphemed or otherwise offended the Ice Mother then he let his blood and poured it into the ice, giving the deity some of his warmth and life. Arflane wondered what particular blasphemy Urquart felt he had committed; though doubtless it was something to do with his hysteria of the previous night.

Arflane nodded enquiringly at the bowl. Urquart shrugged. He seemed to have recovered his composure.

Arflane leaned against the bunk. "What happened last night?" he asked as casually as he could. "Did you offend against the Mother?"

Urquart turned his back and began to pull on his matted

112

furs. "I was weak," he grunted. "I lay down in fear of the enemy."

"It offered us no harm," Arflane told him.

"I know the harm it offered," Urquart said. "I have done what I think I should do. I hope it is enough." He tied the thongs of his coat and went to the porthole, opening it; then he picked up the bowl and flung the blood through the opening to the ice beyond.

Closing the porthole, he threw the bowl back on top of the chest, crossed to grasp his harpoon and then paused, his face as rigid as ever, waiting for Arflane to let him pass.

Arflane remained where he was.

"I ask only in a spirit of comradeship, Urquart," he said. "If you could tell me about last night . . ."

"You should *know*," Urquart growled. "You are Her chosen one, not I." The harpooner was referring to the Ice Mother, but Arflane was still puzzled. However, it was evident that Urquart did not intend to say anything more. Arflane turned and walked into the gangway. Urquart followed him, stooping a little to avoid striking his head on the beams. They went out on deck. Urquart strode forward without a word and began to climb the rigging of the foremast. Arflane watched him until he reached the upper yards, his harpoon still cradled in his arm, to hang in the rigging and stare back at the fire mountains that were now so far away.

Arflane gestured impatiently, feeling offended at the other's surliness, and went back to the bridge.

By evening the ship had been cleaned of every sign of the ash that had fouled her, but the hunting party had not returned. Arflane wished that he had given them more explicit instructions and told them to return before dusk, but he had not expected any difficulty locating a pond. They had taken a small sailboat and should have made good speed; now the *Ice Spirit* would have to wait until they returned and it was unlikely that they would travel at night, which meant that the next morning would doubtless be wasted as well. Arflane was to take the middle watch again and would need to be on duty at midnight. He decided, as the watch rang the four bells terminating the first dog watch, that he would try to sleep to catch up on the rest he had been unable to get the previous night.

The evening was quiet as he took one quick tour around the deck before going to his cabin. There were a few muffled sounds of men working, a little subdued conversation, but nothing to disturb the air of peace about the ship.

Arflane glanced up as he reached the foredeck. Urquart was still there, hanging as if frozen in the rigging. It was more difficult to understand the strange harpooner than Arflane had thought. Now he was too tired to bother. He walked back towards the bridge and entered his cabin. He was soon asleep.

CHAPTER SIXTEEN

THE ATTACK

Automatically, Arflane awoke as seven bells were struck above, giving him half an hour before his spell on watch. He washed and dressed and prepared to leave his cabin by the outer door; then a knock came on the door that opened on the gangway between decks.

"Enter," he said brusquely.

The handle turned and Ulrica Ulsenn stood facing him. Her face was slightly flushed but she looked at him squarely. He began to smile, opening his arms to take her but she shook her head as she closed the door behind her.

"My husband is planning—with Petchnyoff—to—murder you, Konrad." She pressed her hand against her forehead. "I overheard him talking with Petchnyoff in his cabin. Their idea is to kill you and bury your body in the ice tonight."

She looked at him steadily. "I came to tell you," she said, almost defiantly.

Arflane folded his arms across his chest and smiled. "Thanks. Petchnyoff knows it's my turn on watch soon. They'll doubtless try to do it when I'm taking my tour around the deck. I wondered if they had that in mind. Well . . ." He went over to his chest, took out the belt that held his scabbarded flenching cutlass and buckled it on. "Perhaps this will end it, at last."

"You'll kill him?" she asked quietly.

"There'll be two of them. It's fair."

He stepped towards her and she drew away. He put out a hand and gripped the back of her neck, drawing her to him. She came reluctantly, then slid her arms around his waist as he stroked her hair. He heard her give a deep, racking sigh.

"I really didn't expect him to go this far," Arflane said after a moment. "I thought he had some sense of honour."

She looked up at him, tears in her eyes. "You've taken it all away from him," she said. "You have humiliated him too much . . ."

"From no malice," he said. "Self protection."

"So you say, Konrad."

He shrugged. "Maybe. But if he'd challenged me openly I would have refused. I can easily kill him. I would have refused the chance. But now . . ."

She moaned and flung herself away from him on to the bunk, covering her face. "Either way it would be murder, Konrad. You've driven him to this!"

"He's driven himself to it. Stay here."

He left the cabin and stepped lightly on deck; his manner was apparently casual as he glanced around him. He turned and ascended the companionway to the bridge. Manfred Rorsefne was there. He nodded agreeably to Arflane. "I sent Hinsen below an hour ago. He seemed tired."

"It was good of you," Arflane said. "Do you know if the hunting party's returned yet?"

"They're not back."

Arflane muttered abstractedly, looking up into the rigging.

"I'll get to my own bunk now, I think," Rorsefne said. "Good night, captain."

"Good night." Arflane watched Rorsefne descend to the middle deck and disappear below.

The night was very still. The wind was light and made little sound. Arflane heard the man on watch on the upper foredeck stamp his feet to get the stiffness from them.

It would be an hour before he took his second tour. He guessed that it would be then that Ulsenn and Petchnyoff would attempt to stage their attack. He went into the wheelhouse. As they were at anchor, there was no helmsman on duty; doubtless this was why the two men had chosen this night to try to kill him; there would be no witness.

Arflane climbed down to the middle deck, looking aft at the distant but still visible glow from the fire mountains. It reminded him of Urquart; he looked up to see the harpooner still hanging high above in the rigging of the foremast. He could expect no help from Urquart that night.

There was a commotion in the distance; he ran to the rail to peer into the night, seeing a few figures running desperately towards the ship. As they came closer he recognised some of the men from the hunting party. They were shouting incoherently. He dashed to the nearest tackle locker and wrenched it open, pulling out a rope ladder. He rushed back to the rail and lowered the ladder down the side; he cupped his hands and yelled over the ice.

"This way aboard!"

The first of the sailors ran up and grabbed the ladder, beginning to climb. Arflane heard him panting heavily. He reached down and helped the man aboard; he was exhausted, his furs torn and his right hand bleeding from a deep cut.

"What happened?" Arflane asked urgently.

"Barbarians, sir. I've never seen anything like them, skipper. They're not like true men at all. They've got a camp near the warm ponds. They saw us before we saw them . . . They use— *fire*, sir."

Arflane tightened his lips and slapped the man on the back. "Get below and alert all hands."

As he spoke a streak of flame flew out of the night and took the man on lower foredeck watch in the throat. Arflane saw it was a burning arrow. The man shrieked and beat at the flames with his gloved hands, then toppled backwards and fell dead on the deck.

All at once the night was alive with blazing arrows. The sailors on deck flung themselves flat in sheer terror, reacting with a fear born of centuries of conditioning. The arrows landing on the deck burned out harmlessly, but some struck the canvas and here and there a furled sail was beginning to flare. Sailors screamed as arrows struck them and their furs caught light. A man went threshing past Arflane, his whole body a mass of flame. There were small fires all over the ship.

Arflane rushed for the bridge and began to ring the alarm bell furiously, yelling through the megaphone. "All hands on deck! Break out the weapons! Stand by to defend ship!"

From the bridge he could see the leading barbarians. In shape they were human, but were completely covered in silvery white hair; otherwise they seemed to be naked. Some carried flaming brands; all had quivers of arrows slung over their shoulders and powerful-looking bone bows in their hands.

As armed sailors began to hurry on deck holding bows of their own and harpoons and cutlasses, Arflane called to the archers to aim for the barbarians with the brands. Further down the deck Petchnyoff commanded a gang forming a bucket chain to douse the burning sails.

Arflane leant over the bridge rail, shouting to Fydur as he ran past with an armful of bows and half a dozen quivers of arrows. "Let's have one of those up here, bosun!"

The bosun paused to select a weapon and a quiver and throw it up to Arflane who caught it deftly, slung the quiver over his shoulder, nocked an arrow to the string and drew it back. He let fly at one of the brand-holding barbarians and saw the man fall to the ice with the arrow protruding from his mouth.

A fire arrow flashed towards him. He felt a slight shock as the thing buried itself in his left shoulder, but if there was pain he did not notice it in his panic. The flames unnerved him. With a shaking hand he dragged out the shaft and flung it from him, slapping at his blazing coat until the flames were gone. Then he was forced to grip the rail with his right hand and steady himself; he felt sick.

After a moment he picked up the bow and fitted another arrow to the string. There were only two or three brands to be seen on the ice now and the barbarians seemed to be backing off. Arflane took aim at one of the brands and missed, but another arrow from somewhere killed the man. Arrows were still coming out of the night; most of them were not on fire. The silvery coats of the barbarians made them excellent targets and they were beginning to fall in great numbers before the retaliating shafts of Arflane's archers.

The attack had come on the port side; now some premonition made Arflane turn and look to starboard.

Unnoticed, nearly a dozen white-furred barbarians had managed to climb to the deck. They rushed across the deck, their red eyes blazing and their mouths snarling. Arflane shot one and stooped to grasp the megaphone to bellow a warning. He dropped the bow, drew his cutlass and vaulted over the bridge rail to the deck.

One of the barbarians shot at him and missed. Arflane slammed the hilt of his sword into the man's face and swung at another, feeling the sharp blade bite into his neck. Other sailors had joined him and were attacking the barbarians, whose bows were useless at such close quarters. Arflane saw Manfred Rorsefne beside him; the man grinned at him.

"This is more like it, eh, captain?"

Arflane threw himself at the barbarians, stabbing one clumsily in the chest and hacking him down. Elsewhere the sailors were butchering the remaining barbarians who were hopelessly outnumbered.

The noise of the battle died away and there were no more barbarians to kill. On Arflane's right a man was screaming.

It was Petchnyoff. There were two fire arrows in him; one in his groin and the other near his heart. A few little flames burned on his clothes and his face was blackened by fire. By the time Arflane had reached him, he was dead.

Arflane went back to the bridge. "Set all sail! Let's move away from here."

Men began to scramble eagerly up the masts to let out the sails that were undamaged. Others let go the anchor lines and the ship began to move. A few last arrows rattled on the deck. They glimpsed the white forms of the barbarians disappearing behind them as the huge ship gathered speed.

Arflane looked back, breathing heavily and clutching his wounded shoulder. Still there was little pain. Nonetheless it would be reasonable to attend to it. Hinsen came along the deck. "Take charge, Mr. Hinsen," he said. "I'm going below."

At his cabin door Arflane hesitated, then changed his mind and moved along to pass through the main door into the gangway where the passengers had their cabins. The gangway joined the one which led to his cabin, but he did not want to see Ulrica for the moment. He walked along the dark passage until he reached Ulsenn's door.

He tried the handle. It was locked. He leant backwards and smashed his foot into it; the exertion made his wounded shoulder begin to throb painfully. He realised that the wound was worse than he thought.

Ulsenn wheeled as Arflane entered. The man had been standing looking out of the port.

"What do you mean by . . .?"

"I'm arresting you," Arflane said, his voice slurred by the pain.

"For what?" Ulsenn drew himself up. "I . . ."

"For plotting to murder me."

"You're lying."

Arflane had no intention of mentioning Ulrica's name. Instead he said; "Petchnyoff told me."

"Petchnyoff is dead."

"He told me as he died."

Ulsenn tried to shrug but the gesture was pathetic. "Then Petchnyoff was lying. You've no evidence."

"I need none. I'm captain."

Ulsenn's face crumpled as if he were about to weep. He looked utterly defeated. This time his shrug was one of despair. "What more do you want from me, Arflane?" he said wearily.

For a moment Arflane regarded Ulsenn and pitied him, the pity tinged with his own guilt. The man looked up at him almost pleadingly. "Where's my wife?" he said.

"She's safe."

"I want to see her."

"No."

Ulsenn sat down on the edge of his bunk and put his face in his hands.

Arflane left the cabin and closed the door. He went to the door that led out to the deck and called two sailors over. "Lord Ulsenn's cabin is the third on the right. He's under arrest. I want you to put a bar across the door and guard it until you're relieved. I'll wait while you get the materials you need."

When Arflane had supervised the work and the bar was in place with the door chained to it to his satisfaction, he walked down the gangway to his own cabin.

Ulrica had fallen asleep in his bunk. He left her where she lay and went to her cabin, packing her things into her chest and dragging it up the gangway under the curious eyes of the sailors on guard outside Ulsenn's door. He got the chest into his cabin and heaved it into place beside his; then he took off his clothes and inspected his shoulder. It had bled quite badly but had now stopped. It would be all right until morning.

He lay down beside Ulrica.

CHAPTER SEVENTEEN

THE PAIN

In the morning the pain in his shoulder had increased; he winced and opened his eyes.

Ulrica was already up, turning the spigot of the big water-barrel, soaking a piece of cloth. She came back to the bunk, face pale and set, and began to bathe the inflamed shoulder. It only seemed to make the pain worse.

"You'd better find Hinsen," he told her. "He'll know how to treat the wound."

She nodded silently and began to rise. He grasped her arm with his right hand.

"Ulrica. Do you know what happened last night?"

"A barbarian raid, wasn't it?" she said tonelessly. "I saw fire."

"I meant your husband—what I did."

"You killed him." Again the statement was flat.

"No. He didn't attack me as he'd planned. The raid came too soon. He's in his cabin—confined there until the voyage is over."

She smiled a little ironically then. "You're merciful," she said finally, then turned and left the cabin.

A little while later she came back with Hinsen and the second officer did what was necessary. She helped him bind Arflane's shoulder. Infection was rare on the iceplains, but the wound would take some time to heal.

"Thirty men died last night, sir," Hinsen told him, "and we've six wounded. The going will be harder with us so under-manned."

Arflane grunted agreement. "I'll talk to you later, Mr. Hinsen. We'll need Fydur's advice."

"He's one of the dead, sir, along with Mr. Petchnyoff."

"I see. Then you're now first officer and Urquart second. You'd better find a good man to promote to bosun."

"I've got one in mind, sir—Rorchenof. He was bosun on the *Ildiko Ulsenn*."

"Fine. Where's Mr. Urquart?"

"In the fore rigging, sir. He was there during the fight and he's been there ever since. He wouldn't answer when I called to him, sir. If I hadn't noticed his breathing I'd have thought he was frozen."

"See if you can get him down. If not, I'll attend to it later."

"Aye, aye, sir." Hinsen went out.

Ulrica was standing near her trunk, looking down at it thoughtfully.

"Why are you so depressed?" he said, turning his head on the pillow and looking directly at her.

She shrugged, sighed and sat down on the trunk, folding her arms under her breasts. "I wonder how much of this we have engineered between us," she said.

"What do you mean?"

"Janek—the way he has behaved. Couldn't we have forced him to do what he did, so that we could then feel we'd acted righteously? Couldn't this whole situation have been brought about by us?"

119

"I didn't want him aboard in the first place. You know that."

"But he had no choice. He was forced to join us by the manner of *our* actions."

"I didn't ask him to plan to kill me."

"Possibly you forced him to that point." She clasped her hands together tightly. "I don't know."

"What do you want me to do, Ulrica?"

"I expect you to do no more."

"We are together."

"Yes."

Arflane sat up in his bunk. "This is what has happened," he said, almost defensively. "How can we change it now?"

Outside the wind howled and snow was flung against the porthole. The ship rocked slightly to the motion of the runners over the rough ice; Arflane's shoulder throbbed in pain. Later she came and lay beside him and together they listened as the storm grew worse outside.

Feeling the force of the driving snow against his face and body, Arflane felt better as he left the cabin in the late afternoon and, with some difficulty, climbed the slippery companionway to the bridge where Manfred Rorsefne stood.

"How are you, captain?" Rorsefne asked. His voice was at once distant and agreeable.

"I'm fine. Where are the officers?"

"Mr. Hinsen's aloft and Mr. Urquart went below. I'm keeping an eye on the bridge. I'm feeling quite professional."

"How's she handling?"

"Well, under the circumstances." Rorsefne pointed upwards through the rigging, partially obscured by the wall of falling snow. Dark shapes, bundled in furs, moved among the crosstrees. Sails were being reefed. "You picked a good crew, Captain Arflane. How is my cousin?" The question was thrown in casually, but Arflane did not miss the implication.

The ship began to slow. Arflane cast a glance towards the wheelhouse before he answered Rorsefne. "She's all right. You know what's happened?"

"I anticipated it." Rorsefne smiled quietly and raised his head to stare directly aloft.

"You . . ." Arflane was unable to frame the question. "How . . .?"

"It's not my concern, captain," Rorsefne interrupted. "After all, you've full command over all who sail in this schooner." The irony was plain. Rorsefne nodded to Arflane and left the bridge, climbing carefully down the companionway.

Arflane shrugged, watching Rorsefne walk through the snow that was settling on the middle deck. The weather was getting worse and would not improve; winter was coming and they were heading north. With a third of their complement short they were going to be in serious trouble unless they could make the best possible speed to New York. He shrugged again; he felt mentally and physically exhausted and was past the point where he could feel even simple anxiety.

As the last light faded Urquart emerged from below the bridge and looked up at him. The harpooner seemed to have recovered himself; he hefted his lance in the crook of his arm and swung up the companionway to stand by the rail next to Arflane. He seemed to be taking an almost sensual pleasure in the bite of the wind and snow against his face and body. "You are with that woman now, captain?" he said remotely.

"Yes."

"She will destroy you." Urquart spat into the wind and turned away. "I will see to clearing the hatch covers."

Watching Urquart as he supervised the work on the deck, Arflane wondered suddenly if the harpooner's warnings were inspired by simple jealousy of Arflane's relationship with the woman who was, after all, Urquart's half-sister. That would also explain the man's strong dislike of Ulsenn.

Arflane remained needlessly on deck for another hour before eventually going below.

CHAPTER EIGHTEEN

THE FOG

Autumn rapidly became winter as the ship moved northwards. The following weeks saw a worsening of the weather, the over-worked crew of the ice schooner finding it harder and harder to manage the vessel efficiently. Only Urquart seemed grimly determined to ensure that she stayed on course and made the best speed she could. Because of the almost constant snow storms the ship travelled slowly; New York was still several hundred miles distant.

Most of the time it was impossible to see ahead; when the snow was not falling fogs and mists would engulf the great ship, often so thick that visibility extended for less than two yards. In Arflane's cabin the lovers huddled together, united as much by their misery as their passion. Manfred Rorsefne had been the only one who bothered to visit Janek Ulsenn; he reported to Arflane that the man seemed to be bearing his imprisonment with fortitude if not with good humour. Arflane received the news without comment. His native taciturnity had increased to the point where on certain days he would not speak at all and would lie motionless in his bunk from morning to night. In such a mood he would not eat and Ulrica would lie with him, her head on his shoulder, listening to the slow bump of the runners on the ice and the creak of the yards, the sound of the snow falling on the deck above their heads. When these sounds were muffled by the fog it seemed that the cabin floated apart from the rest of the ship. In these moments Arflane and Ulrica would feel their passion return and would make violent love as if there were no time left to them. Afterwards Arflane would go out to the fog-shrouded bridge to stand there and learn from Hinsen, Urquart or Manfred Rorsefne the distance they had travelled. He had become a sinister figure to the men, and even the officers, with the exception of Urquart, seemed uneasy in his presence. They noticed how Arflane had appeared to age; his face was lined and his shoulders stooped. He rarely looked at them directly but stared abstractedly out into the falling snow or fog. Every so often, apparently without realising it, Arflane would give a long sigh and he would make some nervous movement, brushing rime from his beard or tapping at the rail. While Hinsen and Rorsefne felt concerned for their skipper, Urquart appeared disdainful and tended to ignore him. For his part, Arflane did not appear to care whether he saw Hinsen and Rorsefne or not, but made evident efforts to avoid Urquart whenever he could. On several occasions when he was standing on the bridge and saw Urquart advancing he hastily descended the companionway and disappeared below before the second officer could reach him. Generally Urquart did not appear to notice this retreat, but once he was seen to smile a trifle grimly when the door of Arflane's cabin closed with a bang as the harpooner climbed to the bridge.

Hinsen and Rorsefne talked often. Rorsefne was the only man aboard in whom Hinsen could confide his own anxiety. The atmosphere among the men was not so much one of tension as of an apathy reflected in the sporadic progress of the ship.

"It often seems to me that we'll stop altogether," Hinsen said, "and live out the rest of our lives in a timeless shroud of fog. Everything's got so hazy . . ."

Rorsefne nodded sympathetically. The young man did not seem so much depressed as careless about their fate.

"Cheer up, Mr. Hinsen. We'll be all right. Listen to Mr. Urquart. It's our destiny to reach New York . . ."

"I wish the captain would tell the men that," Hinsen said gloomily. "I wish he'd tell them something—anything."

Rorsefne nodded, his face for once thoughtful.

CHAPTER NINETEEN

THE LIGHT

The morning after Hinsen's and Rorsefne's conversation Arflane was woken up by the sound of knocking on the outer door of his cabin. He rose slowly, pushing the furs back over Ulrica's sleeping body. He pulled on his coat and leggings and unbolted the door.

Manfred Rorsefne stood there; behind him the fog swirled, creeping into the cabin. The young man's arms were folded over his chest; his head was cocked superciliously to one side. "May I speak to you, captain?"

"Later," Arflane grunted, casting a glance at the bunk where Ulrica was stirring.

"It's important," Manfred said, advancing.

Arflane shrugged and stepped back to let Rorsefne enter as Ulrica opened her eyes and saw them both. She frowned. "Manfred . . ."

"Good morning, cousin," Rorsefne said. His voice had a touch of humour in it which neither Arflane nor Ulrica could understand. They looked at him warily.

"I spoke to Mr. Hinsen this morning," Rorsefne said, walking over to where Arflane's chest stood next to Ulrica's. "He seems to think the weather will be clearing soon." He sat down on the chest. "It he's right we'll be making better speed shortly."

"Why should he think that?" Arflane asked without real interest.

"The fog seems to be dispersing. There's been little snow for some days. The air is drier. I think Mr. Hinsen's experienced enough to make the right judgment by these signs."

Arflane nodded, wondering what was Rorsefne's real reason for the visit. Ulrica had turned over, burying her face in the fur of the pillows and drawing the coverings over her neck.

"How's your shoulder?" Rorsefne asked casually.

"All right," Arflane grunted.

"You don't appear well, captain."

"There's nothing wrong with me," Arflane said defensively. He straightened his stooped back a little and walked slowly to the bowl by the water barrel. He turned the spigot and filled the bowl, beginning to wash his lined face.

"Morale is bad on board," Rorsefne continued.

"So it seems."

"Urquart is keeping the men moving, but they need someone with more experience to make them do their best," Rorsefne said meaningly.

"Urquart seems to be managing very well," Arflane said.

"So he is—but that's not my point. You know it's not."

Surprised by the directness of Rorsefne's implication, Arflane turned, drying his face on his sleeve. "It's not your business," he said.

"Indeed, you're right. It's the captain's business, surely, to deal with the problems of his own ship. My uncle gave you this command because he thought you were the only man who could be sure of getting the *Ice Spirit* to New York."

"That was long ago," said Arflane obliquely.

"I'm refreshing your memory, captain."

"Is that all your uncle wanted? It would seem to me that he envisaged very well what would happen on the voyage. He all but offered me his daughter, Rorsefne, just before he died." In the bunk Ulrica buried her head deeper in the pillows.

"I know. But I don't think he completely understood either your character or hers. He saw something as happening naturally. He didn't think Janek would come with us. I doubt if my uncle knew the meaning of conscience in the personal sense. He did not understand how a sense of guilt could lead to apathy and self-destruction."

Arflane's tone was defensive when he replied. "First you discuss the condition of morale on board, and now you tell me what Ulrica and myself feel. What did you come here for?"

"All these things are connected. You know that very well, captain." Rorsefne stood up. Although actually the shorter he seemed to dominate Arflane. "You're ill and your sickness is mental and emotional. The men understand this, even if they're too inarticulate to voice it. We're desperately shorthanded. Where we need the men doing the work of two, we find they'll scarcely perform what were their normal duties before the attack. They respect Urquart, but they fear him too. He's alien. They need a man with whom they feel some kinship. You were that man. Now they begin to think you're as strange as Urquart."

Arflane rubbed his forehead. "What does it matter now? The ship can hardly move with the weather as it is. What do you expect me to do, go out there and fill them full of confidence so they can then sit around on deck singing songs instead of mumbling while they wait for the fog to lift? What good will it do? What action's *needed*? None."

"I told you that Hinsen feels the weather's clearing," Rorsefne said patiently. "Besides you know yourself how important a skipper's manner is, whatever the situation. You should not reveal so much of yourself out there, captain."

Arflane began to tie the thongs of his coat, his fingers moving slowly. He shook his head and sighed again.

Rorsefne took a step closer. "Go round the ship, Captain Arflane. See if the sailor in you is happy with her condition.

The sails are slackly furled, the decks are piled with dirty snow, hatch covers left unfastened, rigging badly lashed. The ship's as sick as you yourself. She's about ready to rot!"

"Leave me," Arflane said, turning his back on Rorsefne. "I don't need moral advice from you. If you realised the problem . . ."

"I don't care. My concern's for the ship, those she carries, and her mission. My cousin loved you because you were a better man than Ulsenn. You had the strength she knew Ulsenn didn't possess. Now you're no better than Ulsenn. You've forfeited the right to her love. Don't you sense it?"

Rorsefne went to the cabin door, pulled it open and stalked out, slamming it behind him.

Ulrica turned in the bunk and looked up at Arflane, her expression questioning.

"You think what he thinks, eh?" Arflane said.

"I don't know. It's more complicated . . ."

"That's true," Arflane murmured bitterly. His anger was rising; it seemed to lend new vitality to his movements as he stalked about the cabin gathering his outer garments.

"He's right," she said reflectively, "to remind you of your duties as captain."

"He's a passenger—a useless piece of cargo—he has no right to tell me anything!"

"My cousin's an intelligent man. What's more he likes you, feels sympathetic towards you . . ."

"That's not apparent. He criticises without understanding . . ."

"He does what he thinks he should—for your benefit. He does not care for himself. He's never cared. Life's a game for him that he feels he must play to the finish. The game must be endured, but he doesn't expect to enjoy it."

"I'm not interested in your cousin's character. I want him to lose interest in mine."

"He sees you destroying yourself—and me," she said with a certain force. "It is more than you see."

Arflane paused, disconcerted. "You think the same, then?"

"I do."

He sat down suddenly on the edge of the bunk. He looked at her; she stared back, her eyes full of tears. He put out a hand and stroked her face. She took his hand in both of hers and kissed it.

"Oh, Arflane, what has happened . . . ?"

He said nothing, but leant across her and kissed her on the lips, pulling her to him.

An hour later he got up again and stood by the bunk looking thoughtfully at the floor.

"Why should your cousin be so concerned about me?" he said.

"I don't know. He's always liked you." She smiled. "Beside— he may be concerned for his own safety if he thinks you're not running the ship properly."

He nodded. "He was right to come here," he said finally. "I was wrong to be so angry. I've been weak. I don't know what to do, Ulrica. Should I have accepted this commission? Should I have let my feelings towards you rule me so much? Should I have imprisoned your husband?"

"These are personal questions," she said gently, "which do not involve the ship or anyone aboard save ourselves."

"Don't they?" He pursed his lips. "They seem to." He straightened his shoulders. "Nonetheless, Manfred was right. You're right. I should be ashamed . . ."

She pointed to the porthole. "Look," she said. "It's getting lighter. Let's go on deck."

There were only wisps of fog in the air now and thin sunlight was beginning to pierce the clouds above them. The ship was moving slowly under a third of her canvas.

Arflane and Ulrica walked hand in hand along the deck.

The browns and whites of the ship's masts and rigging, the yellow of her ivory, all were mellowed by the sunlight. There was an occasional thud as her runners crossed an irregularity in the ice, the distant voice of a man in the rigging calling to a mate, a warm smell on the air. Even the slovenliness of the decks seems to give the ship a battered, rakish appearance and did not offend Arflane as much as he had expected. The sunlight began to break rapidly through the clouds, dispersing them, until the far horizon could be made out from the rail. They were crossing an expanse of ice that was bordered in the distance by unbroken ranges of glaciers of a kind Arflane had never seen before. They were tall and jagged and black. The ice in all directions was dappled with yellow lights as the clouds broke up and pale blue sky could be seen above.

Ulrica gripped his arm and pointed to starboard. Sweeping down from the clearing sky, as if released by the breaking up of the clouds, came a flock of birds, their dark shapes wheeling and diving as they came closer.

"Look at their colour!" she exclaimed in surprise.

Arflane saw the light catch the shimmering plumage of the leading birds and he, too, was astonished. The predominant colour was gaudy green. He had seen nothing like it in his life; all the animals he knew had muted colours necessary for survival in the icelands. The colour of these birds disturbed him. The glinting flock soon passed, heading towards the dark glaciers on the horizon. Arflane stared after them wondering why they affected him so much, wondering where they came from.

Behind him a voice sounded from the bridge. "Get those sails set. All hands aloft." It belonged to Urquart.

Arflane gently removed Ulrica's hand from his arm and walked briskly along the deck towards the bridge. He climbed the companionway and took the megaphone from the hands of the surprised harpooner. "All right, Mr. Urquart. I'll take over." He spoke with some effort.

Urquart made a little grunting sound in his throat and picked up his harpoon from where he had rested it against the wheelhouse. He stumped down the companionway and took up a position on the quarter deck, his back squarely to Arflane.

"Mr. Hinsen!" Arflane tried to put strength and confidence into his voice as he called to the first officer, who was standing by one of the forward hatches. "Will you bring the bosun up?"

Hinsen acknowledged the order with a wave of his hand and shouted to a man who was in the upper shrouds of the main-mast. The man began to swing down to the deck; together he and Hinsen crossed to the bridge. The man was tall and heavily built, with a neatly trimmed beard as red as Arflane's.

"You're Rorchenof, bosun on the *Ildiko Ulsenn*, eh?" Arflane said as they presented themselves below him on the quarter deck.

"That's right, sir—before I went to the whaling." There was character in Rorchenof's voice and he spoke almost challeng-ingly, with a trace of pride.

"Good. So when I say to set all sail you'll know what I mean. We've a chance to make up our speed. I want those yards crammed with every ounce of canvas you can get on them."

"Aye, aye, sir," Rorchenof nodded.

Hinsen clapped the man on the shoulder and the bosun moved to take up his position. Then the first officer glanced up at Arflane doubtfully, as if he did not place much faith in Arflane's new decisiveness.

"Stand by, Mr. Hinsen." Arflane watched Rorchenof assemble the men and send them into the rigging. The ratlines were soon full of climbing sailors. When he could see that they were ready, Arflane raised the megaphone to his lips.

"Set all sails!" he called. "Top to bottom, stern to stern."

Soon the whole ship was dominated by a vast cloud of swelling canvas and the ship doubled, quadrupled her speed in a matter of minutes, leaping over the gleaming ice.

Hinsen plodded along the deck and began to retie a poorly spliced line. Now that the fog had cleared he could see that there were many bad splicings about the ship; they would have to be attended to before nightfall.

A little later as he worked on a second knot, Urquart came and stood near him, watching.

"Well, Mr. Urquart—skipper's himself again, eh?" Hinsen studied Urquart's reaction closely.

A slight smile crossed the gaunt harpooner's face. He glanced upward at the purple and yellow sky. The huge sails interrupted his view; they stretched out, full and sleek as a gorged cow-whale's belly. The ship was racing as she had not raced since the descent of the plateau. Her ivory shone, as did her metal, and her sails reflected the light. But she was not the proud ship she was when she had first set sail. She carried too many piles of dirty snow for that, her hatches did not fit as snugly as they had done and her boats did not hang as straight and true in their davits.

Urquart reached up with one ungloved hand and his red, bony fingers caressed the barbs of his harpoon. The mysterious smile was still on his lips but he made no attempt to answer Hinsen. He jerked his head towards the bridge and Hinsen saw that Manfred Rorsefne stood beside the captain. Rorsefne had evidently only just arrived; they saw him slap Arflane's shoulder and lean casually on the rail, turning his head from left to right as he surveyed the ship.

Hinsen frowned, unable to guess what Urquart was trying to tell him. "What's Rorsefne to do with this?" he asked. "If you ask me, we've him to thank for the captain's revival of spirit."

Urquart spat at a melting pile of snow close by. "They're skippering this craft now, between them," he said. "He's like one of those toys they make for children out of seal cubs. You put a string through the muscles of the mouth and pull it and the creature smiles and frowns. Each of them has a line. One pulls his lips up, the other pulls them down. Sometimes they change lines."

"You mean Ulrica Ulsenn and Manfred Rorsefne?"

Urquart ran his hand thoughtfully down the heavy shaft of his harpoon. "With the Ice Mother's help he'll escape them yet," he said. "We've a duty to do what we can."

Hinsen scratched his head. "I wish I could follow you better, Mr. Urquart. You mean you think the skipper will keep his good mood from now on?"

Urquart shrugged and walked away, his stride long and loping as ever.

CHAPTER TWENTY

THE GREEN BIRDS

In spite of the uneasy atmosphere aboard the ship made excellent speed, sailing closer and closer to the glacier range. Beyond that range lay New York; they were now swinging on to a course E. by N., and this meant the end of their journey was in sight. The good weather held, though Arflane felt it unreasonable to expect it to remain so fine all the way to New York.

Across the blue iceplains, beneath a calm, clear sky, the *Ice Spirit* sailed, safely skirting several ice breaks and sometimes sighting barbarians in the distance. The silver-furred nomads offered them no danger and were passed quickly.

Urquart began to take up his old position on the bridge beside the skipper, though the relationship between the two men was not what it had been; too much had happened to allow either to feel quite the same spirit of comradeship.

Leaving twin black scars in the snow and ice behind her, her sails bulging, her ivory decorated hull newly polished and her battered decks tidied and cleaned of snow, the ice schooner made her way towards the distant glaciers.

It was Urquart who first sighted the herd. It was a long way off on their starboard bow, but there was no mistaking what it was. Urquart jabbed his lance in the direction of the whales and Arflane, by shielding his eyes, could just make them out, black shapes against the light blue of the ice.

"It's not a breed I know," Arflane said, and Urquart shook his head in agreement. "We could do with the meat," the captain added.

"Aye," grunted Urquart, fingering one of his bone earrings. "Shall I tell the helmsman to alter course, skipper?"

Arflane decided that, practical reasons aside, it would be worth stopping in order to provide a diversion for the men. He nodded to Urquart, who strode into the wheelhouse to take over the great wheel from the man on duty.

Ulrica came up on deck and glanced at Arflane. He smiled down at her and signed for her to join him. She sensed Urquart's antipathy and for that reason rarely went to the bridge; she came up a little reluctantly and hesitated when she saw that the harpooner was in the wheelhouse. She glanced aft and then approached Arflane. "It's Janek, Konrad," she said. "He seems to be ill. I spoke to the guards today. They said he wasn't eating."

Arflane laughed. "Probably starving himself out of spite."

he said. Then he noticed her expression of concern. "All right. I'll see him when I get the chance."

The ship was turning now, closing with the land whale herd. They were of a much smaller variety than any Arflane knew, with shorter heads in relation to their bodies, and their colour was a yellow-brown. Many were leaping across the ice, propelling themselves by unusually large back flippers. They did not look dangerous though; he could see that before long they would have fresh meat.

Urquart gave the wheel back to the helmsman and moved along the deck towards the prow, taking a coil of rope from a tackle locker and tying one end to the ring of his harpoon, winding the rest of the rope around his waist. Other sailors were gathering around him, and he pointed towards the herd. They disappeared below to get their own weapons.

Urquart crossed to the rail and carefully climbed over it, his feet gripping the tiny ridge on the outer hull below the rail. Once the ship lurched and he was almost flung off.

The strange-looking whales were beginning to scatter before the skull-decorated prow of the huge schooner as, with runners squealing, it pursued the main herd.

Urquart hung grinning on the outside rail, one arm wrapped around it and the other poising the harpoon. One slip, a sudden motion of the ship, and he could easily lose his grip and be plunged under the runners.

Now the ship was pacing a large bull whale which leapt frantically along, veering off as its tiny eyes caught sight of *Ice Spirit* close by. Urquart drew back his harpoon, flung the lance at an angle, caught the beast in the back of its neck. Then the ship was past the creature. The line attached to the harpoon whipped out; the beast reared, leaping on its hind flippers, rolling over and over with its mouth snapping. The whale's teeth were much larger than Arflane had suspected.

The rope was running out rapidly and threatened to yank Urquart from his precarious position as the ship began to turn.

Other whaling hands were now hanging by one arm from the rail, drawing back their own harpoons as the ship approached the herd again. The chase continued in silence save for the noises of the ship and the thump of flippers over the ice.

Just as Arflane was certain Urquart was about to be tugged from the rail by the rope the harpooner removed the last of the line from his waist and lashed it to the nearest stanchion. Looking back, Arflane saw the dying whale dragged struggling behind the ship by Urquart's harpoon. The other harpooners were flinging their weapons out, though most lacked the uncanny accuracy of Urquart. A few whales were speared and soon there were more than a dozen being dragged along the ice in the wake of the ship, their bodies smashing and bleeding as they were bounced to death on the ice.

Now the ship turned again, slowing, and hands came forward, ready to haul in the catches. Ice anchors were thrown out. The schooner lurched to a halt, the sailors descended to the ice with flenching cutlasses to slice up the catch.

Urquart went with them, borrowing a cutlass from one of the hands. Arflane and Ulrica stood by the rail looking at the men hacking at the corpses, arms rising and falling as they butchered the catch, spilling their blood on the ice as the setting sun, red as the blood, sent long, leaping shadows of the men across the white expanse. The pungent smell of blood and blubber drifted on the evening air, reminding them of the time when they had first embraced.

Manfred Rorsefne joined them, smiling at the working, fur-clad sailors as one might smile at children playing. There was not a man there, who was not covered from hand to shoulder with the thick blood; many of them were drenched in the stuff, licking it from their mouths with relish.

Rorsefne pointed at the tall figure of Urquart as the man yanked the harpoon from his kill and made with his right hand some mysterious sign in the air.

"Your Urquart seems in his element, Captain Arflane," he said. "And the rest of them are elated, aren't they? We were lucky to sight the herd."

Arflane nodded, watching as Urquart set to work flenching his whale. There was something so primitive, so elemental, about the way the harpooner slashed at the dead creature that Arflane thought once again how much Urquart resembled a demigod of the ice, an old-time member of the Ice Mother's pantheon.

Rorsefne watched for a few minutes more before turning away with a murmured apology. Glancing at him, Arflane guessed that the young man was not enjoying the scene.

Before nightfall the meat had been sliced from the bones and the blubber and oil stored in barrels that were being swung aboard on the tips of the lower yards. Only the skeletons of the slaughtered whales remained on the stained ice, their shadows throwing strange patterns in the light from the setting sun.

As they prepared to go below Arflane caught a movement from the corner of his eye. He stared up into the darkening scarlet sky to see a score of shapes flying towards them. They flew rapidly; they were the same green birds they had encountered several days earlier. They were like albatrosses in appearance, with large, curved beaks and long wings; they came circling in to land on the bones of the whales, their beady eyes searching the bloody ice before they hopped down to gobble the offal and scraps of meat and blubber left behind by the sailors.

Ulrica gripped Arflane's hand tightly, evidently as unsettled by the sight as he. One of the scavengers, a piece of gut hanging from its beak, turned its head and seemed to stare knowingly at them, then spread its wings and flapped across the ice.

The birds had come from the north this time. When Arflane had first seen them they were flying from south to north. He wondered where their nests were. Perhaps in the range of glaciers ahead of them; the range they would have to sail through before they could reach New York.

Thought of the mountains depressed him; it was not going to be easy to negotiate the narrow pass inscribed on Rorsefne's chart.

When the sun set the green birds were still feeding, their silhouettes stalking among the bones of the whales like the figures of some conquering army inspecting the corpses of the vanquished.

CHAPTER TWENTY-ONE

THE WRECK

There was a collision at dawn. Konrad Arflane was leaving his cabin with the intention of seeing Janek Ulsenn and deciding if the man really was ill when a great shock ran through the length of the ship and he was thrown forward on his face.

He picked himself up, blood running from his nose, and hurried back to Ulrica in the cabin. She was sitting up in the bunk, her face alarmed.

"What is it, Konrad?"

"I'm going to see."

He ran out on deck. There were men sprawled everywhere. Some had fallen from the rigging and were obviously dead, the rest were simply dazed and already climbing to their feet.

In the pale sunlight he looked towards the prow, but could see no obstruction. He ran forward to peer over the skull-decorated bowsprit. He saw that the forward runners had been trapped in a shallow crevasse that could not be seen from above. It was no fault of the look-outs that the obstruction had not been sighted. It was perhaps ten feet wide and only a yard or so deep, but it had succeeded in nearly wrecking the ship. Arflane swung down a loose line to stand on the edge of the opening and inspect the runners.

They did not seem too badly damaged. The edge of one had been cracked and a small section had broken away and could be seen lying at the bottom of the crevasse, but it was not sufficient to impair their function.

Arflane saw that the crevasse ended only a few yards to starboard. It was simply bad luck that they had crossed at this point. The ice schooner could be hauled back, the runners turned and she would be on her way again, hardly the worse for the collision.

Hinsen was peering over the forward rail. "What is it, sir?"

"Nothing to worry about, Mr. Hinsen. The men will have some hard work to do this morning though. We'll have to haul the ship backwards. Get the bosun to back the courses. That'll give them some help if we can catch enough wind."

"Aye, aye, sir." Hinsen's face disappeared.

As Arflane began to clamber hand over hand up the rope Urquart came to the rail and helped him over it. The gaunt harpooner pointed silently to the north west. Arflane looked and cursed.

There were some fifty barbarians riding rapidly towards them. They appeared to be mounted on animals very much like bears; they sat on the broad backs of the beasts with their legs stretched in front of them, holding the reins attached to the animals' heads. Their weapons were bone javelins and swords. They were clad in furs but otherwise seemed like ordinary men, not the creatures they had encountered earlier.

Arflane dashed to the bridge, bellowed through his megaphone for all hands to arm themselves and stand by to meet the attack.

The leading barbarians were almost upon the ship. One of them shouted in a strange accent, repeating the words over and over again. Arflane realised, eventually, what the man was shouting.

"You killed the last whales! You killed the last whales!"

The riders spread out as they neared the ship, evidently planning an approach from all sides. Arflane caught a glimpse of thin, aquiline faces under the hoods; then the javelins began to clatter on to the deck.

The first wave of spears hurt no one. Arflane picked one of the finely-carved javelins up in either hand and flung them back at the fast-riding barbarians. He in turn missed both his targets. The javelins were not designed for this kind of fighting and the barbarians were so far proving a nuisance more than a positive danger.

But soon they began to ride in closer and Arflane saw a sailor fall before he could shoot the arrow from the bow he carried.

Two more of the crew were killed by well-aimed javelins, but the more sophisticated retaliation from the decks of the ship was taking its toll of the attackers. More than half the barbarians fell from their mounts with arrow-wounds before the remainder withdrew, massing for a renewed attack on the port side.

Arflane now had a bow and he, Hinsen and Manfred Rorsefne stood together, waiting for the next assault. A little further along the rail stood Urquart. He had half a dozen of the bone javelins ranged beside him on the rail and had temporarily abandoned his own harpoon, which was more than twice the size and weight of the barbarian weapons.

The powerful legs of the bearlike creatures began to move swiftly as, yelling wildly, the barbarians rushed at the ship. A cloud of javelins whistled upwards; a cloud of arrows rushed back. Two barbarians died from Urquart's well-aimed shafts and four more were badly wounded. Most of the others fell beneath the arrows. Arflane turned to grin at Hinsen but the man was dead, impaled by a carved bone javelin that had gone completely through his body. The first officer's eyes were open and glazed as the grip on the rail that had kept him upright gradually relaxed and he toppled to the deck.

Rorsefne murmured in Arflane's ear. "Urquart is hurt, it seems."

Arflane glanced along the rail, expecting to see Urquart prone, but instead the harpooner was tearing a javelin from his arm and leaping over the rail, followed by a group of yelling sailors.

The barbarians were regrouping again, but only five remained unwounded. A few more hung in their saddles, several of them with half a dozen arrows sticking in them.

Urquart led his band across the ice, screaming at the few survivors. His huge harpoon was held menacingly in his right hand while his left gripped a pair of javelins. The barbarians hesitated; one drew his sword. Then they turned their strange mounts and rushed away across the ice before the triumphant figure of Urquart shouting and gesticulating behind them.

The raid was over, with less than ten men wounded and only four, including Hinsen, dead. Arflane looked down at the older man's body and sighed. He felt no rancour towards the barbarians. If he had heard correctly the man who had shouted, their whale hunt had destroyed the barbarians' means of staying alive.

Arflane saw the new bosun Rorchenoff coming along the deck and signed for him to approach. The bosun saw the corpse of Hinsen and shook his head grimly, staring at Arflane a little resentfully as if he blamed the captain for the barbarian attack. "He was a good sailor, sir."

"He was, bosun. I want you to take a party and bury the dead in the crevasse below. It should save time. Do it right away, will you?"

"Aye, aye, sir."

Arflane looked back and saw Urquart and his band hacking at the wounded barbarians with exactly the same gusto with which they had butchered the whales the evening before. He shrugged and returned to his cabin.

Ulrica was there. He told her what had happened. She looked

134

relieved, then she said: "Did you speak to Janek? You were going to this morning."

"I'll do it now." He went out of the cabin and along the gangway. There was only one guard on duty; Arflane felt it unnecessary to have more. He signed for the man to undo the padlock chaining the door to the bar. The broken door swung inwards and Arflane saw Ulsenn leaning back in his bunk, pale but otherwise apparently fit.

"You're not eating much food they tell me," he said. He did not enter the cabin but leaned over the bar to address the man.

"I haven't much need for food in here," Ulsenn said coldly. He stared unfalteringly at Arflane. "How is my wife?"

"Well." Ulsenn smiled bitterly. There was none of the weakness in his expression that Arflane had seen earlier. The man's confinement appeared to have improved his character.

"Is there anything you want?" Arflane asked.

"Indeed, captain; but I don't think you would be ready to let me have it."

Arflane understood the implication. He nodded curtly and drew the door close again, fixing the padlock himself.

By the time the ice schooner had been set on course again the men were exhausted. A particularly dreamlike atmosphere had settled over the ship when dawn came and Arflane ordered full sail set.

The ship began to move towards the glacier range that could now be made out in detail.

The curves and angles of the ice mountains shone in the sunlight, reflecting and transforming the colours of the sky, producing a subtle variety of shades, from pale yellow and blue to rich marble greens, blacks and purple. The pass became visible soon, a narrow opening between gigantic cliffs. According to Rorsefne's chart the place would take days to negotiate.

Arflane looked carefully at the sky, his expression concerned. There seemed to be bad weather on its way, though it could pass without touching them. He hesitated, wondering whether to enter the gorge or wait; then he shrugged. New York was almost in sight; he wanted to waste no more time. Once through the pass their journey would be as good as over; the city was less than a hundred miles from the glacier range.

As they moved between the lower hills guarding the approach Arflane ordered most of the canvas taken in and appointed six men to stay on watch in the bows, relaying sightings of any obstruction back to the wheelhouse and the four helmsmen on duty.

The mood of dreamlike unreality seemed to increase as the *Ice Spirit* drifted closer and closer to the looming cliffs of ice. The shouts of the bow look-outs now began to echo through the range until it seemed the whole world was full of ghostly, mocking voices.

Konrad Arflane stood with his legs spread on the bridge, his gloved hands gripping the rail firmly. On his right stood Ulrica Ulsenn, her face calm and remote, dressed in her best furs; beside her was Manfred Rorsefne, the only one who seemed unaffected by the experience; on Arflane's left was Urquart, harpoon cradled in his arm, his sharp eyes eagerly searching the mountains.

The ship entered the wide gorge, sailing between towering cliffs that were less than a quarter of a mile away on either side. The floor of the gorge was smooth; the ship's speed increased as her runners touched the worn ice. Disturbed by the sounds, a piece of ice detached itself from the side of one of the cliffs to starboard. It bounced and tumbled down to crash at the bottom in a great cloud of disintegrating fragments.

Arflane leaned forward to address Rorchenof, who stood on the quarter deck looking on in some concern.

"Tell the look-outs to keep their voices down as best they can, bosun, or we might find ourselves buried before we know it."

Rorchenof nodded grimly and went forward to warn the men in the bow. He seemed disturbed.

Arflane himself would be glad when they reached the other side of the pass. He felt dwarfed by the mountains. He decided that the pass was wide enough to permit him to increase the ship's speed without too much danger.

"All plain sail, Mr. Rorchenof!" he called suddenly.

Rorchenof accepted the order with some surprise, but did not query it.

Sails set, the *Ice Spirit* leapt forward between the twin walls of the canyon, passing strange ice formations carved by the wind. The formations shone with dark colours; elsewhere the ice was like menacing black glass.

Towards evening, the ship was shaken by a series of jolts; her motion became erratic.

"It's the runners, sir!" Rorchenof called to Arflane. "They must have been damaged more than we thought."

"Nothing to worry about, bosun," Arflane said calmly, staring ahead. It was getting colder, and the wind was rising; the sooner they were through the pass the better.

"We could easily skid, sir, and crash into one of the cliffs. We could bring the whole thing down on top of us."

"I'll be the judge of our danger, bosun."

The trio beside him on the bridge looked at him curiously but said nothing.

Rorchenof scratched his head, spread his arms, and moved back forward.

The ship was wobbling badly as the sky darkened and the great cliffs seemed to close in on them, but still Arflane made no attempt to slow her and still she moved under full sail.

Just before nightfall Rorchenof came along the deck with a score of sailors at his back.

"Captain Arflane!"

Konrad Arflane looked down nearly serenely. The ship was shuddering constantly now in a series of short, rapid bumps, and the helmsmen were having difficulty in getting sufficiently fast response from the forward runners."

"What is it, bosun?"

"Can we throw out anchor lines, sir, and repair the runners? At this rate we'll all be killed."

"There's no fear of that, bosun."

"We feel there is, sir!" It was a new voice; one of the sailors speaking. From around him came a chorus of agreement.

"Return to your posts," Arflane said evenly. "You have still to understand the nature of this voyage."

"We understand when our lives are threatened, sir," cried another sailor.

"You'll be safe," Arflane assured him.

As the moon rose the wind howled louder, stretching the sails taut and pushing the ship to even greater speed. They jolted and shuddered along the smooth ice of the canyon floor, racing past white, gleaming cliffs whose peaks were lost from sight in the darkness.

Rorchenof looked about him wildly as a precipice loomed close and the ship veered away from it, runners thumping erratically. "This is insanity!" he shouted. "Give us the boats! You can take the ship where you like—we'll get off!"

Urquart brandished his harpoon. "I'll give this to you unless you return to your posts. The Ice Mother protects us—have faith!"

"Ice Mother!" Rorchenof spat. "All four of you are mad. We want to turn back!"

"We cannot turn back!" Urquart shouted, and he began to laugh wildly. "There's no room in this pass to turn, bosun!"

The red-bearded bosun shook his fist at the harpooner. "Then drop the heavy anchors. Stop the ship and give us the boats and we'll make our own way home. You can go on."

"We need you to sail the craft," Arflane told him reasonably.

"You *have* gone mad—all of you!" Rorchenof shouted in increasing desperation. "What's happened to this ship?"

Manfred Rorsefne leaned forward on the rail. "Your nerve has cracked, bosun, that's all. We're not mad—you are merely hysterical."

"But the runners—they need attention."

"I say not," Arflane called and grinned at Urquart, slipping

137

his arm around Ulrica's shoulders, steadying her as the ship shook beneath them.

Now the wind was howling along the canyon, stretching the sails till it seemed they would rip from their moorings. *Ice Spirit* careered from side to side of the gorge, narrowly missing the vast ragged walls of the cliffs.

Rorchenof turned silently, leading his men below.

Rorsefne frowned. "We haven't heard the last of them, Captain Arflane."

"Maybe." Arflane clung to the rail as the helmsman barely managed to turn the ship away from the cliffs to port. He looked toward the wheelhouse and shouted encouragement to the struggling men at the wheel. They stared back at him in fear.

Moments later Rorchenof emerged on deck again. He and his men were brandishing cutlasses and harpoons.

"You fools," Arflane shouted at them. "This is no time for mutiny. The ship has to be sailed."

Rorchenof called up to the men in the shrouds. "Take in the sail, lads!"

Then he screamed and staggered backwards with Urquart's massive harpoon in his chest; he fell to the deck and for a moment the others paused, staring in horror at their dying leader.

"Enough of this," Arflane began. "Go back to your posts!"

The ship swerved again and a rattling sound came from below as the steering chains failed momentarily to grip the runner platform. The ice cliffs surged forward and retreated as the helmsmen forced *Ice Spirit* away.

The sailors roared and rushed towards the bridge. Arflane grabbed Ulrica and hurried her into the wheelhouse, closed the door and turned to see that Urquart and Rorsefne had abandoned the bridge, vaulting the rail and running below.

Feeling betrayed, Arflane prepared to meet the mutineers. He was unarmed.

The ship seemed now completely at the mercy of the shrieking wind. Streamers of snow whipped through the rigging, the schooner swayed on her faulty runners. Arflane stood alone on the bridge as the leading sailors began to climb cautiously towards him up the companionway. He waited until the first man was almost upon him then kicked him in the face, wrestling the cutlass from his grasp and smashing the hilt into his skull.

A sheet of snow sliced across the bridge, stinging the men's eyes. Arflane bellowed at them, hacking and thrusting. Then, as men fell back with bloody faces and mangled limbs, Urquart and Rorsefne re-emerged behind them.

Urquart had recovered his harpoon and Rorsefne was armed

with a bow and cutlass. He began, coolly, to shoot arrows into the backs of the mutineers. They turned, confused.

The ship rocked. Rorsefne was flung sideways; Urquart barely managed to grasp at a ratline for support. Most of the sailors were flung in all directions and Arflane slipped down the companionway, clinging to the rail and dropping his cutlass.

Once again the ship was racked by a rapid series of jerks. Arflane struggled up, his jacket torn open by the wind, his beard streaming. With one hand he held the rail; with the other he gesticulated at the sailors.

"Rorchenof deceived you," he shouted. "Now you can see why we must get through this pass as fast as we can. If we don't the ship's finished!"

A sailor's face craned forward, his eyes as wild as Arflane's own. "Why? Why, skipper?"

"The snow! Once caught in the main blizzard we are blind and helpless! Loose ice will fall from the cliffs to block the pass. Snow will gather in drifts and make movement impossible. If we're not crushed we'll be snowbound and stranded!"

Above his head a sail broke loose from its eyebolts and began to flap thunderously against the mast. The howl of the wind increased; the ship was flung sideways towards the cliff, seemed to scrape the wall before it slid into the centre of the gorge again.

"But if we sail on we'll smash into a cliff and be killed!" another sailor cried. "What have we to gain?"

Arflane grinned and spread his arms, coat swirling out behind him, eyes gleaming. "A fast death instead of a slow one if our luck's really bad. If our luck holds—and you know me to be lucky—then we'll be through by dawn and New York only a few days' sail away!"

"You *were* lucky, skipper," the sailor called. "But they say you're not the Ice Mother's chosen any more—that you've gone against her will. The woman . . ."

Arflane laughed harshly. "You'll have to trust my luck—it's all you have. Lower your weapons, lads."

"Let the wind carry us through. It's our only chance." The voice was Urquart's.

The men began to lower their cutlasses, still not entirely convinced.

"You'd be better employed if you got into the shrouds and looked to your sails," Manfred Rorsefne shouted above the moan of the wind.

"But the runners . . ." a sailor began.

"We'll concern outselves with those," Arflane said. "Back to work lads. There'll be no vengeance taken on you when we're through the pass, I promise. We must work together—or die together!"

The sailors began to disperse, their faces still full of fear and doubt.

Ulrica struggled through the wheelhouse door and struggled along the dangerously swaying deck to clutch Arflane's arm. The wind whipped her clothes and the snow stung her face. "Are you sure the men are wrong?" she asked. "Wouldn't it be best . . . ?"

He grinned and shrugged. "It doesn't matter, Ulrica. Go below and rest if you can. I'll join you later." Again the ship listed and he slid along the deck, fighting his way back to her and helping her towards the bridge.

When she was safely below he began to make his way forward, leaning into the wind, the snow stinging his face and half-blinding him. He reached the bows and tried to peer ahead, catching only glimpses of the cliffs on both sides as the ship rocked and swerved on its faulty runners. He got to the bowsprit and stretched his body along it, supporting himself by one hand curled in a staysail line; with the other he stroked the great skulls of the whales, pressing his fingers against the contours of cranium, eye sockets and grinning jaws as if they could somehow transmit to him the strength they had once possessed.

As the snow eased slightly ahead he saw the black outlines of the ice cliffs in front of him. They seemed to be closing in, as if shifting on their bases, crowding to trap the ship. It was merely a trick of the eyes, but it disturbed him.

Then he realised what was actually happening. The gorge really did narrow here. Perhaps the cliffs had shifted, for the opening between them was becoming little more than a crack. The *Ice Spirit* would not be able to get through.

He swung himself desperately along the bowsprit, conscious only of the careering speed of the ship, gasped and staggered across the deck till he reached the great gland of the steering pin and seized the heavy mallet that was secured beside it, began swinging at the emergency bolt. Urquart swayed towards him; he turned his head, bellowing across the deck.

"Drop the anchors! For the Ice Mother's sake, man—drop the anchors . . !"

Urquart raced back along the deck, finding men and ordering them to the stanchions to knock out the pegs that kept the twin blades of the heavy anchors clear of the ice.

Arflane looked up, his heart sinking. They were nearly into the bottleneck; there was hardly a chance now of saving the ship.

The bolt was shifting. Driving his arms back and forth, he swung the mallet again and again.

Suddenly the thing flew free. There was a high-pitched

140

squealing as the runners turned inwards, ploughshare-fashion; the ship began to roll and shudder violently.

Arflane raced back along the deck. He had done all he could; now his concern was for Ulrica's safety.

He reached the cabin as the ship leaped as if in some monstrous orgasm. Ulrica was there, and her husband beside her.

"I released him," she said.

Arflane grunted. "Come on—get on deck. There's little chance of any of us surviving this."

There was a final violent crash; the ship's shuddering movement subsided, dying away as the heavy anchors gripped the ice and brought her to a halt.

Clambering out on deck Arflane saw in astonishment that they were barely ten yards from the point where the ship would have been dashed against the walls of the cliffs or crushed between them.

But *Ice Spirit*'s motion had not ceased.

Now the great schooner began to topple as her port runners gave out completely under the strain, snapping with sharp cracks. With a terrifying groan the vessel collapsed on to her side, turning as the wind caught the sails, flinging her crew in a heap against the port rail.

Arflane grabbed Ulrica and curled his hand around a trailing rope.

His one concern now was to abandon the ship and save them both. He slid down the line and leapt clear on to the hard ice, dragging the woman with him away from the ship and against the wind.

Through the blizzard he could see little of either the cliffs or the bulk of the schooner.

He heard her crash into the side of the gorge and then made out another sound from above as pieces of ice, shaken free, began to slide downwards.

Eventually he managed to find the comparative shelter of an overhang by the far wall of the gorge. He paused, panting and looking back at the broken ship. There was no way of telling if any of the others had managed to jump free; he saw an occasional figure framed near the rail as the curtain of snow parted and swirled back. Once he heard a voice above the wind. It sounded like Ulsenn's.

"He wanted this wreck! He wanted it . . !"

It was like the meaningless cry of a bird. Then the wind roared louder, drowning it, as a great avalanche of ice began to fall on the ship.

The two huddled together under the overhang, watching *Ice Spirit* as she was crushed by the huge collapsing slabs, jerking like a dying creature, her hull breaking, her masts cracking and splintering, disintegrating faster than Arflane could ever have believed; breaking up in a cloud of ice splinters and swirling snow against the towering, jagged walls of the ice mountains.

Arflane wept as he watched; it was as if the destruction of the ship signified the end of all hope. He pulled Ulrica to him, wrapping his arms about her, more to comfort himself than for any thought for her.

CHAPTER TWENTY-TWO

THE TREK

In the morning the snow had stopped falling but the skies were heavy and grey above the dark peaks of the glaciers. The storm had subsided almost as soon as the *Ice Spirit* had been smashed, as if destroying the ship had been its sole purpose.

Moving across the irregular masses of snow and ice towards the place where the gorge narrowed and where the main bulk of the wreck had come to rest Arflane and Ulrica were joined by Rorsefne and Ulsenn. Neither man was badly hurt, but their furs were torn and they were exhausted. A few sailors stood by the pile of broken fibreglass and metal as if they hoped that the ship might magically restore itself. Urquart was actually in the wreck, moving about like a carrion bird.

It was a cold, bleak day; they shivered, their breath hanging white and heavy on the air. They looked about them and saw mangled bodies everywhere; most of the sailors had been killed and the seven who remained looked sourly at Arflane, blaming his recklessness for the disaster.

Ulsenn's attitude to Arflane and Ulrica was remote and neutral. He nodded to them as they walked together to the wreck. Rorsefne was smiling and humming a tune to himself as if enjoying a private joke.

Arflane turned to him, pointing at the narrow gap between the cliffs. "It was not on the chart, was it?" He spoke loudly, defensively, as much for the benefit of the listening sailors as anyone.

"There was no mention of it," Rorsefne agreed, smiling like an actor amused by his lines. "The cliffs must have moved closer together. I've heard of such things happening. What do we do now, captain? There isn't a boat left. How do we get home?"

Arflane glanced at him grimly. "Home?"

"You mean to carry on, then?" Ulsenn said tonelessly.

"That's the most sensible thing to do," Arflane told him. "We're only some fifty miles or so from New York and we're several thousand from home . . ."

Urquart held up some large slivers of ivory that had evidently come from broken hatch covers. "Skis," he said. "We could reach New York in a week or less."

142

Rorsefne laughed. "Indefatigable! I'm with you, captain."
The others said nothing; there was nothing left to say.

Within two days the party had traversed the pass and begun
to move across the wide ice plain beyond the glacier range. The
weather was still poor, with snow falling sporadically, and the
cold was in their bones. They had salvaged harpoons and
slivers of ivory to act as poles and skis; on their backs they
carried packs of provisions.

They were utterly weary and rarely spoke, even when they
camped. They were following a course plotted from a small
compass which Manfred Rorsefne had found amongst the
things spilled from his shattered travelling chest.

To Arflane space had become nothing but an eternal white
plain and time no longer seemed to exist at all. His face, hands
and feet were frostbitten, his beard was encrusted with particles
of ice, his eyes were red and pouched. Mechanically he drove
himself on his skis, followed by the others who moved, as he
did, like automata. Thought meant simply remembering to eat
and protect oneself from the cold as best one could; speech
was a matter of monosyllabic communications if one decided
to stop or change direction.

From habit he and Ulrica stayed together, but neither any
longer felt any emotion for the other.

In this condition it would have been possible for the party
to have moved on, never finding New York, until one by one
they died; even death would have seemed merely a gradual
change from one state to another, for the cold was so bitter
that pain could not be felt. Two of the sailors did die; the
rest of the party left them where they fell. The only one who
did not seem affected by exhaustion was Urquart. When the
sailors died he had made the sign of the Ice Mother before
passing on.

None of them realised that the compass was erratic and that
they were moving across the great white plain in a wide curve
away from the supposed location of New York.

The barbarians were similar in general appearance to the
ones who had attacked them after the whale killing. They
were dressed all in white fur and rode white, bear-like creatures.
They held swords and javelins ready as they reined in to block
the little party's progress.

Arflane only saw them then. He swayed on his skis, peering
through red-rimmed eyes at the grinning, aquiline faces of the
riders. Wearily he raised his harpoon in an attitude of defence
but the weight was almost too much for him.

It was Urquart who yelled suddenly and flung one harpoon
then another, swinging his own weapon from his shoulder as
two barbarians toppled from their saddles.

Their leader shouted, waving to his men; they rode swiftly down on the party, javelins raised. Arflane thrust out his own harpoon to defend Ulrica but was knocked backwards by a savage slash across the face, losing his footing in the snow. A blow on his head followed and he lost consciousness.

CHAPTER TWENTY-THREE

THE RITES OF THE ICE MOTHER

There was pain in Arflane's head and his face throbbed from the blow he had received. His wrists were tied behind him and he lay uncomfortably on the ice. He opened his eyes and saw the barbarian camp.

Hide tents were stretched on rigid bone frames; the riding bears were corralled to one side of the camp and a few women moved about among the tents. The place was evidently not their permanent home; Arflane knew that most barbarians were nomads. The men stood in a large group around their leader, the personage Arflane had seen earlier. He was talking with them and glancing at the prisoners who had been bound together at the wrists and lay sprawled on the ice. Arflane turned his head and saw with relief that Ulrica was safe; she smiled at him weakly. Manfred Rorsefne was there and Janek Ulsenn, his eyes tightly closed. There were three sailors, their expressions wretched as they stared at the barbarians.

There was no sign of Urquart; Arflane wondered vaguely if they had killed him. Some moments later he saw him emerge from a tent with a small, obese man, striding towards the main gathering. It seemed then that Urquart had somehow gained their confidence. Arflane was relieved; with luck the harpooner might find a way to release them.

The leader, a handsome, brown-skinned young man with a beak of a nose and bright, haughty eyes, gesticulated towards Urquart as he and the short man pushed through the throng. Urquart began to speak. Arflane gathered that the harpooner was pleading for his friends' lives and wondered how the man had managed to win favour with the nomads. Certainly Urquart was considerably taller than any of them and his own primitive appearance would probably impress them as it impressed all who encountered him. Also, of course, he had been the only one to attack the barbarians; perhaps they admired him for his courage. Whatever the reason there was no doubt that they were listening gravely to the harpooner as he spoke, waving his massive lance in the direction of the captives.

Eventually the three of them—the leader, the fat man and Urquart—moved away from the other warriors and approached Arflane and the rest.

The young leader was dressed all in fine white fur, his hood framing his face; he was clean-shaven and walked lithely, his back held straight and his hand on the hilt of his bone sword. The fat man wore reddish furs that Arflane could not identify; he pulled at his long, greasy moustachios and scowled thoughtfully. Urquart was expressionless.

The leader paused before Arflane and put his hands on his hips. "Ha! You head north like us, eh? You are from back there!" He spoke in a strange, lilting accent, jerked his thumb towards the south.

"Yes," Arflane agreed, finding it difficult to speak through his swollen lips. "We had a ship—it was wrecked." He eyed the youth warily, wondering what Urquart had told him.

"The big sleigh with the skins on poles. We saw it—many days back. Yes." The youth smiled and gave Arflane a quick, intelligent look. "There are more—on top of a great hill—months back, eh?"

"You know the plateau of the Eight Cities?" Arflane was surprised. He glanced at Urquart, but the harpooner's expression was frozen. He stood leaning on his harpoon, staring into the middle distance.

"We are from much further south than you, my friend," grinned the barbarian leader. "The country is getting too soft back there. The ice is vanishing and there is something yielding and unnatural beneath it. We came north, where things are still normal. I'm Donal of Kamfor and this is my tribe."

"Arflane of Brershill," he replied formally, still confused and wondering what Urquart had said at the barbarian conference.

"The ice is really melting further south?" Manfred Rorsefne spoke for the first time. "It's vanishing altogether?"

"That's so," Donal of Kamfor nodded. "No one can live there." He gestured with his hand. "Things—push up—from this soft stuff. Bad." He shook his head and screwed up his face.

Arflane felt ill at the idea. Donal laughed and pointed at him. "Ha! You hate it too! Where were you going?"

Arflane again tried to get some sign from Urquart, but the man refused even to meet his eye. There was nothing to gain by being secretive about their destination and it might capture the barbarian's imagination. "We were going to New York," he said.

Donal looked astonished. "You seek the Ice Mother's court? Surely no one is allowed there . . ."

Urquart gestured at Arflane. "He is the one. He is the Mother's chosen. I told you that one of us is fated to meet Her and plead our case. She is helping him reach Her. When he does, the melting will stop."

Now Arflane guessed how Urquart had convinced the barbarians. They were evidently even more superstitious than the whaling men of the Eight Cities. However, Donal was plainly not a man to be duped. He nudged the fat man's shoulder with his elbow.

"We do what this Urquart says to test the truth, eh?" he said.

The fat man chewed at his lower lip, looking bleakly at Arflane. "I am the priest," he murmured to Donal. "I decide this thing."

Donal shrugged and took a step back..

The priest turned his attentions from Arflane to Ulrica and then to Manfred Rorsefne. He glanced briefly at the sailors and Janek Ulsenn, began to tug at his moustaches. He moved closer to Urquart and laid a finger on his arm. "Those are the two, then?" he said, pointing at Ulrica and Rorsefne.

Urquart nodded.

"Good stock," said the priest. "You were right."

"The line of the highest chiefs in the Eight Cities," Urquart said. "No better blood—and they are my kin." He spoke almost proudly. "It will please the Ice Mother and bring us all luck. Arflane will lead us to New York and we shall be welcome."

"What are you saying, Urquart?" Arflane asked uneasily. "What sort of bargain have you struck for us?"

Urquart began to smile. "One that will solve all our problems. Now my ambition can be fulfilled, the Ice Mother mollified, your burden can be removed, we win the help and friendship of these people. At last it is possible to do what I have planned all these years." His savage eyes burned with a disturbing brilliance. "I have been faithful to the Mother. I have served Her and I have prayed to Her. She sent you—and you helped me. Now She gives me my right. And I, in turn, give Her Hers."

Arflane shivered. The voice was cold, soft, terrifying.

"What do you mean?" he asked. "How have I helped you?"

"You saved the lives of all the Rorsefne clan—my father, his daughter and his nephew."

"That was why you befriended me, I thought . . ."

"I saw your destiny, then. I realised that you were the servant of the Ice Mother, though at first you did not know it yourself." Urquart pushed back his hood, revealing his bizarre hair and his dangling bone earrings. "You saved their lives, Konrad Arflane, so that I might take them in my own way at my leisure. The time has come for vengeance on my father's brood. I only regret that he cannot be here, also."

Arflane remembered the funeral outside Friesgalt and Urquart's strange behaviour when he had flung the ice block down so savagely into old Pyotr Rorsefne's grave.

"Why do you hate him?" he asked.

"He tried to kill me." Urquart's tone was distant; he looked away from Arflane. "My mother was the wife of an inn-keeper. Rorsefne's mistress. When she brought me to him, asking him to protect me as is the custom, he had his servants carry me on to the ice to expose me. I heard the story years later from her own lips. I was found by a whaling brig and became their mascot. The tale became known in the top-deck taverns and my mother realised what had happened. She sought me out and found me eventually when I was sixteen years old. From then on I planned my revenge on the whole Rorsefne brood. That was more than a score of years ago. I am a child of the ice— favourite of the Ice Mother. The fact that I live today is proof of that." Urquart's eyes burned even brighter.

"That's what you told these people to make them listen to you!" Arflane whispered. He tested the thongs holding his wrists together, but they were tied tightly.

Urquart moved forward, ignoring Arflane. He drew his long knife from his sheath and stooped to cut the lines tying Ulrica and Manfred to the rest. Ulrica lay there, her face pale, her eyes incredulous and terrified. Even Manfred Rorsefne's face had become grim. Neither made a move to rise.

Urquart reached out and pulled the trembling woman to her feet, sheathed his knife and grabbed Rorsefne by the front of his tattered coat. Manfred stood upright with some dignity. There was a movement behind Arflane. He turned his head and saw that Ulsenn's hands had come free. In cutting the thongs, Urquart had accidentally released the man. Donal pointed silently at Ulsenn, but Urquart shrugged disdainfully. "He'll do nothing."

Arflane stared up unbelievingly at the gaunt harpooner. "Urquart, you've lost your reason. You can't kill them!"

"I can," Urquart said quietly.

"He must," the fat priest added. "It is the bargain he made with us. We have had bad luck with the hunting and need a sacrifice for the Ice Mother. The sacrifice must be the best blood." He smiled a trifle sardonically and jerked his thumb at Donal. "We need this one—he is all we have. If Urquart performs the ritual then the rest of you go free; or we come with you, whichever we decide."

"He's insane!" Arflane tried desperately to struggle to his feet. "His hatred's turned his brain."

"I do not see that," the priest said calmly. "And even if it were true it would not matter to us. These will die and you will not. You should be grateful."

Arflane struggled helplessly on the ice, half-rising and then falling back.

Donal turned with a shrug and the priest followed him, pushing Ulrica and Manfred Rorsefne forward. Urquart came last. Ulrica glanced back at Arflane. The terror had left her eyes and was replaced with a look of helpless fatalism.

"Ulrica!" Arflane shouted.

Urquart called without looking at Arflane, "I am about to cut your chains. I am paying the debt I owe you—I am freeing you!"

Arflane watched dumbly as the barbarians prepared for the ritual, erecting bone frames and tying the captives to them so that they were spreadeagled with their feet just above the ice. Urquart stepped forward, cutting expertly at Manfred's clothing as he would skin a seal until the young man was naked. In a way this was a merciful action, since the cold would soon numb his body. Arflane shuddered as he saw Urquart step up to Ulrica and begin to cut the furs from her until she, too, was bare.

Arflane was exhausting himself in his struggles to get to his feet. Even if he could rise there was nothing he could do, for the thongs held his wrists. As a precaution there were now two guards standing nearby.

He watched in horror as Urquart poised the knife close to Manfred Rorsefne's genitals; he heard Rorsefne shriek in pain and thresh in his bonds as Urquart cut his manhood from him. Blood coursed down the young man's thighs and Rorsefne fell forward, head hanging limply. Urquart brandished his trophy, hands reddened with blood, before tossing it away. Arflane remembered the old, savage customs of his own people; there had not been a ritual of this kind performed for centuries.

"Urquart! No!" Arflane screamed as the harpooner turned to Ulrica. "No!"

Urquart did not appear to hear him. All his attention was on Ulrica as, with her eyes mad with fear, she tried unsuccessfully to shrink from the knife that threatened her breasts.

Then Arflane saw a figure leap up beside him, grab a javelin from one of the guards and impale the man. The figure moved swiftly, turning to slice at Arflane's bonds with the sharp tip of the javelin while the other guard turned bewilderedly. Arflane was up then, his fingers grasping the guard's throat and snapping his neck almost instantly.

Ulsenn stood panting beside Arflane, holding the bloody javelin uncertainly. Arflane picked up the other spear and dashed across the ice towards Urquart. As yet no one had seen what had happened.

Then the priest shouted from where he sat and pointed at Arflane. Several barbarians leapt up, but Donal restrained them. Urquart turned, his eyes mildly surprised to see Arflane.

Arflane ran at him with the javelin, but Urquart leapt aside and Arflane only narrowly missed sticking the weapon into Ulrica's body. Urquart stood breathing heavily, the knife raised; then he moved his head slowly towards the spot where his own huge harpoon lay, ready to finish the pair after the ritual.

Arflane flung the javelin erratically. It took Urquart in the arm. Still Urquart did not move, but his lips seemed to frame a question.

Arflane ran to where the many-barbed harpoon lay and picked it up.

Urquart watched him, shaking his head bewilderedly. "Arflane . . .?"

Arflane took the lance in both hands and plunged it into the harpooner's broad chest. Urquart gasped and seized the shaft, trying to pull the weapon from his body. "Arflane," he gasped. "Arflane. You fool! You kill everything . . ." The gaunt man staggered backwards, his pain-filled eyes still staring unbelievingly; and it seemed to Arflane then that in killing Urquart he killed all he had ever held to be valuable.

The harpooner groaned, his great body swaying, his ivory ornaments clattering as he was racked by his agony. Then he fell sideways, attempted to rise, and collapsed in death.

Arflane turned to face the barbarians, but they did not move. The priest was frowning uncertainly.

Ulsenn ran forward. "Two!" he called. "Two of noble blood. Urquart was the man's cousin and the woman's brother!"

The barbarians murmured and looked questioningly at their priest and their chief. Donal stood up, rubbing his clean-shaven chin. "Aye," he said. "Two it is. It is fair. Besides, we had better sport this way." He laughed lightly. "Release the woman. Attend to the man if he still lives. Tomorrow we go to the Ice Mother's court!"

Ulrica wept like a child as they cut her down. Arflane took her gently in his arms, wrapping her in her ripped furs. He felt strangely calm as he passed the stiff corpse of Urquart and carried the woman towards the tent that the priest led him to. Ulsenn followed him, bearing the unconscious body of Manfred Rorsefne.

When Ulrica lay sleeping and Manfred Rorsefne's wound had been crudely dressed, Arflane and Janek Ulsenn sat together in the close confines of the tent. Night had fallen but they made no attempt to rest. Both were pondering the bond that had grown between them in the few hours that had passed; both knew in their hearts that it could not last.

CHAPTER TWENTY-FOUR

NEW YORK

It took them two weeks to find New York and in that time Manfred Rorsefne, his nervous system unable to withstand the shock it had received, died peacefully and was buried in the ice. Konrad Arflane, Ulrica Ulsenn and Janek Ulsenn rode in a group, with Donal and his fat priest close by; they had learned to ride the huge bears without much difficulty. They moved slowly, for the barbarians had brought their tents and women with them. The weather had become surprisingly fine.

When they sighted the slender towers of New York they stopped in astonishment, Arflane felt that Pyotr Rorsefne had been peculiarly uneloquent in describing them. They were magnificent. They shone.

The party came to a straggling stop and the bears scratched nervously at the ice, perhaps sensing their riders' mixed feelings as they looked at the city of metal and glass and stone soaring into the clouds. The towers blazed; mile upon mile of shining ice reflected their shifting colours and Arflane remembered the story, wondering how tall they must be if they stretched as far below the ice as they did above it. Yet his instincts were alarmed and he did not know why. Perhaps, after all, he did not want to know the truth. Perhaps he did not want to meet the Ice Mother, for he had sinned against Her in many ways in the course of the voyage.

"Well," Donal said quickly. "Let's continue."

Slowly they rode towards the many-windowed city jutting from the ice of the plain. As they moved nearer Arflane realised what it was that so disturbed him. An unnatural warmth radiated from the place; a warmth that could have melted the ice. Surely this was no city of the Ice Mother? They all sensed it and looked at one another grimly. Again they came to a halt. Here was the city that symbolised all their dreams and hopes; and suddenly it had taken on a subtle menace.

"I like this not at all," Donal growled. "That heat—it is much worse than the heat that came to the south."

Arflane nodded. "But why can it be so hot? Why hasn't the ice melted?"

"Let us go back," said Ulsenn. "I knew it was foolish to come here."

Instinctively Arflane agreed with him; but he had set out to reach New York. He had told himself that he would accept whatever knowledge the city offered. He had to go on; he had killed men and destroyed a ship to get here and now that he was less than a mile away he could not possibly turn back. He shook his head and goaded his mount forward. From behind him came a muttering.

He raised his hand and pointed at the slender towers. "Come —let's go to greet the Ice Mother!"

The riding bear galloped forward; behind him the barbarians began to increase their speed until all were galloping in a wild, half-hysterical charge on the vast city, their ranks breaking and spreading out, their cries echoing among the towers as they sought to embolden themselves. Ulrica's hood was whipped back by the wind; her unbound hair streamed behind her as she clung to her saddle. Arflane grinned at her, his beard torn by the wind. Ulsenn's face was set and he leaned forward in the saddle as if going to his death.

The towers were grouped thickly, with barely enough space between the outer ones for them to enter the city. As they reached the great forest of metal and glass they realised that there was something more unnatural about the city than the warmth that came from it.

Arflane's mount's feet skidded on the surface and he called out in amazement. "This isn't ice!"

The stuff had been cunningly made to simulate ice in almost every detail, but now that they stood on it they could tell that it was not ice; and it was possible to look down through it and make out the dim shapes of the towers going down and down into darkness.

Donal cried: "You have misled us, Arflane!"

The sudden revelation had shocked Arflane as much as the others. Dumbly, he shook his head.

Ulsenn charged forward on his mount to shake his fist in Arflane's face. "You have led us into a trap! I knew it!"

"I followed Pyotr Rorsefne's chart, that was all!"

"This place is evil," the priest said firmly. "We can all sense that. It matters not how we were deceived—we should leave while we can."

Arflane shared the priest's feeling. He hated the atmosphere of the city. He had expected to find the Ice Mother and had found instead something that seemed to stand for everything the Ice Mother opposed.

"Very well," he said. "We turn back." But even as he spoke he realised that the ground beneath them was moving downwards; the whole great plain was sinking slowly below the level of the surrounding ice. Those closer to the edge managed to leap their clumsy animals upwards and escape but most of them were left in panic as the city dropped lower into what was apparently a huge shaft driven into the ice. The shadows of the shaft's enormous sides fell across the group as they milled about in fear.

Arflane saw how Donal and Ulsenn were staring at him and realised that he was to be their scapegoat.

"Ulrica," he called, turning his mount to plunge into the mass of towers with the woman close behind him. The light grew fainter as they galloped through the winding maze; behind they heard the barbarians, led by Ulsenn and Donal, searching for them. Arflane knew instinctively that in their panic they would butcher him and probably Ulrica too; they had to stay clear of them. He had two dangers to face now and both seemed insuperable. He could not hope to defeat the barbarians and he could not stop the city sinking.

There was an entrance in one of the towers; from it streamed a soft light. Desperately he rode his beast through it and Ulrica came with him.

He found himself in a gallery with ramps curving downward from it towards the floor of the tower far below. He saw several figures lower on the ramps; figures dressed from head to foot in red, close-fitting garments, wearing masks that completely covered their faces. They looked up as they heard the sound of the bears' paws in the gallery, and one of them laughed and pointed.

Grimly Arflane sent the creature half-sliding down one of the ramps. He glanced back and saw that Ulrica had hesitated but was following him. The speed of the descent was dangerous; twice the bear nearly slid off the edge of the ramp and three times he nearly lost his seat on the animal's back, but when he reached the floor of the tower the masked men were gone.

As Ulrica joined him, looking in awe at the strange devices that covered the walls, he realised that the city was no longer in motion. He stared at the things on the wall. They were instruments of some kind; a few resembled chronometers or compasses while others were alive with flickering letters that meant nothing at all to him. His main interest at that moment was in finding a door. There seemed to be none. Was this, after all, the court of the Ice Mother and the red-clad creatures ghosts? From somewhere came faint laughter again, then from above an echoing yell. He saw Ulsenn riding rapidly down the ramp towards him; he was waving a flenching cutlass while Arflane had only a javelin.

Arflane turned to look into Ulrica's face. She stared back at him then dropped her eyes as if in consent.

Arflane rode his bear towards Ulsenn as the man lunged at him with the cutlass. He blocked the blow with the javelin but the blade sheered off the head of the spear, leaving him virtually defenceless. Ulsenn swung clumsily at his throat, missed and was taken off balance. Arflane plunged the jagged shaft into his throat.

152

Ulrica rode up, watching silently as Ulsenn clutched at the wound, then fell slowly from the back of the bear.

"That is the end of it now," she said.

"He saved your life," Arflane said.

She nodded. "But now it is over." She began to cry. Arflane looked at her miserably, wondering why he had killed Ulsenn then and not earlier, before the man had had the chance to show that he could be courageous. Perhaps that was why; he had, towards the end, become a true rival.

"A fine piece of bloodshed, strangers. Welcome to New York."

They turned. A section of the wall had vanished; in its place stood a thin figure. Its overlong skull was encased in a red mask. Two eyes glittered humorously through slits in the fabric. Arflane jerked up his javelin in an instinctive movement. "This is not New York—this is some evil place."

The figure laughed softly. "This is New York, indeed, though not the original city of your legends. That was destroyed by a single bomb almost two thousand years ago. But this city stands close to the site of the original. In many respects it is far superior. You have witnessed one of its advantages."

Arflane realised he was sweating. He loosened the thongs of his coat. "Who are you?"

"If you are genuinely curious, then I will tell you," replied the masked man. "Follow me."

CHAPTER TWENTY-FIVE

THE TRUTH

Arflane had wanted the truth; it was why he had originally agreed to Rorsefne's scheme; but now, as he stared around the luminous chamber, Ulrica's arm on his, he began to feel that the truth was more than he could accept. The red-masked figure left the room. The walls gleamed blindingly bright and a seated man appeared at the far end of the chamber. He wore the same red garments as the other, but he was almost a dwarf and one shoulder was higher than the other.

"I am Peter Ballantine," he said pleasantly. His pronunciation was careful, as if he spoke the words of a language he had recently learned. "Please sit down."

Arflane and Ulrica seated themselves gingerly on the quilted benches and were startled as the man's chair slid forward until he sat only a foot or two away from them. "I will explain everything," he said. "I will be brief. Ask questions when I have finished."

There had been a full-scale nuclear war. When it was over the human race was all but gone and the majority of the sur-

vivors were in the areas largely unaffected by any direct attack
—the polar bases of the South Antarctican International Zone
where Russian, American, British Commonwealth, Scandina-
vian and other research teams lived; and Camp Century, the
city the Americans had established under the Greenland ice
cap. Nature, unbalanced by the war, had swiftly begun to draw
a healing skin of ice over her ruined surface. What had precipi-
tated the ice age was primarily the bombs and the sudden
change in the various radiations in the atmosphere. The men
of the two polar camps had communicated for a while by
radio but the radiation was too great to risk personal contact.
For one reason and another, forced by their separate circumstances, the two groups of survivors had chosen different ways
of adapting to the change. The men of the Antarctic learnt to
adapt to the ice, making use of all their resources to build
ships that could travel the surface without need of fuel, dwell-
ings where one could live without need of special heating
plants. As the ice covered the planet, they moved away from
the Antarctic, heading towards the Equator until, at length,
they reached the plateau of the Matto Grosso and decided that
here was an ideal location for permanent camp. In adapting
to the conditions they had neglected their learning and within
a few hundred years the creed of the Ice Mother had replaced the second law of thermodynamics which had shown
logically what the people now believed instinctively—that only
ice eternal lay in the future. Perhaps the adaptation of the
Antarcticans had been a healthier reaction to the situation
than that of the Arcticans who had tended to bury themselves
deeper and deeper into their under-ice caverns, searching for
scientific means of survival that would preserve the way of life
they knew.

Among the last messages to be sent by the Arcticans to the
Antarcticans was the information that the northerners had
reached the stage where they could transport their city-complex
further south and that they intended to site it in New York.
They offered help to the Antarcticans, but they refused it,
stripping their radios to make better use of them. They had
grown to feel easy with their life.

So the Arcticans refined their science and their living conditions until the city of New York was the result, and having
done this did what mankind had done in the past and won-
wondered why they had to adapt any further to the environment when it was now possible to adapt the environment to
suit themselves. They developed techniques capable of driving
back the ice and revealing the surface of the healed planet as it
had existed two thousand years before. The rapid growth of the
ice could now just as rapidly be reversed; this they were doing
with special instruments sited in selected locations on other
continental land masses than their own. At the same time they

were conducting biological experiments to produce animals that would help develop the new ecology; the green birds were one example. These would replace the ice-dwelling creatures, most of which would not have time to adapt to the rapid change in climate.

"It will take at least another two hundred years before any great area of land is cleared," Peter Ballantine explained. "We are using the continent of Africa as our main experimental area. The results make us optimistic. Africa was never entirely ice-bound and there was wild-life there which helped us considerably in our biological experiments."

Arflane and Ulrica had received the information almost expressionlessly. Arflane felt that he was drowning; his body and mind were numb.

"We welcome visitors, particularly from the Eight Cities," Ballantine continued. "Whereas the animals will not be able, for the most part, to adapt, your people of course will easily survive." He glanced at them and added thoughtfully, "Physically at any rate."

Arflane looked up at him then. "You would destroy our whole way of life," he said, without rancour.

"Your way of life is no more natural than ours, enclosed as we are in our mechanical womb, sharpening our brains and forgetting our bodies. We are physically enfeebled, all of us, but mentally strong. Your people are almost better balanced, for minds can be nurtured more easily than bodies."

Arflane nodded gravely. "But there are many of us who do not want what you offer. I am one."

"We offer only knowledge. What is wrong with that?"

"I don't know," Arflane said slowly. "Nothing, I suppose. I can see that future generations will benefit from it—but, you see, I'm not adapted here," he tapped his heart and then his head, "to believing that there will be many future generations. I believe in the ice eternal, the doctrine that all must grow cold, that the Ice Mother's mercy is all that allows us to live."

"But you can see how wrong that idea is," Ballantine said gently. "Your society created those ideas to enable them to live the way they did. They needed them, but they no longer need them now."

"I understand," Arflane said. The depression that filled him was hard to overcome; it seemed that his whole life since he had first saved Rorsefne had led to this point. Gradually he had forsaken his old principles, allowing himself soft emotions, taking Ulrica in adultery, involving himself with others; and it was as if by forgetting the dictates of the Ice Mother he had somehow created this New York. Logically, he knew the idea was absurd but he could not shake himself clear of it. If he had lived according to his code, the Ice Mother would be comforting him, not Peter Ballantine disturbing him; if he had listened to Urquart, last of the Ice Mother's true followers, and gone with him, they would have found the New York they expected to find. But he had killed Urquart in saving Ulrica's life. 'You have killed everything,' Urquart had said as he died. Now Arflane understood what the harpooner had meant. Urquart had tried to change his course for him, but the course had led inevitably to Peter Ballantine and his logic and his vision of an earth in which the Ice Mother was dying, or already dead. If he could find Her . . .

Ulrica Ulsenn touched his hand. "He is right," she said, "that is why the people of the Eight Cities are changing—because they sense what is happening to the world. They are adapting in the way that animals adapt, though most of the animals—the land whales and the like—will not adapt in time."

"The land-whales' adaptation was artificially stimulated," Ballantine said with some pride. "It was an experiment of ours that was incidentally beneficial to your people."

Arflane sighed again, feeling completely dejected. He rubbed his sweating forehead and tugged at his clothes, resenting the heat of the place. He turned and looked at Ulrica Ulsenn, shaking his head slowly, touching her hand gently. "You welcome this," he said. "You represent what they represent. You're the future, too."

She frowned. "I don't understand you, Konrad. You're being too mysterious."

"I'm sorry." He glanced away from her and looked at Ballantine as he sat in the moving chair, waiting patiently. "I am the past," he said to the man. "You can see that, I think."

"Yes," said Ballantine sympathetically. "I respect you, but . . ."

"But you must destroy me."

"It does not need to be seen in such dramatic terms," Ballantine pointed out reasonably.

"I have to see it so," Arflane sighed. "I am a simple man, you see. An old-fashioned man."

"You need time to think," Ballantine told him. "We will find accommodation for you both while you do so." He chuckled. "Your barbarian friends are still chasing around on the surface of the city like frightened lice. We must see how we can help them. In their case our hypnomats will doubtless be of more use than conversation."

CHAPTER TWENTY-SIX

NORTH

The next day Peter Ballantine walked in the artificial gardens of the city with Ulrica Ulsenn. Arflane had looked at the gardens and declined to enter. He sat now in a gallery staring at the machines which Ballantine had told him were the life-giving heart of the city.

"Just as your ancestors adapted to the ice," Ballantine was saying to the woman, "so you must re-adapt to its disappearance. You came north instinctively because you identify the north with your homeland. All this is natural. But now you must go south again, for your own good and the good of your children. You must give your people the knowledge we have given you; though it will take time they will gradually come to accept it. If they do not change they will destroy themselves in a reversion to savagery."

Ulrica nodded. "I see . . ." She looked with growing enjoyment at the multitude of brightly coloured flowers around her, sniffed their scents in wonder, her nostrils the keener for never having experienced such perfume before. It made her feel lightheaded. She smiled slowly at Ballantine, eyes shining.

"I realise Arflane is disturbed just now." Ballantine continued. "There is a lot of guilt in his attitude; but there is no need for him to feel this. Literally—no need. There was a need for all those inhibitions, but now it does not exist. That is why you must go south again, to tell them what you have learned."

Ulrica spread her hands and indicated the flowers. "This is what will replace the ice?" she said.

"This and much more. Yours and Arflane's children could see it if they wished to journey even further south. They could live in a land where all these things grow naturally." He smiled, touched by her childlike enjoyment of his garden. "You must convince him."

"He will understand," she said confidently. "What of the barbarians? Donal and the rest?"

"We have had to use less subtle and possibly less lasting methods on them. We have machines that can mould the mind, teach it to think new thoughts. We have used these on the barbarians. Some of the new thoughts they will forget after a while, but with luck many will remain. They will help spread the ideas."

"I wish Arflane had not refused to come here," Ulrica said. "I'm sure he would like it."

"Perhaps," said Ballantine. "Shall we return to him?"

When Arflane saw them come back he rose. "When you are ready," he said distantly, "I would like to be taken back to the surface."

"I have no intention of keeping you here against your will," Ballantine said. "I will leave you together now."

He left the gallery. Arflane began to walk back to the apartment that had been set aside for them. He moved slowly, Ulrica beside him.

"When we go back to Friesgalt, Konrad," Ulrica said, taking his arm, "we can marry. That will make you Chief Ship Lord. In that position you will be able to guide the people towards the future, as Ballantine wants us to. You will become a hero, Konrad, a legend."

"I do not trust legends," he said. Gently he took her hand from his arm.

"Konrad?"

He shook his head. "You go back to Friesgalt," he told her. "You go back."

"What will you do? You must come back with me."

"No."

The city rose to ground level and they disembarked. A storm was beginning to rise over the iceplains. The wind whistled through the tall towers of the city. Peter Ballantine helped Ulrica into the cabin of the helicopter that would take her most of the way back to Friesgalt.

There was a general confused bustling as the barbarians mounted up and began to turn their steeds towards the south. With a wave Donal led his men away across the plain.

Arflane watched them as they rode. There were skis on his feet, two lances in his gloved hands, a visor pushed up from his face; on his back was a heavy pack.

Ulrica looked out from the cabin. "Konrad . . ."

He smiled at her. "Goodbye, Ulrica."

"Where are you going?" she asked.

He gestured into the distance. "North," he said. "To seek the Ice Mother."

As the rotors of the machine began to turn he pushed himself around on his skis and dug the lances into the ice, sending his body skimming forward. He leaned into the wind as he gathered momentum; it had begun to snow.

The helicopter bumped as it rose into the air and tilted towards the south. Ulrica stared through the glass and saw him moving swiftly northwards. His figure grew smaller and smaller. Sometimes it was obscured by drifting snow; sometimes she glimpsed him, the lances rising and falling as he gathered speed.

Soon, he was out of sight.

Neutron Star

LARRY NIVEN

Larry Niven is one of the brightest new talents in science fiction and the title story of this collection won him the 1966 Hugo Award.

The seven other stories are thronged with superbly original characters and whole races of creatures, such as grog, thrint and bandersnatchi, inhabiting worlds like LookItThat, Down, Jinx – an entire galaxy of planets with their own histories, ecologies and cultural epochs.

A Sphere SF Classic   35p

A Selection of Recent Science Fiction
Published by Sphere Books